Brigit's Pawn

By
Sean Mooney

Dedicated to those who try and fail and then try again.

Chapter 1

When I'm alone, when it's quiet, when there is nothing but the sound of my breathing and the beating of my heart, I find myself inevitably falling into the abyss of memories that is my mind. I'm not an egotist by nature – I tell myself. I realize self-reflection is not something done solely by me or even great minds alone. We all swim in the sea of memory, surfing the good times and drowning in the bad. My mind, or any mind I suppose which has been around as long as mine, or who's seen and done the things I've done, who has regrettably lived the exciting life that I've lived – let's say I find myself drowning more often than surfing. It always begins, not surprisingly, at the beginning, from that first minute when I looked up into the awaiting eyes of those who would so dramatically set in motion the pieces of that great machine that is my existence. I can remember smiling. I can remember warmth and safety. I can remember asking, "Who am I?" - something I still have trouble with. I recall, with blissful delight, the sheer happiness that washed over me as my virgin eyes blinked up at the radiance above me – blurred as it was in those first few moments. To set the tone for what was about to come, I can even remember the first words spoken to me – those first sobering and mildly insulting words.

My cell phone rattles against the wooden tabletop as the silent alarm I had set goes off. It rouses me from my introspection. It's not something I enjoy having chained to my hip, but it was a present – the sort of present that's a message. New ones keep showing up, too. You'd think he'd get the hint and stop trying since I tend to burn through a few each year. But, then again, I suppose I'm the one who should be taking the hint. *What's that line? Get living or get dying?* I really should decide one of these days.

I scan the lecture auditorium. I can tell some certainly feel as if this is the end for them. Heads are down – some have assumed the "I give up" position. I always like to give an exam right before a big break as my mind is on food, and that doesn't usually put me in the mood to teach. Besides, it's the perfect chance to catch up on all of those articles I've been meaning to read – if only I had spent the last hour reading. I was about two paragraphs into an incredibly dull explanation on Mayan beadwork when my mind began to wander – leading me to my past. A place I visit all too often. My fault, really. It is the subject I teach – the past, that is, not specifically my own. It is, I realize, much like putting the town drunk in charge of the liquor store.

I pick up my phone, verify the time is correct with the wall clock over the door, and stand. I write on the blackboard behind me, with the last nub of a piece of chalk, *Ten minutes, finish up your thoughts*. As always, there's a ripple of groans and then a flurry of pen on paper – or, for the technologically savvy, the tappity-tap-tap of fingers as they race over the keys of their laptops. I smile as I always do. Freshmen lectures were all the same, filled with those who had yet to realize the simple truth of knowledge. By this point, either you are finished with the exam or you are *finished* with the exam. You either knew it, or you didn't. No final sentence or paragraph, no matter how eloquently phrased, is going alter the grade that the previous fifty minutes had gotten you. Ah, but these were freshmen college students, and most were eager to impress – most still believed that good deeds and well-meaning effort would bring them the rewards they deserved. We all believe this at one point – I believed it at one point. With the final minutes ticking by, several fresh faces are startled by a stiff gust scraping branches against the windows.

It's an icy November, even by mid-Atlantic standards. Unfriendly as it is, as I glance away from the gray beyond the windows and back at the stadium seating, I catch a few frustrated, some angry, faces on my students – making for a chilly interior as well. This does not faze me. I'm not their friend, and I have no wish to be – in fact, I try very hard to keep walls up between us. I've given them everything from long, detailed lectures to near-impossible deadlines, and even unfashionable clothes and general untidiness. It is all designed to send the message: STAY AWAY. Alright, the untidiness is a life choice. A comb rarely touches my hair. I wander into a barber perhaps four times a year, and shaving is something I do only because I hate the idea of a beard only slightly more than the effort in keeping clean-shaven. Although my intent is to be shrugged off, I suspect that I filter into various conversations as the punch line of some jokes.

I check my phone: five minutes. At two minutes, I note the time on the board with a reminder that typed essays needed to be e-mailed. I count off the final seconds in my head and stand. "Alright, stop your work." I take the last sip of my tea as the shuffle of bodies washes down the stairs towards me. There are always questions as students hand in papers, and like some record skipping at the end of a song, every year the questions are the same. I answer almost automatically, "Yes. No. Maybe next semester." I look up from accepting papers and am face to face with a student I did not recognize – yet he seems familiar. "I'm sorry, what was that?" I study his face intently.

"I said that was easy, although that question on Stonehenge was a bit misleading. I aced it. Don't even bother grading it." He lifts his head a little, turning his nose up. "It's great, that feeling, you know, that feeling when you know something others don't. It's like finding something, a secret something – or maybe it's more like uncovering something that someone thought was hidden."

I ignore the gloating and smugness. The boy himself has my attention. He seems normal enough. The boy is thin, perhaps five and a half feet, with neat, short, white-blond hair and a crooked smile. He doesn't say anything further and moves on, replaced by a tall, athletic-looking girl who, if she doesn't play basketball or volleyball, it's a crime. She tries to speak, but I'm already moving towards the door. "Just ah, put it in an e-mail and leave your paper on the stack," I say quickly over my shoulder as I speed through the doorway and out into the hallway.

The light is blinding after the dimness of the low-level track-lighting I usually keep the lecture hall bathed in. I blink. I don't see him. The corridor is a T-intersection; to the left and right, it ends with a door to a stairwell and the emergency exits. Ahead are a few glass cases highlighting local and college historical pieces, a short set of wide stairs, and then the main door – two oak and iron-hinged behemoths that date to when this section of the building was still a church. I rush forward through the narthex, ignoring the looks from students, and put all of my weight against the old church doors. Even before stepping out into the veiled sunlight, I knew – honestly -before I even left the lecture hall, a part of me knew that there would be nothing for me to find.

I slow to a stop and take in a deep breath of crisp late autumn air. I scan the tree-dotted and building-lined campus before me. There are six other Georgian style buildings in sight and a number of bundled students. I catch a glimpse of the white-blond, vaguely familiar teen vanishing into a loosely packed group crossing the street. A breeze gusts up, turning chilly air into biting cold, but regardless, I stiffly move forward across the stage to the low wall that made for a railing on the slate-topped porch. My sweater, warm, but no match alone for the cold, at least not for long, is pressed against me by the wind. All of my senses are fully awake. I look out on the campus before me. It might be nothing, but the hairs on the back of my neck begin to stand up – and I know it's not because of the chilly air.

Omens: the interpretation of natural and or everyday events to ascertain the more profound meaning – if there is one – of life. It takes years of study, meditation, and experience to begin to approach the level of wisdom and understanding necessary to derive meaning from the mundane. Omens, much like scrying, are like walking into a dark room and describing things based solely on what they felt like when you bumped into them. Sometimes it's easy, you bump into a volcano, but unless you have a volcano going off in your backyard when yesterday there wasn't one, such natural events are hard to read as having a subtext. Everyday events are even harder to interpret. It's not an exact science – and some would argue it's not science at all - but as a rule of thumb, it might be an omen if it is something you pass by every day, something you see a hundred times but never take notice of, and then suddenly you notice it. At this very moment, I'm noticing a lot.

Time slows down. I can almost hear each individual leaf rustling in the wind, each footfall, each breath. A bird – a finch – with a beak full of dried grass, flies off ahead of a pack of students coming in its direction. It finds a perch in the tree next to the stage where I stand. A leaf falls from that tree, landing at my feet. Landing next to a crack in the slate of the porch next to my feet. A twig bisects the crack. The crack and twig create a shape very reminiscent of the symbol algiz.

And then it begins to rain.

I make my way inside. Much of the hallway's traffic has cleared, so I have an unobstructed walk back to the lecture hall. The papers are mostly in a neat pile; beside them is a smaller additional pile of handwritten notes from various students. I'll look at those later, but right now, it's four-thirty, I have no more classes today, and I'm pretty sure I need to be someplace else right now.

I pile the notes, exams, articles, and my phone into my satchel and, with coat in hand, head for the door. I halt as I enter the hallway once again. As I stand there surrounded by the wooden display cases, the vaulted ceiling, the soft blue of the walls, and the faces of previous professors long since forgotten looking down on me, I'm suddenly struck by the feeling that this might be the last time I walk through this hallway. There's a sense of finality. I was sent here five years ago. Rarely do I ever know ahead of time why I am being sent to a location, and often it is years before the reasons for my assignment become clear. You learn to stop asking questions – well, you learn to stop asking questions out loud – well, you learn to stop asking questions out loud to *Them*. They want blind obedience. Eventually, They beat obedience into you – the rest I fake. I try not to grow attached – I try.

Eyes shut, I take a step and break free of my melancholy. I heave against the behemoths and step out into the gray. The rain is light but steady. I circle the Humanities building and make my way down a side street and away from campus. I'm not happy about any of this. Except the rain. I love the rain and the gray. I'm not happy about this feeling I have deep in my gut that my reason for being here is about to be revealed – and that usually ends with an assignment elsewhere. I need a drink, and I need to clear my head. And I'm not sure which I want to do first.

My walk comes to a halt as I wait for a car to pass before crossing a street. I know what I should do, and I know what I want to do – well, I've narrowed it down to two choices. I look up. Eyes closed against the rain that feels like tiny icy spears stinging my face. In that moment, I realize two things: that I'm furious with my knee jerk, Pavlovian run-home-and-wait-for-instructions response, and I forgot my umbrella in the classroom.

The car splashes by, and I pick up my pace. I usually enjoy my walk home, but when your brain is divided between regret, irritation, trying to ignore the shivers, and being equally infuriated at yourself and the Powers-That-Be, it tends to drain the love out of life. I live near the edge of town, which, despite being a college town, isn't that big. Even in clear weather, I manage the walk in about fifteen minutes. My quick pace, driven by icy rain and a sudden need to be someplace, anyplace else, has me home in just under ten. I reach for the garden gate, and again I'm overwhelmed by that unwanted sense of nostalgia. It's as if I'm not really here, but living a memory.

For just a moment, I linger with my hand on the wooden fence. I built it myself – in fact, I handmade, crafted, each pointed piece of white picket fence surrounding the small front yard. The house itself is also small; it's almost lost among the acre of trees around it and in the back. I have neighbors; the Martins, with their three kids, to the left, and the Keans, recently married, to the right. Across the street is a small park. Both families are polite and quiet, and I can count on one hand the number of times we've run into each other. Still, they wave when we see each other in passing, so that's nice. I have a better relationship with their cars – the sedan and minivan in the driveways tells me that all the families are home. It seems it's an early day for everyone.

I take a breath and push through the gate and up onto the porch. My door opens with a slight creak that I purposefully keep forgetting to oil. I drop my coat and bag near the front door and stand as I drip onto the slate floor of my living room. My instincts are on fire, and I was sure someone would be waiting for me. But I'm wrong. The house is silent. But it's still there, that feeling of being watched, of expecting someone to pop around the corner. I check the bathroom, bedroom, and kitchen before allowing myself to relax.

I flop onto the couch and exhale deeply. I stare at the near-empty bookshelves and blank walls. I'm certain something is out of sorts. It's not often that my instincts lead me astray. I don't believe it. No. This is where *They* want me. And that makes me very angry. I can't wait. I need to blow off some steam before the boss gets here. Leaving will probably mean trouble.

Two minutes tick by before I settle on a decision.

I need to think, and if I'm right – despite feeling foolish, I still think I am – I decide that I'm not a dog. I'm not going to sit here and wait for instructions. My mood has pushed me into being rebellious. I need to clear my head, and that means going out. "Come and find me," I grumble and pull myself up from the couch. I step over to the shelves near the bathroom and stare at the line of books at eye level, their spines neatly aligned. Out of the three built-in bookshelves around the living room, it's the only one with books on it. I filled it with books from the bargain bins of bookstores and the "please take" cart at the library. Most I've read, some are junk I've added to fill in the shelf. I have always meant to fill in the rest of the shelves. It's always on tomorrow's list of things to do – but tomorrow never seems to come. I press on *A Tale Of Two Cities*. There's a soft, almost imperceptible click. The floor behind me lifts up, revealing a stone staircase.

A hunt is what I need.

Chapter 2

I need to think. To clear my head. I stare deeply into the darkness of the narrow stone steps leading down. Here, where I stand, is my house, but below, that's where I live. It's difficult to make out any but the first three steps. I hadn't turned a light on when I arrived, and the heavy curtains were still drawn. However, just enough diffused gray light filters into the living room around the curtains to outline the shadows.

I hesitate.

Strictly speaking, I wasn't allowed to do what I was about to do – what I, in truth, have been doing for a very long time. I'm not sure if *They* are aware of the fact that I continue with my hobby. I'm a professor – a disguise, really. I'm also a hunter, but that's just another disguise – a distraction. Both give me the semblance of purpose. I've gotten the impression over the years that *They'd* rather keep me in a box – only to set me loose as needed. Yet, many of my assignments require blending in – not infiltration as much as being non-descript – so I'm often granted temp work. This, however, *this* has been the one consistency while waiting for whatever trap I was a part of to spring. That I'm occasionally caught and punished has never really deterred me.

I try to keep my worlds separate, partly because modern and ancient practices don't entirely mix and partially because when I step below, I become a different person. It's not that the past and the present can't play well together, but, much like oil and water, it takes a lot of shaking to get them to mix. It's an energy thing. Technology uses energy. Magic takes energy.

I empty my pockets. My keys, a pen, and a small notepad are set on the bookshelf. I pause. I measure my irritation. I need to make a full transition. I need to shed as much of this negative energy as I can. My shirt comes off, followed by my shoes, sweater, all my clothing – all of which make a pile at my feet. I'm naked, both in presence and in spirit. "Professor no more." Being naked isn't, strictly speaking, necessary, but I feel the storm of rage in my mind and know this is a time when it is very much necessary. I catch my reflection in the mirror across the room. I see a man, but I know it is not a man. It wants to be a man. It tries to be a man. My thoughts of earlier today circle back – *who am I?* A question I have been asking myself in ever growing frequency these last few years.

Today, a teacher.

Tomorrow, a plumber.

Soldier.

Scribe.

Student.

Always different. Always changing. And I always give myself fully over to my role - that way, at least while I'm pretending I'm someone else, I can for a short time feel like I have control, like I have a purpose. As I said, I need to clear my head.

I close my eyes as I take a step. When I open them, I can feel the mantle of the professor fully slip away. The stairs are cold, and the air is even colder as I move deeper into the below. I know I reach the bottom not because I can see, but purely from memory. "Solas coinnle," I command, and several candles respond with *pfts* and crackles as they awaken. There is a small semicircle of a recess in the wall at the bottom of the stairs; wherein sits a glass vial the size of a golf pencil. I let my fingers glide over the edge of the niche and try to force some hope into my mind. Next to this, and hanging from a cast iron hook near my head, is a heavy brown cloak. I quickly dress in it – the weight and warmth are welcome.

As I turn to face the room, I flip the hood up. "Tine," I say. From across the room, there's a spark and a whoosh of the sudden consumption of air as the hearth fills with fire. I take in a deep breath – I enjoy the scent of damp earth - and slip my feet into my pink, overly fluffy bunny slippers. My prize possessions. They are the very first things I ever ordered online. I look down on them with satisfaction and pride. They are warm and comfy, and I don't care a rat's ass that they probably make me look ridiculous. I shuffle further into the workroom. The bookshelves behind the desk are lined with an abundant amount of reading and research material – this has always comforted me, knowledge. As a boy, I didn't have books, but my father's stories filled that role. But, this day, that comfort does not come.

"He's early," a deep growl resounds within the chamber.

"Or late," the bubbly voice is bookended by what passes for giggles.

I wait for the third though I am relatively sure nothing will be said – it always pays to be polite. "It's raining," I say.

"Something, you are assuming, we are somehow not aware of."

I bow my head slightly to the grumpy voice. "Not in the least. I just meant I made my way home in a hurry because of the rain."

"I like rain - it tickles. How can you not like the rain?"

I smile. "I'm afraid I gain very little from the rain."

Red, Blue, and Green are companions of a sort. I learned a long time ago that trees have a voice. They love poetry and spend days reciting their own works to each other and, on occasion, a human verse. I learned to listen to them as a child – something that almost always requires physical contact. But it wasn't until much later that I learned to speak with them. And even then, as now, there's a lot of guessing and assumptions I have to make on what they actually mean. I glance over to the far wall beyond the small stone circle. Placed upon three separate roots are three softly glowing stones, each flat, a little smaller than my palm, and carved with the kenaz symbol.

"As he has said before, and you would know if you'd -" Red begins.

"Maybe if you stop and just stand in it," Green interrupts.

"This is what I'm talking about," Red barks.

"I'm just trying to help. Maybe he needs to experience the," Green giggles, "joy of being all drippy wet."

I enjoy listening to Green. She exudes cheer, and right now, I'm in dire need. "It's not a lack of experience -" I try to speak up, but the argument continues.

"You do this all the time," Red's voice bristles, "talking over others. Interrupting. Forgetting."

I lift an eyebrow. Forgetting is a rather harsh tree insult. As they begin to argue, I step over to the heavy oak table that takes up most of the small room's left side. I've never worried about offending my companions by having wooden furniture. Trees are practical, logical, and what we see of them is only the tip of the iceberg. They've never been happy with humans, but they at least give us the same regard as squirrels, birds, or beavers. Behind the desk are shelves recessed into the earth, surrounded in thick roots, where books and jars are stacked and crammed along every available space. On the table are two glass bowls, along with more jars of various liquids and ingredients.

As I consider my materials, I am vaguely aware of their bickering, but it's nothing I'm not used to by now. Blue usually steps in long before I grow tired of the chatter.

When I arrived here five years ago, the first thing I did was to grow my basement. Although deep and large, the house's basement is filled with too many modern trappings to be of use to me. Roots and earth make up my walls, and there isn't a pipe or electrical socket to be found. I asked permission from the largest tree in my new yard in preparation for the construction – a very tall and round pine. After completion, I thanked it and found it had a lot to say. He was the first – Red. The stones help translate for me, but in truth, the tree picks the voice, which, on many occasions, has left me wondering how and why they choose which voice to use. Within days I was told others wanted to speak – which was odd because although a chatty bunch, they regard humans as insects. Apparently, I had made a good impression. Green followed. And finally, Blue. And despite the occasional mention of *the others,* no one else has asked to be heard. I'm sure they have names, but it's rude to ask a tree that question. In my youth, I'd call them by their type. I learned the hard way that "type" was a human designation, and besides, to call Green "Willow" was as wrong as referring to someone by their skin color or a body feature. Moreover, names never mattered as somehow they always know which of the three voices I'm speaking to.

I contemplate the two glass bowls on the desk. One has a handful of small stones and the other has finger-length twigs. *I'm running low.* I think to myself so as not to draw attention to my actions. I know it will take a full day to resupply myself with a decent amount of magic. I grumble inwardly at the word.

I hate using the word magic, possibly because it has become such a silly word – not something taken seriously. You mention magic to someone, and their mind is instantly drawn to Las Vegas and images of top hats, handkerchiefs, and large props. I grew up with the notion of this energy that surrounds us, albeit unnamed – a force. It just – was, is. I think about my ancestors and wonder how they would feel about me, describing something as ethereal as this force as a type of background radiation, but that's how I think of it.

"Conduits and crafters," I mutter as I continue to contemplate the jars, wondering if I should put this outing off and do some work instead.

"What was that?" Red grumbles.

There's an irritated sigh from Green.

Caught. "I was just musing. Wizards and the like are conduits – even the ones that don't need a focusing agent; they can draw upon radiation and perform great feats." I use my most boring, stilted, lecture voice in the hopes they'll lose interest in me and go back to arguing. "Witches and their like are crafters. They lack the ability to access the magic on their own, but can craft items that draw in power, which they can then use. Of course, the problem is that once the item has been crafted, anyone can use it. This has led to many, many problems and ushered in giving magic its bad name. History -"

"So many funny words, so defined," Green interrupts.

"There. You did it again."

I smile as their voices turn on each other.

But now I can't stop my thoughts. History – it's a drug to me. I feel the need to mention to myself - because no one else is listening - that I'm not blaming any one group specifically for magic's bad name. There have certainly been bad apple wizards who have done nothing to help the cause. And Las Vegas, they have started calling it the "art of illusion". My kind – my mind stops, and I sigh - *my own kind. What am I?* Green would tell me not to be so defined. To sway with the wind. I shuffle away from the table in the direction of the large armoire.

A voice breaks over the discordant jabbering in the background. "Trouble."

The voice is calm and quiet – a whisper of a child with an English accent. Instantly the arguing comes to a halt. I'm not sure where Blue came up with the English accent, but I'm mostly sure he is the young oak in the front yard. There's a brief moment of utter silence. I picture Red, Green, and Blue, huddling in a corner and whispering to each other in my head.

"Is there something you're not telling us?" Red growls, his voice coming from all around me.

"There are a great many things I haven't told you." I stand still, hoping they get back to their argument.

"Aedan, dear, your bark is showing," Green spoke.

That's one of my more favorite tree phrases. Their language is that of images, so when translated into spoken, a lot is lost. "Your bark is showing" could refer to being upset or an acknowledgment that your true self is showing – which is also a complicated tree concept. The thing is, trees can't lie. Before humans, they had no concept of it. They exist in a collective but with individual thoughts, but I've never been able to figure out if their link is physical or metaphysical. In any event, because they have so little experience with lying, I can, on occasion, sidestep uncomfortable questions. "I was just thinking about going out."

They instantly spoke at once – they hadn't bought it.

"Aedan," Green's voice becomes apparent as the other two drop away. "Aedan, we saw you looking at your balls."

"Rounds," Red corrects.

"No, it's balls," Green's coquettish, matter-of-fact tone is laced with just a hint of irritation. "Rounds, that's a... shape,"

"Balls are a shape," Red argues back.

"No, silly, balls are a thing like, like -"

As Green searches for a word, Blue cuts in, "Bowls," he says shortly, "it's bowls – round is the shape, and balls are the thing."

There's quiet for just a handful of seconds – long enough that I feel that if I move slowly, I may get away without being noticed. I don't want to worry them, especially since I don't know if there really is anything worth worrying about.

"That's not right," Red says dismissively.

"Are you sure?" The lilt at the end of Green's question suggests she doesn't think Blue is correct.

There's another quiet pause. I assume their minds are mingling. I take the opportunity to open the armoire. I press my palms against the wooden surface. It's made of ash and is a smoky slate color. The doors are lined in runes, etched there by my hand. I read them silently: *To your protection and health. There is no fear, only strength, determination, and skill. Let reason guide you, and let your heart be the light.* I write primarily in runes for no other reason than it was the first language I learned to write in. Besides, I do enjoy the look of it. The simplicity of lines. The right angles and slants. It's almost mathematical.

I reach quickly for the handles and pull open the doors. A dark forest green coat – a duster by name - hangs within. Strapped to each door is a bracer of various daggers. On the floor of the cabinet are two small baskets. "I shall impersonate... a man," I whisper to myself. I remove the heavy brown robe I'm wearing, fold it neatly, and place it into one of the empty baskets. I follow this by placing my bunny slippers into the other empty basket. As I'm reaching for the green coat, the voices again address me.

"We have decided," Green spoke cheerfully, "that they are called bowls."

"Yes," Red grumbles.

"Thank you," Blue says with pride.

"And," Green continues, "that you are unsure of the season."

That imagery I understand. They've used it to refer to me on multiple occasions. The phrase means that I am aware of what's going on but am stubbornly refusing to accept it. They know I'm lying or trying to hide something. The thing is, you can't out wait a tree - they're a patient bunch. I don't want to linger, so I press on with my plans by lifting the duster from its hook. "I'm not sure," I have many years behind me, and honestly, these last five will live on in my memories as some of my most cherished. A lot of that is due to Red, Green, and Blue. "I can't be certain until it happens, of course, but I think I'll be moving on soon." Their silence is heartbreaking. I repress the urge to cry and dress in the coat.

The sleeves are wide and edged in gold thread, which weaves around the cuff into an intricate knotwork. The bottom half is left loose, and from the waist up, the garment cinches in snugly, with aged copper buttons holding it closed; it billows rather dramatically when I run. As I finish pushing the last of the nine buttons through its corresponding loop, the transformation is complete. I feel it. It's more than just a mental change; a tingle ripples along my flesh from head to toes.

When it subsides, I glance up at the mirror at the back of the armoire. I'm not me anymore. My face, thin and pointed, is now much more square with the appearance of tree bark. I have grown a beard the color and texture of soft forest moss while my hair - much longer now, nearly to my shoulders – resembles the coarse and stringy Spanish moss. I'd crafted the look at a time when forests dominated the landscape, but it served just as well hiding in the shadows of this era of concrete and steel. I'd pass for human from a distance, but up close, there's no resemblance.

My physical change isn't limited to skin and hair. Padded leather gloves form around my hands – though my fingers are left bare. Soft, black, linen and leather pants and a heavy set of boots, now clothe me. On a small shelf on the inside of the cabinet rests a wooden cylinder about six inches long, two inches in diameter, and decorated with runic carvings. I place that in a large side pocket. I next grab two daggers from the line of them along the doors – a boleen, which I slide into its sheath on the right side of my abdomen, and a dirk, with the pommel of a silver falcon head, into the sheath along my thigh. I move away from the armoire and back to the oak desk. I reach into the glass bowls and carefully choose several stones and twigs, placing each into one of a dozen small, hidden pockets around my coat. I leave the rest, reminding myself again of the need to resupply. I step over to the low encircling wall – also etched in runes – that borders the round, shallow, stone pit at the center of the room. I stand for just a moment with my eyes closed.

"Dig deep," Red breaks the silence.

"And reach high," both Blue and Green finish.

I bow.

At the center of the stone ring is a carving of a raven. I tap it now with the toe of my boot and wait as the floor opens up.

Chapter 3

Now exposed, the tunnel had a gentle slope that went further underground for about five feet before leveling off and then slowly rising again to the exit at the back of my property. It was about an acre and a half walk through limestone darkness. But first, there was a choice to be made. *Cat? Mouse? Dog?* Of course, I knew that magic in and of itself was not deadly; however, I also knew that water, in sufficient quantity, will kill you. And I was about to dive headfirst into the deep end of magic. All of us, my brothers and sisters and I, we all have more or less the same talents, but each of us also has one thing that we are really, really, good at.

I'm a shapeshifter. I think proudly. Even before I was chosen, I enjoyed a special connection with animals. I called upon them in battle. My headdress was in the likeness of a falcon. My ax swung with the might of a bear. Of course, in those days, I drew upon their energy to emulate their abilities; these days, I draw upon energy to become them. But it's dangerous. Probably one of the deadliest forms of magic – well, any of the magics that cause transition can be trouble. The danger of shapeshifting is losing yourself and simply evaporating. Tremendous focus is necessary to carry over the thought, the image, of what you are changing into. It's a guide. You've become rolled out cookie dough, and that image is your cookie cutter. I make it a point to remind myself of all of this because my conscious and subconscious are playing volleyball with my irritation, which may make the transition into and out of a form difficult. But sometimes fun trumps rules. I suppose it's like knowing that too many cherries can give you the runs, but you eat too many anyway because they're so yummy.

"And it's not as dangerous as teleporting." I mumble in defense of my overeating of cherries. I recall that one time I tried teleporting – and how badly it had gone. *Never again.* Although occasionally I will use portals – but they make a lot of noise.

I open my mind, drawing in all of the energy in the room, flooding my body with that harmless background radiation. My skin begins to tingle and then itch, which oddly becomes a tickle, followed by a sense of weightlessness as every molecule of my being is dissolved into the ether like sugar into water.

I am a swirl. One with the magic. All that I am - my body, my clothes, my weapons, my supplies - all are pin-pricks of light without meaning. I need to give them meaning. Those points of light reform into quarks within moments, then atoms, then elements, then molecules, and then cells.

There's a flash of light. There's always a flash of light, which differs in intensity depending on the size of the change. I'm a cat. What I had been now comprising a ghost image in my mind and an invisible - nearly invisible - aura around me. Like millions of moons circling a planet. I'd pass for a cat, but if someone paid a little too much attention to me, they'd sense something odd about me – might even catch a glimpse of a slight waver about my body. It seldom comes to that, however, as I try to stick to the shadows and the time limit. You can lose yourself in your form and stay lost for a long time. But it's a welcomed misplacement, calming, simple, fun – when it isn't forced on you.

Bad memories of a harsh punishment bubble to the surface. It gives me pause – for the length of a heartbeat. I lightly step down. The tunnel surrounds me with nearly three feet above and about me. I occasionally ventured out in larger forms. I move down the passageway, soon coming to a thick root wall that parts easily, and of its own accord, as I approach. A light rain dampens the mouth of the tunnel and my fur. As I trot out into the wet I notice the night had taken the chill of the day and made it cold. I hear the rustle of the roots behind me as they close to hide the tunnel. I gallop towards a tall tree, the tallest tree in fact – Red. I claw my way to the top branches where I hunker down onto a twisted limb to survey the land below me briefly. *Sometimes it's better to ask forgiveness than permission.*

I leap away from the safety of Red's outstretched arm. My body is the epicenter of a silent explosion and then an implosion marked by a flash of light. I'm a bird – a falcon. With a screech, I flap to give myself altitude and head east. My house is about a twenty-minute flight west of the city of Philadelphia. Not my home, but I was with the city at its founding and feel a certain amount of fondness for it. And, as cities tend to be, it's a draw for a horde of unsavory elements, and thus, a constant source of reason to engage in my hobby. I want to lose myself in my work – forbidden as it is by *Them*. *Well, more like against orders*. I hadn't been told to patrol, but then again, I haven't been told not to patrol either. Sit down. Stand up. Go here. Go there. Don't draw attention to yourself. The mission is what matters. Wait for orders. *Wait for orders. They* knew, *They* must have known before I was even chosen that waiting is not something I do well. So, really, this is on *Them*, not me.

A portal would have been quicker. I've been to the city hundreds of times; it would have been no trouble. But portals are noisy and leave a lot of wake. Besides, I like to fly. I pass through the rain in about ten minutes and am into the city after another ten minutes. I don't know if the term "acting shady" translates into bird form, but I keep looking over my wings to make sure nothing is following me. I don't know why I'm so worried. I try to calm my self, but something is still tingling my senses, like a fly on a spider web. But am I the spider or the fly? *You have time*, I remind myself. *A quick run out and back again, They'll never know.*

I've noticed that They have a harder time tracking me or finding me when I change. It's as if They are looking for Aedan, and when I'm not him, or even when I am him, because who the hell am I, They can't lock on. Of course, when They do, questions follow about why They couldn't find me. *I've got time.*

I come in for a landing on a three-story low rent. I twitch my head this way and that before stepping behind a chimney. In a flash, I'm me again. I feel lighter. Actually, I'm heavier now, but lighter in a Zen-like way. My troubled mind is already quieter. "You have time, enjoy this." I lean my head back and inhale and exhale slowly. There's the thrill. I'm not saying this serves an addiction – but I'm not not saying that either. "Rebelling, at your age? Why is this still exciting?" I tell myself it serves a purpose. *They* focus on the Big Bad, but little bads are important too and need to be dealt with. But, "Don't draw attention to yourself," I mutter as I stand and cross to the edge of the building.

That's a big rule – bigger, I think, than "wait for orders", or at least that's always been my impression. So, again, this is on *Them*, not me. I crouch down and let all my senses out for a run. Magic – *I wish I had a better word for it* – it's all around us, but when you draw it to you, or when you pass from one plane or dimension to another, it clings to you. You create a wake, and ripples, like a swimmer. Given time, it will pass, but while it swirls around you, it can be spotted like tire tracks in the dirt by a trained eye.

I'm better than a trained eye – I've got trained everything, and a ripple isn't the only tell. Much like the flash with shapeshifting, depending on what you do with it, using that energy to manipulate the physical world has other side effects. Smells, sometimes sour, sometimes sweet, and sound, often a faint crackle like static, can give you away. If you're a casual user or an innocent traveler among dimensions, you've got nothing to fear. But if, on the other hand, you're up to no good – it's how I find you. I try not to hunt in the same location too many times in a row – it draws attention. But this is a good spot. The theater is a few blocks away and a couple of run-down, but excellent places to eat, so even though it's a chilly night and it's a neighborhood where you keep both eyes open while walking, it remains a busy place.

Cars and people pass below me. The sounds of the city grow sharper as night completely asserts itself. I'm looking for trouble. I want it. I need it. I'm looking forward to a fight. The anticipation is euphoric. My senses tingle. The sudden spike in the sour scents around me tells me something is afoot.

A shuffle below me catches my attention. Almost falling over each other in their haste, three men advance down the alley towards the main road. "Quiet!" Echoes up the walls.

"Shush!"

"You shush!"

"Both youse shut up."

A giggle pulls my focus up the alley to a young couple. They're stopped at the mouth of the alley. Bundled against the chill with coats, hats, and each other. They hang on each other, enjoying the night and the prospects of more to come – a large dumpster blocks their view of the oncoming danger. Their pause grows into a linger, and, given the long kiss and groping hands, I'm not entirely surprised when they sidestep into the alley using the brick wall for support. The three from the other direction are slow and crouching like lions stalking a gazelle, and fall silent as they approach the dumpster. I wait to be sure.

A car with a blinding set of headlights approaches. The couple shades their eyes and takes half a step back further into the alley to avoid the intense light as the car drives by. The couple rubs their eyes and laugh – about the absurdly bright lights, or maybe over the embarrassment of being spotted.

Before better judgment can take root, the three pounce. With a nimbleness that belied his ample frame, the shortest of the three leaps up onto the dumpster and bounces over the heads of the young couple, landing on the sidewalk just in front of them. He produces a handgun and gestures for the two to move further into the alley, his two companions making sure the lovers comply.

I have my proof. I step off the edge of the building; my hand slips into my sleeve as I speed towards the ground. With a quick flick, I send a small, flat stone ahead of me. It strikes the cement with a clink. A rush of air whooshes up towards me, catching me as I fall and easing my descent. I step out of the vortex as it dissipates in a gust that sends trash and debris down the length of the alleyway. It wasn't a quiet entrance, but I wasn't going for one. I hold still as the three begin to whisper among themselves.

"That was not nothin' -"

"Go, I've got this."

Shuffling follows as the group moves further inward. The wind had toppled some of the boxes and trashcans, and I can see that one of the muggers has broken off to investigate the strange noise. Obviously not a fan of horror movies – but then again, when your life is a horror movie.

I remain still. The darkness obscures me. I watch as the one makes his way down the alley, his head twitching, his eyes darting. Up ahead, the usual terror banter plays out. The woman cowers on cue, pleading for her life, offering everything, even her virtue, if they let them go. The boy, silent, but brave despite the odds, has planted himself firmly between the girl and their foes.

The mugger approaching me is in a dark jumpsuit like a mechanic would wear. In fact, I can see now that his name is displayed in an easy-to-read script within a white oval. I wait a moment more and then whisper, "Sammy."

Sammy turns sharply, but before he can register how the darkness has spoken his name, I attack. I rush forward and plant a palm strike in the middle of his chest. Sammy stumbles back but remains on his feet. I follow up with a sidekick that sends him reeling and toppling onto his rear. The noise grabs the attention of his friends, all of whom come running at me. I reach into my sleeve and pull out a thin stick about the length of my thumb.

Before I can do anything with it, there's a crack, and a bullet hits my chest. I allow myself to fall back, vanishing once more into the din of the alley.

"What was that!? Dan, Andy, did you see him?" Sammy shouts from the ground.

"Get on your feet and stop embarrassing yourself." The man with the gun shoves Andy. "Get him up. We've got work to do."

While their attention is on Sammy, I creep a few steps closer. It's time to know what I'm dealing with. I lift my hand, the motion catches Dan's attention, and he fires again. This time the bullet goes way wide. I snap the twig and open my palms. The pieces begin to glow and levitate, become a small glowing orb, which suddenly races forward and explodes in a flash when it strikes Dan.

In the wake of the light, all three of the muggers double over in pain. Within seconds, they begin to change. Their clothes tear. Arms and legs elongate. Shoulders become bony. Their facial features become sharp, each with a pointed and prominent chin. Their flesh takes on a reddish-brown hue. I recognize them at once.

These are cambions - the offspring of a human and a succubus or incubus. They're born looking like humans; often, as children, they'll have a mean streak, but they become fully aware of what they are at puberty. Young ones tend to, though not always, travel in packs. Their one goal: impregnate humans to spread their demon spawn. They are fast but not abnormally strong. About twelve feet stand between me and the couple, both of which, out of fear or misplaced curiosity, have not moved from where they've tucked in next to the dumpster. The twitching and moaning come to an abrupt stop.

Dan's long talons, good for slashing, were not especially fit for holding a gun. He awkwardly shakes off the firearm and then looks up. As it turns out, they all look up and right at me. With their human form suppressed, they had full access to their other demon skills – which meant much better night vision and a nose for magic. I had forgotten about that. Dan lets loose a screech, very reminiscent of a command, which echoes down the alley. Sammy and Andy rush forward and are on me before I can blink. They tackle me, howling into my face, but hold off on inflicting pain.

Dan approaches.

The thing about cambions is that they're all out of proportion. Their heads are too small. Their arms and legs too long. Fingered talons made for hooking, stabbing, and ripping. A tall, crooked body made to loom over prey. In all, they're made to ensnare and engulf while they rape and impregnate you. They aren't made for wrestling, and their enlarged genitals make for easy targets. I kick as Dan comes within striking distance. As he roars and stumbles back, I pull and roll to my right, dumping Sammy onto Andy.

I'm on my feet. Leading them away is not an option; at one will remain behind to finish the work they had started. So, I place myself between the couple and them. Again, it's Sammy and Andy who come at me first – there's hardly a chance to raise my hands to block the first swipes. Claws rake over my forearms and face. I feel a jab at my side, but it fails to penetrate my coat. I duck the second onslaught, slide back, and spin forward with an elbow to Sammy's face, which drives his head into the brick wall. I then grab him by the neck and fling him into Andy.

Dan is suddenly in my face. A grin is a human facial expression. On a cambion, it's grotesque. It's a moment before the pain registers. His claws dig into my side. He reaches up to strike with his free hand, but I catch it. We strain against our opposing strengths. And then, in a surprise to the both of us, I head-butt him. I feel his bony forehead cut into me – for his part, his surprise gives me a better opening. I bring up my knee fast and hard, catching him just under his ribcage. He drops back, gasping for air. I stumble away from the wall. As I do, I reach into the pocket with the wooden cylinder and pull it out. I touch two of the runes, and there's a soft click, like gears locking into place. Then, the cylinder extends into a six-foot staff.

"You're not winning this," I say – well, huff with an extremely gravelly voice. I'm winded. That stab had taken a lot out of me, on top of which it's now burning. They don't buy the stern tone. They laugh – the demon version of such a thing – and charge. I brace and swing fast. I parry one claw, a second, a third. I strike back, clubbing - Sammy, (I'm not sure - I'd lost track) on the head hard enough that he falls to the ground. I'm body checked into the wall by another one, but duck the fury swipes meant for my face. I bring my staff up between his legs, hit and push the cambion into his friend, who is just now pulling himself up from the ground. I press another rune on the shaft, and a point forms at one end. I aim and let loose. The spear skewers them both. In unison, they howl. They drop to their knees. The air around them wavers, and then darkness envelops them.

The one I assume to be Dan stares at me. Nothing precedes the explosion of speed. One second he's six or seven feet away, and then, that same second, he's at my throat. We struggle, him trying to wrap himself around me, and me, pulling at his limbs and punching as I can. We spin - a deadly dance - eventually falling away from one another. I hit one side of the brick alleyway and he the other. He charges. This time I flick out my boleen and dive forward to meet him. I catch him across the throat. I feel the hooked knife-edge catch, and then I yank – his head is almost pulled from his body. His body refuses to drop. I approach from behind and use the boleen to finish the job. His head comes away easily. His body, like that of his companions, wavers and then vanishes in darkness.

I take a step back. The night isn't over just yet. During the fight, any fight, you're focused on your target, but on a subconscious level at least you are aware of your surroundings. I couldn't help but notice how the couple didn't run during any of the open windows I had given them. I see why now. I turn and step towards the couple. I'm doing my best not to look battered, and I don't want to startle him any more than he already has been, so I hold back a few feet. "You should go," I say.

The young man nods but is unable to move because the young woman has stayed put.

"It's over," I command. I'm in no mood for the staring contest, so I reach for her. At the same time, she pushes the young man away and springs for me. Her body contorts into its true form. She lunges for my chest, with her fingers rapidly becoming knives, but I'm ready, and I drive the boleen down onto her head, cleaving it in two. Her body hits me, shifting me back a few steps, but my hands firmly wrap around the handle of my knife planted in her skull and push the blade down firmly. The body quivers, and then she and the gore vanish as did her companions'.

They'd be back, eventually, maybe. They'll be new to their "hell" and will find many much larger, much meaner creatures to deal with on their journey back to this realm – assuming a gatekeeper even allows them back. "Hmm?" I examine the spot where the female had stood before me. I pass my hand through the air. I sniff. *Or maybe not their first trip to the homeland.* I stiffly make my way over to where the males had been dispatched. There's pain as I stoop to touch the cement of the alley floor. *They had jobs – I think they've been here a while.* So many questions starting with "why" scroll through my mind. *But first.* I step over to the young man and offer a hand to him. He's dazed and confused. "You're safe," I was going to add a few more comforting statements – even had all my words ready - but as he gets to his feet, he catches a good look at my face.

I look the way I do because it protects my skin, but also in case I am spotted while on an excursion like this; I mean who's going to believe anyone who retains the presence of mind to go to the police. In this case, however, after witnessing what he did, it's too much for him. He yells, stumbles back, and runs for his life.

"There isn't enough therapy," I mutter in sympathy. Granted, the nightmares he will undoubtedly have are better than the fate that cambion had in mind for him, still - no "thank you." It hurt my feelings. Which I immediately forget as pain claws up my side as I turn. I inhale sharply. My face and arms are sore, but my side burns with pain, and taking in that deep breath did not help. I'm pretty sure a rib is broken; the bleeding has slowed and will stop in a few more minutes – the magic of the coat speeding up my healing abilities. But the pain will last a bit longer – and I am not entirely upset by that.

I place my hand over the wound and press. A fresh wave of agony washes over me, and I close my eyes as I sigh both in relief and discomfort. I feel the need to remind myself that I'm not a masochist. The hunt gives me the semblance of control, but the pain reminds me I'm alive – that I'm actually a part of this world of blood, brick, and smartphones. I'd savor longer, but it's time to go.

What had been their plan? I wonder. A female cambion is rare, rarer still for her to be working with a pack of male cambion. *Did that young man have the misfortune of gaining the attention of two separate groups? Or possibly they were from the same family unit?* The idea was probably to rape that poor guy several times to make sure he'd be a carrier. Human biology is pretty good at resisting being implanted, hence the reason for engulfing and holding on, or in this case, a gangbang. Once they were sure he was infected, they'd have him impregnate the female cambion and then set him loose to unwittingly spread the spawn to others. *Still, family unit or not - to be working together like that.* And then a scarier thought comes to me: *How had so many been allowed to cross over? Something's not right.* I resist the voice in my head reminding me that I'm here avoiding being sent on a mission.

But, my avoidance had worked out. That man would have a normal life, regardless of the expense of his future therapy sessions. I knew it had worked out for the best. "You did good, Aedan," I mentally pat myself on the shoulder. It had worked. I'm sore – and I'll be sore for a few days, but I feel better — more clear-headed. I set the boleen back in its sheath and stiffly bend to retrieve my staff. I touch runes, shrinking it back down to its cylinder size.

It's then that I hear the clapping.

Chapter 4

The sound doesn't seem to be coming from any one direction. It echoes off the walls of the alley, first sounding like it's ahead of me and then behind. And then I feel the crackle of something powerful, something big, pushing itself into our world. I hold the wooden cylinder tightly, my fingers ready. A figure steps out of a shadow. It's the boy from earlier this afternoon - hoodie, jeans, and all. His clapping abruptly comes to a halt. He takes a step in my direction but fades out of sight – and a breath later, fades back with hardly two feet between us. He looks up at me. His hood back just far enough for me to see his face. Despite the pale skin and white-blonde hair, his expression is dark, his eyes hold me in a death stare of seriousness.

And then he smiles.

My blood runs cold. Every ounce of me cries out in unanimous fear – *Run!* But you don't run when you're caught in the gaze of a leopard. You stand perfectly still and hope they lose interest. There's a silence between us. I grow more nervous the longer it goes on. And, damn me, but this triggers my defense in such situations. "Is this like a therapy session where you're waiting for me to speak first?" I flick my free hand between us.

I sense his will but am powerless to move. Like water pulling away from the shore only to swell into a wave and crash back against the land, he throws me back with a thought. I hit the brick wall hard and land with a groan. The pain in my side erupts, but I no longer savor its reminder of life. I blink and cough. I'm momentarily dazed, and it takes a second before I realize the cylinder has rolled free. Against him, it would have done little, but there was comfort to have it in my hand. From the ground, I hold up a hand in peace and bow my head. "Great Lugh, how may I be of service?" I show all deference in my tone. Lugh finds this amusing.

"You know, I waited for you to follow me this afternoon. I waited and waited until I realized not even you would be taking so long. I assumed then that you didn't understand my rather obvious clue. So I went back to that school of yours, only to find that you weren't there either."

"I got distracted."

"Obviously." Lugh snorts and comes halfway closer. "I looked for you - this close it was hard not to catch your scent - and then, what do I spy coming out of your hovel, but a cat that wasn't a cat." He waggles his finger back and forth.

I'm annoyed and in a great deal of pain. I can't help myself. "My life is my own as long as it doesn't interfere with any tasks given to me."

"Slave!" Lugh snaps and thrusts a finger at my chest. "Is that what you think? That you have something that we have not given to you?"

A dagger of ice shoots at me; it strikes my right shoulder and pins me to the brick. Despite his diminutive stature, I'm terrified. Out of all of *Them*, Lugh is the one I fear the most – for good reason. If he were human, he'd be on a regiment of lithium and olanzapine.

"Here I am," his tone is calm again, almost playful. He looks around, frowning at his surroundings. "Only to bring you a message... a warning," he sighs, "To take time out of my day to remind you..."

His eyes come back to my own, and in a blink, he rushes towards me. I cringe. But no attack comes. Instead, he spins himself around and slides down the wall to sit next to me.

"I know we haven't been the best of friends, you and I. But I think you'd be a little more grateful for me coming out of my way to see you." He "playfully" fist-bumps my shoulder – the one with the ice shard. "Here," he waves his hand, and the ice melts, but the wound remains. "Better?" He pats my head.

From somewhere, I find the courage to grit my teeth and stand. "Thank you." I keep my head bowed. "Please, what is your message?" I feel the surge of power again and brace for it, but it dissipates. Apparently, he changed his mind. Instead, he stands and takes me by my shoulders.

"Daddy's in town, club and all."

I blink in disbelief. *He never walks among the mortals, not since the Formorians.*

Lugh smirks and cocks his head to the side. "He's seen something in that cauldron of his, something he doesn't like, something in the ether," his fingers dance majestically. "Someone's breaking the rules - or is going to break the rules." He winks and steps back.

This feels like a trap. *Why tell me? Is he even allowed to tell me? What's he up to?* "And you felt I needed to be told this?"

Lugh scoffs and lifts his arms to indicate the alley.

"I -" I try to defend my actions but don't get far.

"I spend a great deal of my valuable time keeping an eye on you, your brothers and sisters, making sure you all remain aware of your place." He points a finger at me. "Keep your mind on the task at hand. Get it done. Now, rather than later. Do you understand?"

"I -" I try again.

"Unless "thank you" is the very next thing you're going to say - shut up." He waits a moment and then, with a disappointed frown, tuts and raises an eyebrow.

Belittled and annoyed, I decide I don't need to defend my actions and instead press the issue he has brought up. "Keeping an eye? More like informing on us. We have served -" he cuts me off with a raised finger to his lips. His anger pulses. I brace again, but again the power dissipates. In its place, he laughs.

"I see why she likes you so much. And, point of fact," his eyes go dark, "not all of you have served faithfully." He pauses and smiles broadly, "Which is why I'm here." He nudges my wounded shoulder again. "It's better for everyone that someone keeps an eye on you lot. Oh, the shouting and finger pointing when one of you steps out of line. So I take the time," he lays a hand gently on his chest and makes a solemn expression. "It's a burden that I gladly suffer. Besides, I like our little visits." He bends so he can look into my downcast eyes. He smiles. "Aww, still a little sore from last time?"

I don't answer.

"You left me little choice."

You've already pushed your luck, I tell myself. *What the hell.* "Thank you, Mighty Lugh, but if there's something of importance that I need to know, I'm sure Brigit will tell me – without the games." There's almost no warning this time.

"You are indentured to *us*!" He shouts. Fingers dig into my chest as he lifts me and slams me face-first into the concrete ground. "You have no life, but that which *we* give you," he seethes and brings his foot down onto my back.

"Which is it," I cough, "slave or indentured? Because they're not the same thing."

He kicks me, and I roll more than halfway down towards the back of the alley. He leaps and comes down next to me. His hands are on me again, this time digging into my back. I sail through the air and stop when my face meets a brick wall. If this is it, I'm going down fighting. My mind claws its way out of the fog of pain. My limbs tremble with adrenaline, but also because I'm pretty sure my brain is misfiring after that hit. I get myself to my feet, somehow, and face him.

His hands ball into fists and become engulfed in flames.

I'm not sure who's more surprised that I block his punch. For just a moment, his flaming fist scorching my hand, we stop and stare at each other - and then he head butts me. I fall to the ground. Lugh looms over me, his presence far exceeding the small college boy before me. In a swift motion, he lifts his hands to strike – but then stops. We both, he first and then I, become aware of someone at the mouth of the alley. A pleasant humming and the sound of hands rummaging around in a trashcan reach us. I can't place the tune, but his humming comes to a crescendo as he lifts something he likes out of the can and holds it aloft.

Lugh pauses and regards the homeless man for a moment and then, accepting the distraction, changes his mind about killing me and steps back. He pulls his hood back up and drives his hands into his pockets. "Don't mess up, Aedan. Do exactly as you are told. Your mission is your own. The burden is yours. You never know which of your brothers and sisters are against you, so I suggest getting it done and quickly." He then points at himself. "All-knowing. All-powerful. We're all watching you. All the time." In a flash and a whirling vortex, he's gone. I wait until the trash in the alley settles before I pull myself to my feet. I retrieve my cylinder. The homeless guy has wandered or run off. I wondered what he had seen. I don't expect him to go to the police any more than that poor young man.

The scuffle with Lugh has taken a lot out of me. And I don't mind showing it – especially since I'm the only one around. *Sit and wait until I'm strong enough to change?* I look up the walls of the alley. No windows, but between the two fights, there has been a lot of noise. I don't want to wait around for someone brave enough to investigate now that things have quieted down. *I could teleport...No.* There are many ways of getting around when you can tap into that level of energy known as magic, each with its own dangers, limitations, and drawbacks. A portal will do - not as discrete, but it will do. I limp to the end of the alley. A utility hole cover, a brick wall, and two wooden crates stacked on top of one another in front of a rusty door blocked any further movement. I fish around in my sleeve, feeling for one of the tiny pockets. I pull out another small stone, this one about the size of a chalk stick. I learned this spell from an old German woman. She hated leaving her house.

I draw a circle on the brick wall with the stone and then press it against the center of that symbolic gesture with the palm of my hand. "öffnen," I whisper. I step back as the wall ripples out from where the rock remains pressed against the wall. There's a crack, like that of the edge of an ice cliff giving way. And then a rumble, followed by a second crack. Electric arcs of purple sprawl out from the center and along the wall. Within the circle I have drawn, the bricks begin to spiral in on themselves, with each brick grinding against the other until a tunnel forms. I worry about the wall's integrity, but as this is probably the first time anyone has pushed a portal through this location, I let it go. I take a quick glance over my shoulder. This is not a quiet or subtle way of travel. I lean to my left and touch the wall of the building. "Sorry," I say. The occupants of these two buildings are going to have to deal with oddness for a bit. I wasn't worried. They'll chalk it up to a haunting or the building being old, or just plain ignore it. In a couple of days it will be forgotten. I close my eyes, take the very important deep breath, and step into the tunnel.

My next steps are in my backyard. I look behind me to make sure the portal closes. It's an unpleasant way to travel – lots of pulling and stretching. I often wonder why Erna used it. I don't linger. My yard is well protected from eyes, and the neighbors aren't the nosy types, but a small sonic boom might be enough to catch their attention. So I rush inside through the backdoor that leads into the kitchen. I take a breath that feels like the first one in a while. Lugh was not playing around. His presence all but confirms what I've been feeling. Though I don't usually see him before I see Brigit – *he did seem particularly irked and impatient.* The plate of cookies on the counter tempts me, but I need to get out of uniform. In a few steps, I'm through the living room and down the stairs to my workroom. I unbutton my duster – the corresponding clothing dissolves into motes of light that are absorbed by the green coat – and hang it on its hook in the armoire. The calm I had found in those few moments after my fight with the cambion is returning.

"Oooh, you look like you've lost a few branches. Stood against the storm, though, very nice." I picture Green with a coy, sexy smile – but then again, that's how I always picture Green.

"Sap," Red says gruffly. "Sap for gashes."

He always offers me sap when I come home injured. I'm not sure if that's a tree thing or just a Red thing. "I'll be fine. Thank you." I dress in my robe and bunny slippers.

"Much too quickly. I enjoy your bark. So like a sapling, yet aged like a deep root. It confuses and intrigues me." Green twitters in what passes for a laugh.

"Someone's here," Blue says, not so much in alarm but more as a "by the way".

Lugh - is my initial thought. The night is already feeling endless. I sigh at the loss of my calm. I scramble up and carefully set the door closed behind me as I enter into my living room — *round three, fight*.

Though not who I expected to find in my living room, I'm not entirely surprised. She's beauty in form. She's turned so I can only see her back, a lovely piece of creation, strong lean muscles framed by the open back of her short, black cocktail dress. Her arms, like her back, are firm, slender, yet most obviously feminine. Her raven-black hair just reaches her shoulders. As she turns, I see that her face is buried behind my copy of *The Count of Monte Cristo*. Her eyes, crystal blue and piercing, appear above the lip of the book. It's picturesque.

"I've been looking for you."

Her words, quiet but powerful, full of authority, and none of the arrogance. I don't react until she snaps the book shut. I hope she didn't see me flinch. "Brigit," I say, "looking lovely as always."

"Of course," she says, her accent lyrical. She doesn't say anything further as she turns to put the book back on the empty shelf behind her.

"Interesting reading?"

She doesn't answer.

It worries me that she's looking at the pile of clothing I had left on the floor. And then I catch her glance at my cut and bruised face - and I'm sure she notices the gash on my side because my robe is hanging open. I want to, but don't move, for fear it will draw more attention. At the moment, the plan is to pretend everything is fine and hope she doesn't ask about my very obvious wounds. I start to sweat. I recall the time my father had caught me in the woods with Aideen – he laughed and thought no more on it, but we were embarrassed. Brigit isn't laughing, but that does not change the fact that I'd been caught doing something naughty. I try to find that fire of indignation that had swelled within me while Lugh was interrogating me, but there isn't even a flicker. As always, she makes me feel like that insecure, skinny teen boy from so long ago.

"Nice slippers," she smiles and comes forward to sit on the left side of the couch.

That smile – playful or knowing? My throat is tight. I swallow and find my voice. "Wh-what, these old things?"

She pats the seat next to her.

I casually close my robe and come around the couch, but don't sit next to her; instead, I sit on the furthest cushion.

"I have an assignment for you."

This is curious. "Delivering it in person? A pleasant surprise -"

"Not that unusual," she says quickly, her eyes darting to the door. She turns to the side table and brings back the pad of sticky notes and a pen. "I like to keep tabs on our... agents," she speaks as she jots something down. She pulls off the top note and hands it to me.

"Wissahickon, 3," I read aloud. "That's all?"

A brief expression of nervousness passes across her face as I say this – it was momentary, but definitely there. "As I've said before, that is all the information you get. It's not all the information I have." She drops the pad and pen on the cushion between us. "We can't make it too easy for you, now can we?" She smiles, her eyes catching mine – holding them, I find I can't look away. "Don't go thinking above your station now. It's enough for you to know that there is more going on than what I tell you." She gives a slight nod.

I have a snarky comment ready, but she stands up abruptly and moves towards the door. Her steps, powerful without being forced, her heels clicking over the wood and slate floor, seem to echo without end.

"It should be fast. In fact, the quicker, the better in this case. Do what you need to make sure you get a positive outcome. You understand me?" Her eyes are both stern and pleading.

Slightly different advice from what Lugh had given me. Less emphasis on – you are alone. Doom. Doom. Doom. Do I tell her that he paid me a visit? She's a god, she must know. I nod, confused – this has been a very odd night - something tells me not to speak. There are only a few times in all the years I've know her where Brigit has looked worried, and this is one of those times.

And that's it. The visit is over just that quickly. She returns my nod, opens, and shuts the door behind her. I'm after her within a heartbeat. Anger, frustration, it's all there. Always simmering, boiling since Lugh knocked me around. I had sensed this was coming. Feared it – as I always do. Like walking down a long, dark hallway, knowing something is going to jump out at you from the shadows, waiting for it to happen, and then it does. You know it's coming, prepare for it, and you still jump. You still feel scared, stupid, and relieved at the same time. I want more than just a jump scare; I deserve more. I open the door, knowing there would be nothing on the other side except the misty night. I shut the door and turn my back to it. I glance at the note I had left on the arm of the couch. "Wissahickon, 3 – what the hell am I supposed to do with that?" Despite the urgency of her request, I give serious thought to procrastinating.

Chapter 5

Thought becomes action as my mind and body cry out for alcohol. *Procrastination is my favorite pastime* – I think, as I stand before my chosen temple of inebriation. It's a three-story green and white building near the end of a block in South Philly. There are no windows at street level. Next to the double door is a faded white wall where the word ALAN'S, is written in bright green script outlined in brown and yellow. The intricate swirls and lines of the logo are impressive and eye-catching – and they should be, as I painted them. There's a single light above the door, but otherwise, the street is dark. The occasional car drives by.

I can hear the faint sound of cheering. I steel myself and cross the street. As I open the door, the muffled noises become a wave that forces me to pause before walking through. Well placed lighting, a couple of wall-mounted screens, subtle bar decorations, and an excited crowd glued to the sets greet me – this is a happy place. I wonder why I favor it so much. The bar itself takes up less than a quarter of the room. The rest of the ample space is filled with a small, just off the floor, handmade stage, some dance space, and a number of tables. It's easy to make out the bar's former incarnation as a restaurant.

There's an unused corner, where the mahogany bar bends to meet the wall; here, a single stool is left unattended. This is my seat. I'd claimed it years ago, and the owner has been kind enough to indulge me. The bar itself has only one other guest, a tall, thin man with at least three day's worth of scruff on his face. Alan, the owner, is there. He chats up the guy while refilling his mug of beer. It's an odd scene only because the pair are so removed from the other patrons' constant noise and motion and the two waitresses in the background. They stand out like an island in the open ocean, seen but easily overlooked. But I suppose no odder than the cliché tall, dark, and handsome guy in the long coat sitting in the corner – the navy-blue sweater and jeans - both of which have seen better days – perhaps taking away some of my mystique. But hey, odd things happen in bars. "Did I just think of myself as handsome? Yes, I did. Now stop talking to yourself."

Alan steps away from the scruffy guy and notices me. I nod. He grabs a glass and a bottle of amber-colored mana from under the bar and heads in my direction. "Rough night, I see." He says as he spots the still healing claw marks across my face. The tumbler is set down, and he fills it with whiskey. "On-call?" he asks.

"No Drew tonight?" I need more to drink before I talk about tonight, so I avoid the question by putting my foot in my mouth.

Alan's face sinks. "No, um, he's – no, not tonight."

Shit, strike one. "Sorry. Off again?"

"Maybe,"

While he's making up his mind on whether or not he's going to tell me more, I down the whiskey. Pleasant warmth washes over me. Whiskey is whiskey, you're not going to mistake it for rum or beer, but within the family, when you compare whiskey to whiskey, the differences are telling. I call this particular member: Dignified. While my eyes are closed and savoring, I tap the bar.

Alan pours me another. "You know, I didn't even hear you come in," he says by way of avoiding my question, "That guy over there, he's funny. He has this dry, observational humor." He glances over his shoulder and then back at me and spoke, this time in almost a whisper. "He's sad, though. My guess is troubled past."

"Bartender's intuition?" I ask, and down the second glass – I tap the bar again.

Alan sighs, a shadow of concern falling over his face, but refills the glass. "I'd ask him over, but I know you'd hate that. I think the two of you would have a lot in common."

"Trying to set me up?"

"I know better." He smirks.

I draw the glass to my lips, eyes closed, but pause. I hear the distinctive sound of a cap screwing back onto a bottle. Quiet rage grips me. "I only drink when I'm here, but when I'm here, I drink a lot. Leave the bottle." I open my eyes. Alan is wearing a mixture of feelings: hurt and surprise, with a little anger of his own thrown in.

He sets the bottle down. "I'm going to check in with Millie and Georgia," Alan steps away and flags down his waitresses.

Shit, strike two.

The scruffy guy at the bar gets up; I lose him in the crowd. There's a funny thing about being watched that sometimes happens – especially if you don't notice it at first. Even if you overlook the act, the absence can create a sense of something missing, something different, like shifting wind. When I first learned to drive, I had this sense that the instructor was quietly judging me. That's what this felt like, like the instructor stepped out of the car. "I'm doing this my way," I say to whoever's listening. Being watched, not being watched, this does not stop me from finishing my drink – or pouring another.

Stay focused. I remind myself that I'm here to drink to my anger at Brigit. *No. Not even her.* I think, in some ways, she's just as trapped. *It's Lugh, that psychopath.* And I'm not mad at him - I'm scared of him. *What the hell was all that about Father being here? Why tell me? And not jumping at the chance to turn me in? He wasn't that nice the last time he caught me moonlighting.* The memory is not a good one, and I drum on the bar top to chase the images away. *I don't need him reminding me about my obligations.* I raise my glass to my lips but only sip down half. As I place it back on the bar, I wave over Alan – who ignores me and goes about filling an order that Millie has just brought over. So I wave a bit more emphatically. His shoulders slump, and he looks at me with a sour expression. He expands on this with an irritated roll of his eyes as he makes his way back over to me.

"Explain to me again why I care about you?"

"I've had a bad day," I say and sip half again of what's left in my glass.

He fills my glass from the nearly empty bottle. "What was it this time?" Alan checks over his shoulder to make sure no one is within earshot.

"Cambion. Four of them."

He thinks for a moment. "The sex beasts?"

I nod and gulp down the amber mana. I can feel it now; the warmth has become numbness. I've found my calm.

"I didn't realize they ran in packs," Alan rubs the back of his head, "Every time I talk to you, I learn to fear the dark even more."

"Good,"

"Should I be worried?"

"Always."

He hesitates, locking eyes with me for just for a second, before very reluctantly filling my glass again. "I guess you can crash upstairs -"

"Your hospitality will not be necessary," I say, but admit to myself that flying home is going to be interesting. Alan owns the building, and he's the closest thing I have to family. I don't need to crash at his place, but he may need to let me sit until my head clears. He's done so before. His commute to work is better than mine. He lives on the top floor, a very spacious loft. A high traffic day is if he runs into either of his two tenants from the second floor on the way down to the bar.

"At least leave me this last little bit, then. I'm behind on my orders."

I catch his distracted gaze. I reach up and take the bottle from him.

"No, really -"

I hold up a hand to quiet him. A flat stone slides into my hand from up my sleeve. I press it to the bottle. A moment later, there's a glow, which Alan shuffles to the side to block.

"Dude,"

Had anyone been paying attention, I'm sure his attempts to block the light are far more conspicuous. However, the glow subsides, and no one is any the wiser. I hand the bottle back. "Been distracted, hmm?" He turns away and sets the now full bottle back under the bar; his slow return tells me he knows what I will ask about. "Drew?" I look around again, and there's definitely no Drew in the building. *Well, he could be upstairs, but I don't think so.*

"It's not like we were married."

"Two years, though," I forget about my drink and lean in to speak with Alan. "What was it this time?" Alan's on-again-off-again relationship with Drew is honestly the reason I don't have a television. He begins to fidget, but I'm not letting this go – it's impacting my drinking. "Alan, was he stealing from you again?"

"He said he was bored," he blurts and tries to play it off with a smile. "I get it..."

There's more to that, but he doesn't continue. I very much see in his face the scared boy I had first met and not the young man standing before me. I already didn't like Drew, but I'm beginning to hate him now. Alan grabs my glass and downs the whiskey. He doesn't drink whiskey, and it's obvious. Thankfully there's a swell in the crowd's cheering to hide his coughing.

When his breathing becomes normal, I say, "What do you 'get'?" I find his reluctance irritating but hold my tongue. For about three seconds – a record. "Don't make me drag this out of you. I've had a long night, and you're killing my buzz."

He's gripping the glass tightly but sets it back onto the bar top gently. "He's young," Alan shrugs. "He doesn't see the point in a register full of money and not traveling monthly to Costa Rica. He wanted to party, and you know, that's just not me. He wanted a nightly rave; it's a bar, after all, you know – he," Alan's sigh is heavy, "he really hated it when I used the word 'responsibility,'"

I know he doesn't want me to see him cry, so I distract him. I bang my fist on the bar and waggle an angry finger in his face. "Listen to me. You're twenty-four; those two years you have over Drew do not make you an old man. Give Millie a raise and hand over the bar and kitchen to her for a long weekend every once in a while. Also, Drew's an asshole. And third, you're as pale as a ghost. Get some sun. Show yourself off. Have some meaningless sex. And then find yourself someone new. Someone better."

Alan nods soberly as he absorbs the lecture.

I give him a moment and then add, "Do you want me to turn Drew into a frog?"

It catches him off guard. He laughs. "Wait, can you really do that?"

I lift an eyebrow.

He rubs the back of his head. "Man, you've got to teach me some of this stuff."

The fact is, most ordinary people can touch the energy from which magic draws power. Sometimes this is conscious. Sometimes it's unconscious. Usually, it doesn't manifest itself beyond that vague notion we call a gut feeling. But with training – years of training – some light physical manipulation is possible. *It'd probably take me ten years to teach him a simple push spell.* And then I remind myself of how long I've known Alan. "It's not for you." I give him my standard answer to that request. It's probably overly protective, but the ways of magic are dangerous and counterproductive to an old promise.

"So you say."

Although not happy about me denying him, yet again, he's in a much better mood. I press the pressure point behind my ear. I begin to hum. And then I see the odd look Alan is giving me. "What?"

"Why are you humming that?"

"I heard it earlier, been stuck in my head."

"But you don't know what it is?" he laughs.

"Alan," Millie calls.

Alan goes to her and pours several beers.

Perhaps it's seeing Alan's dedication to his job or my conscience, but I start to feel guilty about what I'm doing. The meeting with Brigit plays in my mind. I pull out the note and set it on the bar. She gave me a name and nothing else. It's not that unusual to get so little out of her; still, this is pushing her typical brevity. I grab the empty tumbler and rattle it back and forth, trying to get Alan's attention. He finishes his order and rushes back over to me.

"Yes," he says with impatience.

I set the glass down on the note. "One more for the road. Please."

"Alright," he picks up the whiskey from under the bar and fills my glass.

I almost don't wait for him to finish before I start to raise the glass.

"Wissahickon?"

"Hmm?" I look down at the note. Brigit's neat handwriting now circled in a watermark.

"Are you looking into the missing woman?"

"What?" The glass is at my lips.

Alan looks around under the bar and then sets down a folded newspaper. He flips it open, scans the headlines, and then points to a small article: "Missing Person Along Wissahickon Trail."

I snatch the paper out of Alan's hand and stare at the inked words. "Shit," I set the glass down and run for the door.

Chapter 6

When I'm tasked it's usually at a point where I need to steal something, or disrupt a ceremony, and sometimes there's a fight – usually there's a fight. It's months, sometimes years of waiting, and then a few days of pain, suffering, and near-death experiences. And I'm tired of it. I'm tired of the game. I'm tired of being a weapon. I'm tired of saving the world from gods acting like five-year-olds. But, if Brigit had just told me this had something to do with a missing person – I probably would have procrastinated, but not as much.

My evening after Alan's consisted of a few phone calls and some research. I'm sure canceling my classes came as a welcomed surprise to my students. The next couple of calls I made were less enjoyable. My snooping leads me to a gas station across a busy street from a police station: a squat rectangle made out of yellow brick that hadn't changed much since the nineteen fifties. The newspaper I'd taken from Alan had helped very little – other than getting my butt off of that bar stool. In all fairness, it had given me a name: Becca Trent. A couple of phone calls later, pretending to be a journalist - I'm always surprised at how well that works – I'd discovered the name of the detective in charge of the investigation: Robert Darren. The paper had labeled this as an abduction, but after speaking with Detective Darren over the phone, I had been told the case was being worked as a simple missing person. I gathered by his tone that he wasn't taking the matter very seriously.

So much of my life is working in the dark that I prefer to have a plan when I have the chance. I have a plan – and I wouldn't say I like it. *There are too many uncontrollable variables in play,* but I remind myself that you can't control what the defenders do when storming a castle. With that pep-talk cheering up my confidence, I cross the street and make my way up the stairs to the police station. Just beyond the glass doors is a spacious room with many chairs, several CCTV cameras, and a bank of payphones. At the front, behind a Plexiglas screen, is the desk sergeant. I pick a chair near the bathrooms and wait. And thus, half of my plan is underway.

Detective Darren strikes me as a man who punches a clock, and I guess he will not be dissuaded from lunch no matter his workload. I arrived early to give myself a half hour to be noticed and then forgotten about. I wanted to blend with the background noise. And I wasn't worried about the surveillance cameras – the talisman I'm wearing will make sure there's plenty of static. As to anyone keeping a physical eye on the visitor's area, I doubt they'll see more than a guy in a sweater and jeans. Next to me, the high school kid is undoubtedly more eye-catching in his black duster, black jeans, black t-shirt, and combat boots. Though his mother sitting next to him reduces his badassness. We glance at each other; I smile at his frown.

As I counted on, the shifting numbers of people in the waiting area help - every five minutes, there's a new face, while many of the old faces become more impatient in body language and volume of voice. It's a pageant you can get lost in, and one I'm sure the sergeant behind the desk has grown numb to.

Sooner than I thought, Darren appears through the keypad locked door to the left of the front desk. He's with another officer, but I keep my eyes on Darren. I watch his movement. I memorize his facial features. I had his voice thanks to our phone conversation, and now I have him. He's through the waiting area and out the front door without a single glance at the people seated there. It's enough. I slip out of my seat and into the bathroom. I check to make sure I'm alone and then lock the door and turn off the lights. It won't help much, but every little bit will make it easier. I need to work fast before I lose this moment of privacy.

I pick a stall for some added concealment. *Just like a cat* – I tell myself, but it isn't. Becoming someone else is difficult to do and maintain. It's like the universe knows you're copying someone and ups the entropy. I picture Darren. The transformation begins with a crackle of air. It's a struggle to pull in a continuous flow of magic. The pipes, the porcelain, the mirrors, and the plastic all diffuses the presence of the energy I need to draw upon. I reach out beyond the small restroom's walls like a child at the beach trying to scoop in more and more sand to use in the construction of a castle. It takes longer, but the familiar tingle begins to spread over my body as the slight rattle of pipes starts to become noticeable.

I emerge several pounds heavier, wearing a cheap suit and the face of Detective Darren. Before I take too many steps away from the bathroom I feel something hot against my leg. I check my pockets and give an angry sigh when I pull out my cellphone. The glass is partially melted, and the casing is warped. "Shit," I drop it in the trashcan that's right there and continue on my way. I take my cue from the original and don't make eye contact with anyone, not even the desk sergeant who is busy with a tall woman in very tight jeans at the moment anyway. The next part of the plan will go one of two ways; either someone will open the door as I get there, or it will remain closed.

The door remains closed.

I admit that there's a bit of me who feels guilty for what I'm about to do. I dig into my pocket and pull out a small bit of root about my thumb's size and thickness - a bit of Red he let me cut off. If I'm going to get caught, this will be it. I press the bit of root to the keypad, "Anois." Several things happen at the same time: The lights waver, the keypad sparks, a few startled people scream, the two uniformed cops become very alert, and the desk sergeant calls out to me. I hear him get up from his chair just as the lights give out completely, cutting illumination to just what pours in through the front glass.

I expect hands to grab me, but when none do, I pull open the door and rush through. I'm greeted by two benches that appeared to have been repurposed from a church, and a pair of very confused and frightened teenagers sit twitching in the flickering lights of the bullpen. Desks are arranged around the room with an office for the captain opposite the two holding cells - whose few occupants are quiet and alert. A couple of detectives are at their desks swearing at their unresponsive computers; many have crowded around a single desk.

"Someone hit a pole, knocked out a transformer or something,"

"It's more than that. I'm telling you, we've been hacked."

"I think he's right. Look -"

"It's not working. Looks more like a power surge."

"It's not. It's like it's scrambled,"

Using the confusion, I do a quick scan and find Darren's desk. Its lack of, well, anything, makes it stand out. There's an inbox with folders, an empty outbox, his computer, one pen, and a pad of paper, and that's it. I sit down. It's useless to use the computer to find what I need. I had used an unlocking spell on the keypad. It had unlocked *all* of the locks – passwords, door locks, everything. But magic being what it is, in a place of metal and wires, it's also gone and scrambled the electricals. I hadn't been counting on the computer anyway. Darren didn't seem the type to use one unless he had to. I open the largest desk drawer and find twelve hanging folders, each labeled with a case number. I begin searching the folders.

"They're all missing persons," I mutter, my eyes glancing up to make sure no one had heard. Noble, I suppose, a man with a quest – but it's usually something an officer would handle, at least initially. But it's all Darren seems to cover - just missing persons, and not one of them has progressed beyond the initial interviews. *He hasn't done any follow-up calls, nothing.* I flip through in my quest and come to a folder with a little handwritten note. "Mom thinks boyfriend, but the dad says he's a good boy – go with dad, don't bother with boyfriend." *Not a noble quest, that's for damn sure.* All the folders are like this: names and numbers, notes to make calls or check this or that place out, but there is no indication that he did any of it. As I close each folder and move onto the next, I grow to dislike this man more and more. At nearly the back of the drawer, I locate a folder, as anemic as the rest, with Becca Trent's name. I glimpse at the inside. I don't know why I was hoping for more, but regardless, I don't have time to read it thoroughly.

Time is running out. The magic will eventually work its way out of the building, and everything will be back to normal. I look up, everyone is still distracted. "You don't care." I tell myself. "Just humans being bad to humans. You barely care about your own mission." I stare at the folders in the desk drawer. "Son of a bitch." I growl and reach for the pen and notepad. In big letters, I write: Do everyone a favor, QUIT. I leave the note on the computer. I snatch up Becca's folder and turn to make my escape - and bump right into Robert Darren.

I believe in coincidences. They happen all the time. You plan a trip to New York, and you happen to run into a friend in that great big city who just happened to have also planned a trip to New York. Or you break up with your girlfriend and then find out she's now dating the guy you get your coffee from every morning. Nothing sinister. Nothing twisted. Just life. However, coincidence checks its hat at the door when I'm on the job. Darren had no reason to be back early from lunch; someone is working against me. I can smell it.

Before the surprise can fade, I clamp my hand over his mouth and grab his arm before he can reach for his gun. I'm wearing a Darren suit, but it's still me underneath – and I'm far stronger than the real Robert Darren.

The thing about coincidences, or not coincidences, is that they can work in your favor too. It's just then that the quiet detainees behind the iron bars notice that their cell doors aren't locked and take advantage of everyone with a badge being distracted. I catch the motion out of the corner of my eye and toss Robert into the lead criminal. They collapse in a tangle of arms and legs. I dash for the door. Once I'm outside, I keep walking and allow the disguise to drop away.

Chapter 7

The abduction location is only a few miles from the station, so I walk. I have another reason for walking. If I'm being tracked, if someone or something is acting against me, magic would only make it easier for them to keep tabs on me. *What am I saying, "if"? I'm certain.* I've been tasked. The job is no longer passive; it's active, which means the opposition is on the move. Someone is definitely playing against me. And the thing of it is, I might never find out who it is. Sometimes the end game is a battle, and sometimes it's just the first to find or destroy something. And then it's over. I receive new orders, go undercover, and it all begins again. But that's the way of it. Well, the way of it since the gods realized that directly fighting each other would only mean the destruction of that which they were fighting over. So, instead, I and those like me, get moved around like chess pieces.

Abduction or not, I feel my interest in this task waning the more I think about why I'm on this walk. I pick up my pace as I cut through Pachella Fields – a crowd is enjoying an off-season baseball game – and then over a fence and into the trees.

Wissahickon is a river and the name of the twenty miles or so of trails along that river. According to the file, Becca's backpack had been found south of Pachella Fields, where the trail crosses a wide creek. There are a few pictures and even GPS coords written in some diligent officer's handwriting - not Detective Darren's. The coords are useless to me, but the description and the pictures are a great deal of help. I'm positive I'll know the spot when I come to it, so I continue south along the trail.

It's peaceful, and it's very easy to forget about the city, a stone's throw in any direction. I can't believe I've never taken advantage of these trails before - for a few moments, I forget about the task at hand. This is what I want. I want to disappear into the woods for a hundred years. I want to make my own choices and be my own person. I miss this. The sound of splashing grabs my attention.

"I'll get you," echoes through the trees. I come to a stop as a young couple runs by me. I don't bother with them; flirting has never changed. I'm looking down a gentle slope to the edge of a wide creek. Stones have been placed in the small river, rising just above the waterline, connecting the trail to both banks. I don't need to check the file. I'm here. Even several days after the abduction, I can feel it, smell it. The air is acidic. My eyes begin to water. It's like running into a burning building. Whoever did this wasn't even trying to cover their tracks. The ground is well-worn and a bit soggy in places. Trees are thin near the water's edge, but press in as you move away. A couple of felled trees make for improvised seating. An older man with a six-foot walking stick, wearing red and blue hiking clothes, is just ending his rest as I sit down.

"Kept it warm for you," he smiles and moves off.

Just as he moves out of sight, another man, younger, in shorts despite the chill, come across the river from the other side.

"Hey," he nods as he goes by.

I move to a new location, choosing a young oak to sit under about six feet back from the tree bench. About two minutes later, a pack of four teens comes jogging down the trail, over the river. One waves at me, and then they're gone.

I move again, this time further back, and wait. A young woman comes by a few minutes later; she makes eye contact with me but keeps on her way. Ten minutes follow before another person appears. A middle-aged man, fit, and by his gear and attire, I gather he's an experienced hiker. He doesn't see me at first and then does a slight double-take. He stops.

"Hey, um, what you doing back there?" He asks politely but with interest.

I stand from my squatting position and move towards him. "Don't be concerned," I hold up the folder and tap the police logo. "Detective Darren," I don't look anything like Robert Darren anymore, but this guy doesn't know that. "There's a suspected abduction that took place here several days ago. I was -" I gesture about.

"Looking for something you might have missed?"

"You a cop?"

"No, just watch a lot of crime shows. I did read about this - a college girl, right? Anything we need to be worried about?"

"Yes, and no. We've got plain-clothed officers up and down the trails. If it's more than an isolated incident, we'll catch the guy." I have no idea if any of that is true, but it sounds like a sensible precaution that Darren should have requested.

"Alright then, sorry to bother you, Officer."

We shake hands, and he goes on his way. I think I have everything I need. I go back to the tree bench and sit. I clear my mind. Or try. The area is disturbed. Something had reached through into our world and taken Becca Trent. This whole sitting area is like shattered glass. I feel it poking against my flesh. The scent of it burns my nose and eyes. I take a deep breath and open the folder. According to the report, Becca's backpack had been left right here. Darren's notes indicate that Meredith Trent, Mother, widow, reported her daughter missing. He states that there's no sign of foul play – although he wrote "fowl" play. According to the mother's statement, there had been no fight between them. Darren writes "Mothers and daughters always fight. I suspect this is a runaway. Probably met up with some friends and accidentally left the bag behind, or maybe on purpose to upset the mother. I will follow up with friends." But his notes end there. My guess is the lack of progress prompted mom to go to the news – though it doesn't seem to have lit a fire under Darren's ass.

I look up at the sound of two people approaching. They come down the shallow incline chatting, say hello, and continue on their way. In just my short time here, I'd seen a number of people cross this section of the trail. The longest time between hikers was about fifteen minutes. I check the file. "Last seen about eleven in the morning," I don't have a watch, but I guess the time to be about half past noon. The conditions aren't exact, but "Someone would have seen, or heard something. This had to have been done quickly, really quickly." *Had she been the target or a victim of opportunity?* An attack of opportunity, another word for coincidence, so the same rule applies – which means she was the target. "So, the question is, why her?" I open the file – "A student at Chestnut Hill," I scan my surroundings. There'll be a focal point. Whatever grabbed her came through at some point. I let my senses loose.

A sycamore, behind the tree bench by about four feet, catches my attention. I stopped asking myself a long time ago whether it was my senses that picked things up or whether it was something tickling my senses in order to grab my attention. A mental version of "Hey, over here, stupid." In this case, just in case, I place a hand on the sycamore, "Thank you."

I dig around in my coat pocket until my hand touches the right stone and pull it out. It's a flat two-inch bit of aventurine – green, translucent, glistening. On it, in red paint of my own mixing, is the symbol ansuz. I place the stone on my forehead and press. A tingle of tendrils creeps into my brain. I was told once that this had the effect of turning my eyes a glowing green, so I move fast before another hiker can appear. I step back from the sycamore and almost immediately see a set of footprints; they're glowing a faint purple. The prints are deep, made by something that had waited here for a while, bipedal, and invisible. *No, not invisible...* I get on my knees for a closer inspection. I poke at the imprints – cracked edges, the glow fitting into the surrounding soil, like a puzzle piece. "Phased." *Which would explain the lack of physical evidence – and also the lingering energy trail.*

I step back. The prints move away, in one large stride, towards the bench, and transform. They were now a faint yellow and much bigger, "You're no longer hiding and moving fast now. You come up behind her, have to phase back in, grab her, but," I take a step back. I see now that the bench has been recently moved, like it had been pushed against. "she slipped free. You knocked into the log as you stepped over it." More prints, obliterated by weather and traffic, but clear to my eyes at the moment. All were a faint yellow, still moving fast – forward, back, forward, to the side, back. *She fought you.* "Good for her," but in the end - I stand over a swirl pattern in the ground; it glows a pale blue to my eyes. And, as my eyes and brain are beginning to burn, I gently pull off the aventurine.

I need to process. I sit on the log and cup my head – it hurts — hangover level five at least. I turn my mind away from the pain and try to bring order to my thoughts.

Can change size.

A creature of the forest.

Two legs.

Phased like a spirit.

Or at least magically camouflaged.

Portal travel. But maybe had help there.

A Snatcher? A Spriggan, or Blight, maybe. It fits, but at the same time, it seems unlikely. Snatchers and Spriggans are mischievous for the most part and tend to hide in out of the way places. Blights are crueler; probably would have eaten her. And none are going to be easily convinced to go after a specific person. "You could have nabbed any number of people passing by," I'm mumbling to myself as a woman comes down the lane and across the river. "Yet you picked her. Why?" I nod at the middle-aged woman. Everything she's wearing is new, and she looks uncomfortable in it. She appears to need a break but sees me and keeps going. "Who would be collecting specific humans, and why?" I stand up and pace while I read through the file's limited information one more time – hoping for something to jump out at me. *Nothing.*

I plant my feet and curse. There was a moment of hope that I'd be able to handle this quickly and be done with it. I can already feel that hope spiraling away from me.

I flop onto a bench. "This was a hit. One of three, I'm guessing, based on Brigit's note." I want to move but continue to sit. Options float to mind – I don't like them. I don't like the probable pain with some. I don't like the probable time with others. Then, an idea comes to mind, an idea that bounces between two things that were recently said to me. Lugh told me to keep to the path, no unsanctioned fraternizing. Brigit told me to get it done and get it done fast. "This was a hit," I say to myself again. Get it done and get it done fast. What better way to get it done than to let someone get it done for me, or at least help me get it done faster? *A shortcut. Nothing wrong with a shortcut.* I clear my throat and stand. I shiver at a sudden freezing gust that comes down through the trees. "And when you want to know about a hit, you speak to a gangster." I say out loud and then mutter under my breath, "And for that, I need to prepare."

Chapter 8

My choice could make all of this go away in one conversation. It also has the potential to be extremely dangerous. The potential for violence prompts me to settle a few outstanding responsibilities that I'm sure Brigit would view as unnecessary. I spend the next half a day getting my temp job in order. I don't think I'll be back. In fact, I'm pretty sure of it at this point. I've never returned to a job after a mission. The thing of it is – I've really enjoyed this disguise, and a part of me, a large part of me, wants to pretend for a little while longer that my life is normal. But it isn't. So I left word with the Department Chair that I had a family emergency, wrote an e-mail to the Department Secretary asking that she post it to my classes, and made a phone call to Professor Martin. All of my quarter exams, but one, now consisted of a single question: What did you learn this semester? However, my seniors' only class on ancient funerary practices needed to have their final papers read and graded. I owed Professor Martin a fruit basket or something. I then spent a few hours gathering the supplies I was pretty sure I needed for my trip.

It's now about four in the afternoon, and I find myself over the island of Manhattan – and boy, are my arms tired. I chuckle to myself. *I'm funny, and since I never disagree with that, it's always true.* I set aside my self-congratulations and focus on a place to land. It's a busy city, not unlike any other bustling city – there's always a park or a dark alley to hide in. New York City is full of both, so I've never feared changing upon arrival.

Central Park is a busy park inside a busy city, even in a cold November. Thankfully, there are a hundred places you can go to be alone if you wanted to. It's always such a pleasure to glide into the city locked forest, especially at night. It's like an oasis – which the designers were definitely going for when they built this place, so a job well done.

I land. A man approaches. He's jogging but not dressed for it, and I can't help but wonder about where he's going or where he's running from. Once his back is to me, I change. The scenery tempts me, seriously tempts me, as I begin to wander the park. The trees, the open spaces, they call to me. It's not home; the city's constant thrum is plenty to remind me of that, but it looks like home. And home, especially lately, has been on my mind. At times, the memories consume me, and they are not easily shook. I have this idea that if I could go back to the beginning, somehow, I'd find myself. But it's a foolish notion, and I'm foolish for having it. *There is no past, no future; there is only the mission.* I remind myself of the two things I've been told. Stay the path. Get it done. I feel I'm already off the path. Which is probably no surprise to Brigit. I stop mid-trail and sigh. "Get it done."

Duty calls.

Though, with any luck, I can pass this off. I don't mind playing second fiddle. Let someone else take charge. Let someone else be scrutinized and judged. Let me get back to my life.

"My life," I grunt. "What am I trying to get back to? Playing? Pretending?" *Don't lose your temper. Focus on the goal.* I tell myself.

I find a trail that takes me around to 72nd Street. I cross 5th Avenue, and about three-quarters down the block, I find Manna among expensive apartments and home offices. It's a small ouzeri that mainly serves a large variety of ouzo, coffee, and beer, as well as a short list of superb appetizers, made that day at the discretion of the head chef. I've never eaten here, but Yelp gives it high marks. It's apparently "the place" for authentic, upscale Greek food.

I hesitate going in. *My mission. My burden.* We're told to refrain from involving others because we rarely know who is in opposition. *I think Lugh enjoyed reminding me about this because he gets to rub my face in how alone I am, how alone we all are.* Perhaps it's a coincidence – no such thing right now – but I feel eyes on me as I think his name. It can go unnoticed, but it's unmistakable once you become aware of the feeling - prey in sight of a hunter.

"My mission. My burden." I mutter the mantra drilled into me. "But who am I to say no to a friend if they want to join me? Or to say no if they can get this finished faster." Perhaps it's a coincidence, but as I say this, I feel the pressure of even more eyes on me.

I shake it off and try to look like I'm considering my options – which I am, but not in a "am I hungry for Greek" kind of way. I see a small number of patrons through the window – no dinner rush just yet. At a booth near the front of the establishment, I can make out my contact, though occasionally, his chubby face is blocked by a woman with black hair who sits opposite him.

She abruptly stands up and begins walking my way. She has a powerful stride that diminishes none of the femininity of the well-tailored suit she wears. I'm surprised that I recognize her, but, as I wasn't ready to be recognized, I back down the block a few doors and duck behind a car, pretending like I had dropped something. I peek around the Lexus' bumper, and when I see her moving towards Madison Avenue, I come out of hiding. "What are you doing here, Persephone?" I whisper. A question for another time.

I make my way back over to Manna, and this time, I don't stop at the door. There's a small reception area with a glass podium just in front of a wide arch. A thin woman in a black dress smiles at me as I come in.

"Hello," she says.

I almost don't hear her. The eyes watching over me are suddenly gone, and the departure is momentarily distracting. I look over her shoulder, not in a subtle way. "I'd like to speak with the owner," as an afterthought, I glance at her and add, "Please."

She looks me up and down and deems my jacket, jeans, and sweater – this time a dark green – unimpressive. "Do you have a reservation?"

"I need a reservation to speak with the owner?"

"I mean, um, an appointment."

I'm making her nervous – I understand. She's young, and I do have a fantastic haircut. I smile, but it doesn't help. I put my hands in my jacket pockets, but that only adds to the tension. She's probably thinking I'm going to pull a gun or a knife. Profiling is rude. "He's an old friend."

Before she can say anything, a booming voice sounds from the main seating area. "Anant!" A barrel-chested man with the bronze complexion of a god and the face of a cherub appears. He laughs out loud, opens his arms wide, and scoops me up into a bear hug. He holds the embrace longer than he needs to and squeezes me more than what is considered typically friendly.

"We need to talk," I wheeze out with what little air I still have in my lungs.

"Ah, yes, of course."

For many of us, our accents mellow. You move around so much, picking up habits and ways of speaking from wherever you're stationed. Eventually, that native tongue of yours is vaguely European or vaguely Asian. Gregor had kept his accent. An affectation, I suppose, though Gregor is the type to refuse to be diluted by time and space.

He releases me and thumps my back. I follow him into the main seating area. The décor is not Greek. I know nothing about interior design – let's call it Modern. The room is longer than wide, with booths lining the long walls and a single row of two and four seat tables running down the center. He stops at a booth towards the back but then glances at me for a few long seconds.

"No, I think more privacy."

I nod.

He continues past the bar section and bathrooms into the kitchen, at the back of which is a sturdy, deep brown, wooden door. He opens it and enters.

The office is impressive. It's all wood and leather. Ancient maps of Greece and Greek cities hang on the walls protected by expensive-looking frames. There are three bookshelves, two with books. A third - the center one - is filled with artifacts of his homeland. A bank of three filing cabinets sits along the wall to the left of the handsome desk, and to the right is a marble plinth with a glass top that shields a helmet. It's bronze, with a rounded point covering the top of the head coming down into a faceplate that forks at the mouth and has a curved projection that protects the nape of the neck. It's his own. I'd seen him wear it into battle on several occasions. As I admire the helmet, my eyes fall upon the dent on the left side, where he had taken a blow from Kaumodaki. Thankfully for him, it was not being wielded by Vishnu at the time.

He grunts with amusement, "Ah, yes. Drachenhöhle," the soft leather of his chair creaks as his full weight eases into it. "That was a bloody day."

"And night."

"Indeed." I feel his eyes on me as I stare at the helmet. "Aodhan Anant," he says, almost as if he's trying to convince himself that I'm really here. "Fire and water." He smirks.

It's nice to hear my old name. That person I'd like to get back to. But, I don't allow myself to be distracted by his charming voice. Gregor likes interesting puzzles, and kidnapping is right up his alley. *Play this right, and everyone will go home happy.* Still staring at the helmet, I say, "How you doing, Gregor?"

"I have no complaints. You, my friend Anant, as always, have the face of a man with many." He waggles his finger at me.

That was almost friendly banter, but it has only been a few minutes. I expect things to get worse. *Remember, in and out. Ask your question. Get an answer. This all over with and you can get back to your sham of a life.* I turn away from the helmet and sit in the chair in front of the desk. "I go by Aedan now."

He grimaces, tut-tuts, and shakes his head as he sits back and relaxes in his chair. "You change too much. Always different. Aedan," he tastes the name, "I don't like. It's too simple. Aodhan Anant – it rolls off the tongue. It has power. Aedan," he smacks his lips and makes an unpleasant scowl. "It has no... dynami."

I tell myself not to take the bait. I'm here for information, maybe to pass the buck, not to start a fight. "You have a nice place here." *Be nice. Be nice. Be nice.* "You've been here for fifty years, right? Looks it."

Gregor's iron stare holds me, and I don't give an inch. The silence stretches on for long enough that I begin to think he's going to be very rude and completely ignore my insult.

"You been here before?" he asks without the venom I'm catching from his eyes.

I'm honestly not sure which to address – his beady little eyes or the seemingly innocent question. *Be nice.* "No." *There, that was nice.* "But, I like to know what the family is up to." *That was less nice.* The truth is that Gregor is the only one of my brothers and sisters I know about, and that's purely by accident. I happened to see him the last time I was in New York. Gregor likes to know things. He consumes, savors information like I would a fine meal. And now he knows that I know of his location, and I may have intimated that I know what some of the others were up to.

I don't think he's digesting any of that information at all well. For that matter, how did Persephone know where to find him? That couldn't be sitting well either. I mean as a rule – guideline, really – we don't interact with each other unless we're fighting. Some of us have teamed up very rarely, and by teaming up, I mean our Patrons have told us to play nice with each other. But, never knowing if your Patron is friend or foe with another Patron is an excellent incentive to remain isolated and hidden. However, I have questions, and I don't really want to go elsewhere to look for answers. *Be nice.* "I mean, I don't know how you've done it, but it's a pretty sweet deal." He still says nothing. His angry eyes, however, carry his intent loud and clear. I shrug. "Well, I guess I'll just ask Brigit about it," his eyes widen just a sliver as I say this. *Shit, got cocky.*

He leans toward me. The leather of his chair sighing a little as his weight shifts forward. "I did not realize you and your Patron were on such good terms. That is interesting."

I've known Gregor off and on for many years, too many to bother counting. He misses little. Is never direct. And always has a plan – usually three. I begin to think he keeps his Greek accent less for himself and more because it makes him sound a little like a supervillain. I shiver a little. I suddenly think this is a bad idea - *time to get to the point.* I clear my throat. "Anyway, at the risk of being rude, my friend, I need to ask you something."

Suddenly he laughs and thumps his desk. "As it should be," he laughs again. The tension instantly evaporates but is replaced by my confusion. "Helping each other, giving experience, advice, to those less capable," he stops there and leans again back into his chair, his smile fading. "But, it is not, is it?"

"With reason," I say.

"Of course," he says in a booming voice, his arms wide, "the mission," he points at me and winks.

I lift my arms defensively, "I just wanted to ask you a question. Maybe two," I say with a fake smile. *Is it worth denying I'm on task?*

"You would not be here otherwise?" He shifts in his seat, leaning now to the left and resting his head on his hand. He considers me for a moment. I can see him come to some decision. It's a subtle change – the corners of his eyes are less creased. He shifts again, now resting his elbows on his ample gut and his fingers tent at his lips. "I'm not in the business of giving away anything for free."

What would Brigit say to me? "Lives could be at stake."

Gregor is unmoved.

"Alright, worth a shot," I dig into my pocket and pull out a small, flat, white stone. He tries to hide it, but I can tell he's interested.

"A truth stone?"

I nod. "My own recipe."

"You have my attention."

The stone itself is limestone – it takes nine months of care and attention, a fifty-pound gold block, vinegar, a liar's blood, and an absolute truth to make it a truth stone. "I assume we have a deal."

"Within reason."

"What does that mean?"

"It means, you ask, and I answer, and when I'm finished - I am finished. I get the stone, whether you are happy or not."

"I really don't see that as a fair trade. What's to stop you from lying?"

"You have the stone."

This is true. The stone will vibrate if the holder is told a lie. This one time in Germany, I was interrogating a guy who was dealing in ancient scrolls when he told me a lie so big that the stone burned a hole in my pocket and singed my thigh on its way out the bottom of my pant leg. But, "You know such artifacts do not affect us."

"Ah, right. My mistake. But this changes nothing,"

I sigh and put the stone away. I watch as his eyes follow my hand. He wants the stone; I know he does. I decide to test how much. "Watch your back, Gregor. They enjoy punishing us." It's a threat, but also a warning. Lugh had said Father is in town; it's possible Gregor could be the reason.

"They enjoy punishing you," he chuckles.

Great, I'd become a cautionary tale.

"You must learn rules. Rules," he rolls his Rs as his hands roll in the air, searching for the right words, as I roll my eyes at the theatrics, "are your home. They keep you protected, warm, safely cocooned – that is until you find the door."

I feel I'm losing control of the conversation, so I put on my angry face. "Still, fifty years in the same location -"

"My existence is my concern." His verbal irritation matches his eyes this time.

"I wonder how many of Them would agree, or how many of our own would be happy with your sedentism."

Gregor says nothing.

"Could get ugly," I feel like he's daring me to follow through. I stand to leave.

He nods, "Good to see you, Anant."

Shit. If I'm not going to pass this off than I at least need information, and I don't know anyone else who hears the things Gregor does. I hold my ground - for three seconds and then flop back into the chair, blowing a raspberry of defeat. I know I can't trust him, but I nod in agreement. "What do you know about any abductions in the area?"

"Nasty business, time-consuming, almost never worth the effort. Can you be more specific?"

"Can you tell me about anyone hiring a Spriggan, or a Blight, to grab coeds?" I almost say more but stop myself.

"Spriggans," he tut-tuts again, "those won't listen to just anyone. And Blights won't listen to anyone. You might be able to bribe one. More likely, it was forced."

"Forced?"

Gregor pauses. His hands fold, now resting on his stomach. "We're all afraid of something, Anant. Nature is governed by laws, some rather strict, so I think we can safely assume such a concept is universal."

I blink slowly. "Okay. And you should always stand up to bullies. Are you giving me a pep talk?"

He shrugs.

I sigh, frustrated. "You've got to know something, Gregor. This is what you do." *Shit, pushed too hard* – I can see it on his face. "What about anyone making waves? Whispers of someone summoning the beasts of the aes sidhe and using them as muscle? You talked about fear; that would certainly generate some."

"That was more than one question."

"Come on, Gregor, give me something."

"Begging now? Wonderful."

"What about the normal bumps in the night? Anyone, anything, suddenly not being normal?"

"This conversation -"

"I'm serious."

"So am I."

I pause to find some calm. "I ran into a pack of Cambion, possibly working with one of their females. Looks like they've been here a while – someone's been holding the door open, I think." I cheer a little on the inside as this grabs his attention, but it's only a moment before he regains his composure. That slip makes me think he does know something. I open my mouth to say more, but he shakes his head.

"I think we have said enough," he speaks slowly, that deep rumble, as if he's shouting without opening his mouth wide, punctuates the finality of the conversation. "It was wonderful to see you, Anant." He holds out his hand.

"You didn't answer me!" I rage.

"I believe I did," he says softly.

The office door opens. Gregor isn't surprised by this.

"Have you met my head chef? This is Aela."

I cock my head over my shoulder. She's tall, has eyes the shape of almonds, a heart-shaped face, and high cheekbones. There's little else I can tell about her as the chef's coat and blue bandana hide most of her. "Hey," I say.

Aela says nothing. She doesn't have to. Just then, there's a pulse of energy, strong; it fills the room. It's not something an average person would have seen or felt, but I do. She's flexing her strength. Rude - in a way, it's like a bodybuilder coming up to you and flashing their bicep in your face. Aela appears human, but I'm pretty sure she isn't. I turn my head and find a smirk on Gregor's face. *Out maneuvered. Time to retreat.* I stand up and slap the truth stone down on Gregor's desk. "I'll see myself out."

Chapter 9

I leave fuming. Half a block vanishes before I come to a stop. I plant my feet and stare at the sky. The sun is going down, and it's getting dark and chilly, quickly becoming cold. *That did not go well.* "I'm not taking all the blame for that," I say loudly as a man in an expensive suit walks by. "Hey," I say with a pleasant nod. He gets into the back of a nice-looking black car, although not before scowling at the two service vans – one parked behind him and the other in front. As the man's driver pulls the car away from the curb, I continue on my way, with no destination in mind. *I'm serious.* I think to anyone who may be listening. *I'm not taking all the blame for that. I might have handled Gregor poorly, but Gregor – Gregor is - Gregor is who he always is, and I probably should have been more prepared for that.*

The odd thing is, I don't feel anyone listening. I felt Their attention, or at least someone's attention before going into Manna, but nothing now. It's not unusual to feel Them watching while the end game is in motion – like fans at a tennis match, or couch surfers during a season finale. Gods are a fairly predictable bunch, but when they act strangely, the universe trembles. *Best to get this off my plate as fast as I can.*

I turn at the corner, pausing again. I push my back up against the concrete of the building. I mindlessly watch the traffic on Madison Avenue. "That did not go to plan." I huff. "This was a bad idea. Gregor," my hands rub at my face. *I'm such an idiot.* "Gregor could be the one I'm playing against. Stay calm. Reassess."

I close my eyes and lean my head back against the wall. *What do I know? I know that a creature of the Sidhe has abducted a girl. That there have been three abductions. Actually, no, that was a guess based on Brigit's note. Concentrate on what you know for sure?* And then, rather abruptly, something occurs to me. *Brigit was afraid.* A terrifying thought. *What was it that Gregor had said? That we're all afraid of something. I wonder what Gregor is afraid of? Persephone? If he's smart.* As I remind myself of Persephone, I gently ease away from the wall and begin walking again. "Persephone. A friendly face? At one time." It's dark in the shadow of the building and cold. "No coincidences," I mumble as my pace quickens.

I backtrack to Manna. It's no coincidence that she was here exactly when I show up. *If Gregor can't help or take this off my plate, then perhaps she can* – or at least that's what I think. The truth is that I'm actually curious as to why she was here. There's still a chance I can sense her. We're steeped in exotic energies. They tend to linger like a wake – or perfume. When we put our mind to it, we all can get a vague sense of the others when we're nearby, a blurry picture in our heads. It's not usually much, enough to point in a direction. Of course, the closer we are to each other, the fresher the scent, the better the sense. There are ways to mask your presence - if you're very good - and there are ways to heighten your senses - if you're very good. And I'm very good.

I try to put Gregor out of my mind. And I ignore the voice at the back of my mind telling me how suspicious I appear walking back and forth in front of Manna. After a couple of passes, I pick up the scent. I quickly dig around in my pocket and pull out the smooth bit of aventurine I had used at the abduction site. It glistens in my hand and becomes warm as I draw in just a little of the energy around me, including some of the cast-off from Persephone. I place the stone to my forehead, and tendrils of energy instantly dart into my skull - the world shifts. The cars, the buildings, all the man-made stuff goes gray, lifeless. By contrast, the equidistant trees lining the street and the people are vibrant with a faint glow about them. However, what has my attention is the purplish haze, like dancing smoke, that comes in and out of focus as it snakes its way toward Madison Avenue. I avoid looking at the people and the cars passing me by. As Halloween is long over, glowing green eyes would be more than just a fun scare.

I follow the purple mist around the corner to where I was just recently standing and stop. At the curb, the dancing smoke scatters like dandelion seeds in a stiff gust. There's nothing else to see, and, as it's bad for my health to have the stone pressed into my forehead for too long, I pull it and place it back into my pocket. I examine the curb. *Maybe she crossed the street here? Or perhaps she had a car waiting. Or cab?* There's no way to tell for sure; there's too much motion, too much metal and plastic moving back and forth. The trail is gone. *Failure. Shit.* I stare at the length of concrete where the purple mist dissipated – it gives up no more secrets. My options for quick and easy seem to have evaporated. I'm left with time consuming and painful.

In a fog of thought, I find myself walking back toward Central Park. My feet feel like lead weights. I've tried to get someone else to paint my fence for me, but it's blown up in my face. I still have Darren's report and what I know from the abduction site. Stale breadcrumbs. *I used to be good at this. I used to care. I can't recall when I lost that.* But I'm lying to myself. Because it's not good enough that *They* punish me, I have to punish myself. I do remember. Anger from the memory stiffens my spine. "I can never forget. Or forgive." I step out into traffic without looking and cross to the park.

Just on the other side street, next to the archway to the park, I spot a little girl sitting on a bench. Dark hair escapes from under her blue woolen hat. She's reading - she's reading in the park, near dark, by herself. At least three adults pass her by as I watch her. She gives no indication she's aware of me. I shove my hands into my pockets and say as I walk by, "I know. I know. Get it done."

However, regardless of the urgent mission and the slow start, there's something I need to do – someone I always like to check in on when in Manhattan. I head further uptown towards Carnegie Hill. I decide to walk rather than change or take a cab. The early evening is chilly but pleasant, and besides, I want to give her time. The thing about it is, I never know where to find her. It's a big city, after all, and she's odd - even by our standards. So, her possible whereabouts are always difficult to narrow down. Nevertheless, the trick is not to look for her; she'll find me. I just need to be sure of where I'm going.

I set my mind to thinking about Lodestone and soon arrive. It's a small café just opposite the reservoir. The lighting is set to "mood." The coffee is fantastic. The patrons are mostly aloof writers far more interested in their latest unfinished novels than the other customers. It's an attractive bistro. Like Manna, it's longer than it is wide. At the back, the service counter is empty of customers and stationed by a bored-looking man with a beard. The counters, running the length of the long walls, are mostly empty. I look up at the ceiling because it's my favorite part of this place, in all honesty. The ceiling is a series of pointed arches, the ribs of which come down the walls breaking up the counters into sections about four comfy bar stools long.

I don't need to spend any time looking around because I spot her right away as I step in. There she is, about halfway into the room, head resting at an odd angle against the stone pillar. By today's standards, she looks like just another Emo. But those others - they're all pretenders. She's the original; dressing in heavy, oversized, dark sweaters, tight jeans, and scarfs long before it was cool. As I knew it would be, the clientele is quietly chatting but mostly consumed by their laptops. No one is paying her any attention. Her hand is loosely holding a tall coffee cup, though she hasn't taken a sip the entire time I've been watching. Which, I now realize, has been a creepily long time. I move towards her and notice a second cup – *curious*. It's possible, I suppose, that she is expecting someone else. I'm not sure who else checks in on her. I find myself thinking of Persephone again. *How did she find Gregor? Did she live in the city?* I stop myself there. This is not the time or the place. I need to stay focused as I'm not sure what getting distracted would do to our meeting. Besides, the barista behind the counter has now glanced up at me twice - *best not to draw too much attention.*

I step up beside her. I clear my throat because I have this silly thought that I don't want to startle her. It's foolish, of course. She wouldn't be here if she didn't know I was here. At that moment, her head lifts off the pillar, and she stares at me – the sudden action spooks me, and I flinch. Her mouth partially opens, but there it pauses like she's waiting for me to say something first. "Hello, Cassy." I begin. Her face twitches, and her mouth shuts. It's as if she'd been expecting me to say something else. But that's the way with Cassy. It's always you saying something and her looking at you like you had just messed up your line in a play. "It's been a long time."

"I'm supposed to say that – it's been a long time. Or am I? Oh, but I just did. Wait, has it? Where are we? Are we here?"

There's an acceptance to her words, a confused acceptance. She doesn't question what's in her head; she just says it. But that outward confusion doesn't change the softness or the strength of her voice. It grabs my attention and makes me feel safe, like a neurotic Mother Goose. I have no trouble picturing her in those days, long gone now – and then my pity for her returns because those days of long gone are why she is as she is. I take a reassuring step forward – reassuring for me. "It has been a long time,"

"Are we here?"

"You asked that already," I smile worriedly. "I am. I'm here. This is now." She doesn't respond – her expression, if I'm not mistaken, says, "Shhh. I'm thinking." Which I do for a few moments before asking, "May I sit?"

Cassy sighs as if giving up on a puzzle. "If you say so," she says wistfully as her head rolls to her shoulder.

My mind balks. I'm not sure if that was a yes or a no. I look for another opening. "Is this for me? May I have it?" I point at the cup.

"You will."

Her words are bored and assertive, and I accept them as an invitation to sit down. I take a sip – cinnamon tea. My favorite. "Very nice. Thank you. It's chilly out there, isn't it?"

"I knew one of you would drink it," she says suddenly, quickly, like she is catching up – or trying to rush forward.

Another pause. Like before, like always, I get the impression she's waiting for me. The problem is, I don't know how to respond to that. She's working from a script she's read a thousand times, but I haven't even seen the cover page. "Are you well? Do you need anything?" I don't expect her to respond. In all the years I've known and checked in on her, I've never known her to need anything. It's a mystery I've always been willing to wonder about but not investigate. She's taken care of; that's what I care about.

"I don't know. I lose track."

I take another sip, trying to give myself time to figure out what she's referring to. I decide to move on. "Has anyone else been to see you?" I ask cautiously as I don't want to put her into the middle of anything.

"Ask it!" she snaps. She rubs at her temples and presses her hands against her ears as she squeezes her eyes shut.

The impatient outburst doesn't upset me. "Gregor?" I ask slowly, "Have you seen him? Spoken with him? Or Persephone?"

"Be polite," Cassy's voice has become sweet again.

"I know. I'm trying. I like him, you know – if you can get past the whole not trusting him part." I take a sip of the tea and then lean forward onto the counter. "He's up to something, so the usual, I guess. Still..."

"Trust, until the betrayal,"

"Yes, it does end like that more often than not. Listen, Cassy, about -"

Cassy shifts forward and slaps the counter. "Don't go home." She holds her head and speaks it with such rapidity I get the impression she's jumping ahead.

I don't pretend to understand her mind, but I know fighting what she sees, fighting the order of it, brings her pain. And I wish she'd stop doing that. I give the room a surreptitious scan. A few had looked up but had gone right back to their phones and computers. I smile nervously. When I look back at Cassy, she's drumming her fingers on the counter. Despite her warning tone, my first instinct is to play it off. "I have to, eventually. Go home, that is. All my stuff is there. Besides, I have three trees and two bunny slippers to feed."

Cassy continues to tap at the counter with one hand and press the other against her left ear.

I see the barista looking at me again. He's not happy. I try to change the subject. "You have a good spot here. You can watch a lot of the city walk by that door and the park across the way. The city is its own type of beautiful. Harsh, but welcoming," I turn away from her to look out the front door. "There was this snowy mountain where I grew up – I say was, but it's still there, isn't it? I mean, I'm the one who's moved away. Anyway, I can remember thinking the same thing about it. Harsh but welcoming," I turn back to her. I find her with her forehead on the counter, arms over her ears, her hands entwined behind her head. She seems more irritated than usual, and I'm not sure if I've upset her or if it's something else. "I just wanted to see you. Make sure you're okay." Reluctantly, I start to leave.

Her head picks up, but it's like she doesn't see me. "Sometimes. No. Are we here? Where are we? It's been a long time,"

As she turns away, my heart flutters in that ridiculous schoolboy way. My hand instinctively reaches out, but I pull back – I made that mistake once before. I leave before I upset either one of us any further. The park across the street calls to me, and I plant myself on the first bench I find. There's a man with well-established crow's feet sitting next to me – his odor and worn clothing suggesting he's homeless. He's also drinking from a bottle wrapped in a brown paper bag.

I can see Lodestone, and after a few moments the man joins my gaze. "Shouldn't have asked about Gregor. Should have known better than to push her for information. Revert to form. You can't just visit someone. Business,

business, business," I snap at myself and notice that the man next to me stops in mid-swig. I give him a half smile. "That's what I was like, you know. All business. All questions. Always asking why." The man sitting next to me blinks, taken aback by the tears in my eyes, I think. "That's who I was, and I don't want her to see who I've become."

I look back at Lodestone. We sit in silence for a time until I see her leave. I watch Cassy until I lose track of her in the night and crowd. I lean towards the man next to me. "The thing of it is, she knew that's how that was going to go." I sigh. "You know," I nod at him – he looks at me like I'm speaking a foreign language, "she makes me sad, which makes me not visit until I need something, and then I feel guilty, which makes me sad – it's this whole thing,"

The man holds his bottle to me.

"Thanks, but," I hold up my tea.

He nods politely and sips from his bottle.

"She has nothing and everything. I don't get it. Even though she doesn't look like she needs it, I always want to leave her some money because I don't know what else to do for her. And I want..." I trail off into a sigh. To break the awkwardness I feel from the man's eyes, I take a sip of my tea. "The important thing is, she's surviving. Aren't we all?"

The man chuckles and takes another sip.

"Right," a smile breaks my grimace as I relax a little and recline into the seat. We watch two bicyclists and then a guy on a Segway pass by. "She's not always like this," I silently curse Apollo and then look around nervously– an action the man next to me mirrors. We glance at each other, and when I relax, so does he. We sip from our respective containers.

I catch myself staring off in the direction Cassy had gone. I feel a shoulder nudge my shoulder. "The two of us? No, not really," I read his thoughts, well, not really, I just assume he's thinking the same thing I am. "There was once a time we were inseparable, for ten years at least – and were together for exactly seventy-six hours of those years. I know because I counted. Seconds here. A few minutes there. Once – once, on a beautiful spring day in Scotland, we talked for an hour. She has these moments, shining moments of lucidity, everything about her brightens – and then she's gone again. In those seventy-six hours, we... tempted the fates. As for the rest of the time," I spill some of my tea as I squeeze the cup a little too tightly, "she's trapped, you see, in that space behind her eyes and between her ears. Imprisoned there by a jock who couldn't stand being told no." I finish the tea and set the empty cup between us.

"She told me about it once – the trapped part, not the jock part, well, actually, the jock part too, but -" I'm interrupted by the slosh of booze. "Right, get on with it. Have you ever worn 3D glasses? It's like that, she said, but with each of those colored shadows moving of its own accord and repeating what the one in front has done but with this disorienting time lapse. She walks through life as a ghost. Never knowing what is real and what is a repeat of future actions. Is that explosion happening now or soon? Am I talking with a person or to the thin air where that person will be? Am I being held, or am I remembering being held from a moment in the future? What breaks my heart, what wakes me up at night sometimes, is that she knew. She knew, and either didn't want to change things or couldn't change things. She – we - she knew how things would go, and she did it anyway. I wasn't worth it."

My head tilts forward. I'm feeling sorry for myself, and I hate it. I can feel my companion's eyes on me. "And your line is, no, don't be so hard on yourself." I glance at the homeless man. "But I'm not, and I'm not worth it." I really want to reach for his bottle, and I clench my hands together to stop myself. "I do wonder, when I want to be particularly cruel to myself, if she wonders. If, in those shining moments, she spares any of her precious time as herself to think on it – to think on me." I take a breath. "I hope not. She needs to be happy." I try to leave, but a gentle hand on my arm stops me. He offers me the bottle again. My hand twitches. I want it. I need it. But a promise is a promise. "No, thank you."

He pats my arm and takes a swig.

"You've been very kind to listen to an old man ramble on. Thank you," I sigh and return the gesture by patting his arm. "But I do need to go." This time, I make it to my feet. I turn to him and pull a stone from my pocket. I press Fehu between my palms and close my eyes. There's a soft glow that does not go unnoticed by my bench companion. When I pull my hands apart, there are a few twenty dollar bills - I just robbed a bank, and I don't feel bad about it. "Here," I hand the money to him, which he takes without question.

His expression of glee and astonishment makes me wish I could do more. But there are rules, and I've already bent several of them.

Back to work.

Chapter 10

On my flight back to Philly, the weather conditions went from cold to frigid and breezy. I try a flyby. I do. But between the cold, and my mind being on Cassy, I can't help but seek solace from the only other person who's ever come close to matching those feelings. I tell myself I just need to know he's there and safe. I've been his guardian for ten years. Cassy and I were together for ten years. A decade. Even by mortal standards, not that long, but we lived in those ten years. We were like children hiding in the garden, ignoring mother's call to come in for dinner. I try to tell myself that the darkness that befell the world wasn't our fault – I mean, the world is always in danger, but it got dark, really dark. And then They found us, and things got worse – for us at least. I don't know what *They* did to her. I tried to take the blame.

And that quickly, the flyby turns into a visit. I'm distracted by the tango between sadness and longing and don't realize I've sat down at first. I blink, and it feels like the first time in an hour.

"Hey," Millie says. "Back with us?"

I don't remember the tumbler being placed in front of me – I don't remember Millie being the one to serve me. I can smell and taste that I'm not being served the good stuff. "Where's Alan?"

She sets the bottle of whiskey down and slides it towards me. It's mostly empty. "In the office."

Something in her tone tells me the bargain brand whiskey is a punishment. I nod and top off my glass. She steps away to the other end of the counter to wash a few mugs. The bar is near empty, a slow night. *Slow nights worry the boy, even though the place does profitable business the rest of the time. He's probably brooding in the office.* I decided to poke my head in, but first, I empty my glass. As I'm setting the tumbler down, the door to the office opens. "Shit," I say under my breath.

He stops when he sees me. For a moment, there's an expression of joy, followed by relief, but then his mouth settles into a frown. More or less, my relationship with everyone – ever - summed up in about ten seconds. I lift my glass to him because it seems like a fun and safe gesture. His frown deepens. "Shit," I say, smiling. Still, he heads my way, so it can't be all bad.

69

He comes around the bar and sits on the stool next to mine. He sets down an accordion folder on the mahogany top. His eyes work me over, and I smile. "Been here long, I see," he says.

Both our eyes dart to the bottle. "Alan,"

"Save it."

"It's been a bad night,"

"Isn't it always?"

"Really bad."

"You just walked out," he blurts.

I assume he's talking about how I left last time – as I recall, it's how I tend to leave all the time, so I'm not sure what's got him so upset.

"You always just go. You're here, and then you're gone. And it's not like I can contact you. You never answer your phone."

"Kind of melted it today anyway."

He slowly shakes his head in anger – he'd given me that phone as a present. He'd given me every phone as a present. "Here I sit, never knowing if you're going to ever walk through that door again."

"I can't change that." That appears to have been the wrong thing to say. Alan is physically biting his lip in order not to say something. "You look like you could use a drink," I say cheerily as I push my glass over to him and pour him some whiskey. He drinks with his eyes for a few moments and then looks back over to me. He doesn't flinch when I lean over and reach for a glass from the shelves under the bar. I sit back with a beer mug in hand, which I fill halfway with whiskey. "Do we need to have this conversation again?"

He picks up the tumbler and sips - and then coughs. "Ugh! Why?" He sets the glass back in front of me.

We seem to have hit a turning point, so I try to steer the conversation in a different direction. "Expanding the business?" I nod at the folder on the bar.

He hesitates and places a hand on the folder. "I want to help."

Nope. Walked right into it. Shit. "No." I laugh as I take a sip because he must be joking, as we've had this conversation so many times.

"I'm not an expert, but I've got skills -"

"No."

"I do. Look." Alan quickly unwinds the cord and opens up the accordion compartments. "You can't do things -"

"Alan, we've talked about this. No. This is a bad idea." He's not listening and continues to pull out stacks of stapled pages.

"Listen. You can't use computers,"

My pride is momentarily hurt, and this shifts my focus. "I can."

"Alright. Can, but don't."

"I choose," I emphasize because I feel the distinction is important, "not to use computers."

"Why?" He asks, a knowing grin on his face. When I don't answer, he goes on. "Right. After you left, I decided to follow a hunch based on that note you had. Look. At least look at it."

"I made a promise. I won't have you getting involved in this – any of it. Once you do," I pause to drink. "Once you do, you become a part of the game, a piece on the board, a target."

"I'm a target anyway."

"You're not. I've worked hard -"

"To keep me out of it. I know," he cuts in over me. "The name change. School. This bar. You've done a lot to shield me by recreating me."

"I always asked for your input." I gesture with the mug, sloshing some of the contents onto the floor. "I always asked you what you wanted."

"You did. And I am grateful. Especially for the sticking around."

"Well, you were so young when we first met – I couldn't have left you, even if I had wanted to. And I didn't want to."

"Aedan, I doubt I could ever thank you enough for everything you've done. For your protection. For being there for me..."

We've only ever talked about what happened to his parents once. He's never brought it up again, ever. This was coming very close to hitting on that topic. I hold my breath for the 'but' I know is coming.

"...but, I am a target, whether you like it or not. I'm in your life."

At this, my head turns to face him.

"I'm in your life. I like to think I'm a part of it." He smiles uncertainly – a hint of mistiness in his eyes. "If whoever you're playing against knows you, they know me. I'm a target. I might as well help you keep me safe."

My eyes close, and I turn away.

"Aedan -"

"No." The room shakes, and there's an echo of a boom very reminiscent of a tractor-trailer hitting a large pothole. The scattered patrons all look up but soon go back to their drinks and conversations.

Alan begins to stuff his pages back into the slots of the folder.

I stand up. I have drunk enough that the room spins for a moment as I get to my feet. I try to speak but can't – and like a coward, head for the door. At the threshold, I stop and rush back to the bar. I grab the folder and place a hand on Alan's head. We don't speak, but the tension isn't there. I take that as a good sign and leave before I can ruin it.

The flight home is wobbly. When I land, I nearly stumble forward onto my face. I take a second to steady myself, and as I do, I let my senses take a look around. The house is quiet - no unfamiliar energy. None of the wards have been triggered. I take a deep breath and burp – I feel my face pucker at the taste of bile and after whiskey. "Might have overdone it." My words are only slightly stilted. I head for my back door, which annoyingly keeps swaying.

I stop for some cookies in the kitchen. There'd been a party the other day for one of the other professors, and someone had made snickerdoodles. I made sure to leave with a dozen. I peel back the plastic wrap. I stuff one – a little stale but delicious - and munch on the second as I shuffle toward the living room, nearly knocking over a lamp as I turn it on. I make it to my couch and flop into it. I stare at the accordion folder on my lap.

My conversation with Alan plays in my mind. *Maybe he's right. Maybe it is too late. Maybe he is a target. Maybe he's always been a target.* All these years, just knowing me, being a part of my life, has put him in danger. "Francine, Dominic – sorry," Apparently, I'd never been able to keep that promise. I've just been lucky. But that doesn't sit right. Luck, like coincidence, when the game is in play, neither applies. Something else has been at work here. Something has shadowed Alan's presence, protected him when I couldn't – maybe, possibly. *Shit, if this is true* – it's like finding out your door is actually made of paper. *My wards are good, but if this is true, then... What? I don't know.*

I can't get my mind to focus. The room keeps swimming – which probably has more to do with the bottom shelf whiskey Millie had been pouring me. My fingers drum on the folder. I want to open it. The moment feels momentous, and I can't decide if that's because of the booze or me being dramatic. The clock on the wall ticks by; it's the only sound in the house. It's strange, but I'm sure contemplating my next move has made the folder feel heavier. Its weight on my lap is noticeable. "Stop being dramatic." I push myself out of my slouched position. My fingers tug on the cord holding the folder shut. I feel like I'm standing on a cliff edge. This, what I'm about to do, it feels like a point of no return. Change is in the air. It's not just my imagination. My senses, like the hairs of an arm, tingle. I drop the cord. "Brigit?" I ask shakily. I'm afraid to look around. I don't feel her, or anyone, but that doesn't comfort me. I set the folder aside and go to the window. I'm tip-toeing as if I'm trying not to wake up dad. I gingerly pull the curtain back, barely enough for me to peek at the street - nothing but darkness and quiet.

One of the reasons I picked this street to live on was how dark it is at night. This section of the town had missed out on much of the modernization done during the eighties and nineties. And, as much of my activity is at night, the dark is welcomed. This night, however, the ambiance is a bit much. I let the curtain fall back into place. My palms rub at my eyes. The clock on the wall tells me it's only ten. I'm exhausted. "Okay," I say to the fog of dread, "Okay, I'll sleep on it." I don't make it to the bedroom as my couch is very comfy.

A thunderous knock startles me awake.

In a moment of panic and paranoia, I reach for the folder. It's still there on the cushion beside me. While I'm catching my breath, there's another knock – even more determined. My fingertips linger on the manila as I get up to answer the door. The creak of the door and my smiling face welcome the two officers on the other side. A thin, yet fit young man with a bad mustache and his friend with a much larger waistline and dark sunglasses greet me. "Yes?" I keep my smile, but my mind is anything but friendly. They're wearing the local uniforms - nothing on the surface to get my hackles up, and yet - I don't know everyone in town. I do try to note law enforcement – easier to avoid that way. Neither of these guys is familiar. I take a surreptitious glance over their shoulders – no cop car. There's a beat-up, faded green sedan I don't recognize in the street. *Not the typical patrol car, but let's not panic just yet.*

"Sir, are you Mr. Aedan Anant?" the younger cop asks.

The this-is-no-good list continues to grow. He pronounced my name "Uh-non" - no one ever gets my last name right on the first try. Also, his accent is all wrong. He's trying to hide it, but I hear Jersey in there. Could be nothing – could be something. "Yes. What is this about?"

The young man with the unfortunate mustache smiles and asks politely, "May we come in for a few minutes?"

I step back. They step over to the couch, and I can't help myself. My eyes flick to the folder on the cushion. I've never had a good poker face. I see the larger of the men notice, and I clear my throat as I shut the door. "You haven't told me what this is about yet." The larger officer circles my couch, examining it and the room around it. He's not a local, I'm sure. He's walking like a man who's walked a crime scene or two. But, there's an air of familiarity. I feel like I'm trying to remember a dream.

"Do you mind if we ask you, sir, where you were yesterday?" The larger man, his beer belly making the buttons of his shirt scream in pain, speaks.

Another bell goes off in my head. That was a Philly accent, and he wasn't even trying to hide it. He catches me staring at him.

"Sir," he says aggressively.

Mustache raises a hand and smiles; Beer Belly is annoyed by this but reluctantly holds his tongue. "Mr. Anant, allow me to be blunt. Were you in New York City yesterday around four?"

Their odd dynamic has my mind spinning. The older one has the air of a seasoned cop. The younger one – his tone, his stance, it's too casual. Even a rookie – especially a rookie – would not be leaning on the back of my couch to ask me a question. *And what the hell is up with that Cheshire grin?* I see no reason to lie to them. "I was in New York yesterday, although I'm not positive of the time."

"And what were you doing in the city at that time?" Mustache asks.

Beer Belly hikes his belt, grimacing with discomfort, and begins to circle again around my couch.

"Visiting a friend."

"Would that be a Mr. Gregor Eidonis?"

Beer Belly is now between me and the door, and the couch is between Mustache and me.

"Would it interest you to know that Manna was gutted by a fire last night? And that we have video of you casing the joint just a few hours earlier."

"What?" The distraction works, I don't notice Beer Belly move towards me until he's almost standing right next to me. They want me talking. They want me distracted. They're not writing any of this down. They're not cops. And with that, the cloud blocking my memory parts. He's out of his detective garb and those sunglasses Clark Kented me, but that's the face of Robert Darren.

"I think you should come with us, sir," Darren sneers into my ear.

I haven't brushed my teeth yet. I haven't had a piss. I haven't even had a shower. I'm not a coffee drinker, but I prefer long morning showers. So I'm certainly not going anywhere with these guys.

"Dave, grab the folder," Darren orders and then lunges for me.

I spin out of his hands and throw myself into my couch, which skids back into Dave, doubling him over. There's a gunshot as I flip myself over the back of my couch and dash into the kitchen.

"No guns!" I hear Dave shout.

"We were told not to kill him. Nothing was said about not hurting him," Darren shouts back as he heads for the kitchen – at which point he comes face to face with a frying pan. The large man drops to the floor.

I enter the living room, frying pan in hand.

I see the options Dave is considering cross his face: Grab the folder. Grab me. Shoot me. Run for the door.

"Time for you to answer some questions," I say and take a step.

Dave decides to make a run for the door, but before he's taken two steps, the frying pan hits him in the side of the head.

I glance at the body on the living room floor and at the feet of the other body halfway into my kitchen. "Shit."

Getting both Darren and Dave into the backyard isn't too tricky. Typically, I'm not too worried about my neighbors. My yard is protected from a casual glance, and, besides, it's early. The kids will be at school. Parents will be at work. Except Mrs. Martin, who works from home – and I can hear her on her back porch. She's on the phone talking to someone about hearing a gunshot. Hopefully, it's a friend or relative. I need to get rid of the bodies, and doing so in the backyard is the best option. I secure the hands and feet of the faux cops and wait. But Mrs. Martin seems content to stand on her back porch. So, not wanting to wait any longer, as quietly as I can, I slap Darren awake.

As his eyes open, I clamp my hand over his mouth. "Who sent you?" I wait for a second and then remove my hand.

"Kill me. I'm not saying a thing." He struggles against the vines I had conjured up. And then his eyes dart in the direction of Mrs. Martin.

This time, I pinch his broken nose and press my hand against his mouth. "I know you're thinking of screaming for help. So, firstly, coward. I didn't call out for help, now did I? And, what would your thug friend think of you? But before you do, you should really think that through. You're way out of your jurisdiction, in what I'm guessing is a stolen uniform. I don't think it's going to be much help for you to call out." I pull my hands away. He remains silent. "Good boy." I straddle him and plant my bottom on his gut. "So, tell me, Detective Robert Darren, is this you quitting, or is this just a side hustle?"

"I," he starts, but then I see the clarity. "You," he says in an angry whisper. "I'm going to -"

"Shhh, I'm thinking," I say and slap him on the forehead. "You're human. We don't use humans all that often, so whoever hired you wanted you to get close – and is possibly trying to remain unseen by the Others. Which is against the rules. The game's in play. Your boss is very naughty. That's interesting. And you know where I live. How did you manage that?" Darren looks away from me. *Seriously, though, how had they managed that?* Darren begins to struggle. "Shh," I close my eyes for a second and clear my thoughts. There it is – a presence. *Someone's watching.* Before I can get anywhere else with this, I see Dave begin to stir. I'm not sure I'll be able to convince both of them to stay quiet. Darren's smile catches me. "What?"

"The eyes always give it away. While we're waiting for you to be outnumbered, what's in the folder, Aedan?"

The only comeback I can think to say is, "Shut up." I bounce off his gut and stand up. And then something finally goes my way. Mrs. Martin goes back inside. Wasting no time, I use a travel stone, draw a large circle around the two bodies, and then place my hand at the center of that circle. "Öffnen," I say and step back. The ground ripples, and there's a thunderous crack as purple arcs of electricity spark out from the circle. The grass and dirt begin to swirl, and Dave and Darren sink into that swirl. It's not the best way to travel, and it's limited by places that I've been to, but I'm good at setting up portals, so *happy trails*. They'll be safe in Darren's precinct. After a few seconds, all is quiet. And Mrs. Martin storms back out onto her porch. "It sounded like lightning just struck my backyard," she says into her phone, but I don't stick around to listen to the rest of that conversation.

I'm not sure how much time I just bought myself. "How did they know where to find me?" I scratch at the back of my head as I reenter my kitchen. "It's hard enough for one of us to track another, and for one of us to give that information out to humans – that's just not done," I say to the eight snickerdoodles on my counter. "I think I'm racing to catch up." I pop a cookie into my mouth. "I need answers." I storm into the living room and reach for the folder – but stop. "I need answers." My hand hovers over the manila. "But not this way." *Is he a target? I can't take the chance.* I turn and pull on *A Tale of Two Cities*.

I don't bother with undressing or the robe, and I almost forget to give the notch in the wall, with its tiny glass vial, a brush for luck. I slam, rear first, into the chair behind my desk and set my hands, fingers spread, onto the desk. The abductions. Demons acting oddly. Humans in the game. None of those matters. *They know where I live.* "Now you have my attention." *How did they find me?* "Persephone..." I exhale as I lean back.

"What did he say?" Green asks, in a whisper that's not a whisper.

"He's thinking. Now do be quiet," Red scolds.

"He's acting strangely. I think he's got rot."

"He does not."

Green giggles, but I'm not sure whether at me or at having fun with annoying Red. "He's in the wind, for sure."

"That we can agree on," Red states.

"What is this word, 'Persephone?'" The quiet sound of Blue's English accent drifts across the chamber.

I let out a sigh. Sometimes I regret giving them a voice. "I am thinking. Or trying to. Or I was trying to think, but now I think I need to find someone."

"So many words," Green's exasperation brings a smirk to my face.

"Persephone?" Blue asks.

"Yes."

"We can help," they say in unison.

I lean forward and rub the back of my neck with my hands. "Thank you, but," I struggle with my words. I have no idea how to make them understand this. In as much as the runes that give them voice translates their thoughts and images into words I'll have a better chance of understanding, the stones do the same for my words into their language. But their concept of war, good and evil, are alien to what I am dealing with. They don't understand cruelty the way I do. This is not their fight. This is my fight. I am general, soldier, spy, and standard-bearer, and I will not have them dragged into something dangerous that they can't possibly understand.

Worry-filled anger swells within me, and I feel my face turn red. I ignore the small voice inside me, suggesting I might be misplacing my rage. I close my eyes. "This is not for you." In the silence that follows, I get up in a huff. Misplaced or not, I'm still angry. I don't look; I don't care if anyone is still watching. I thump the desk and move to the armoire. I take the leather satchel resting on the floor against the side of the closet and begin stuffing my battle gear into it. The cloak, daggers, cylinder staff, and even my slippers, before pulling back. And then I hear Red's bristled tone.

"A forest is more than one."

"We know things."

The hurt in Green's voice has me picturing her with pouty lips and arms tightly folded over her chest. "Yes. And yes. But when lightning strikes a member of your forest, can you help them fight the fire?" I wait, but no answer comes. The silence feels different this time. It's like their consciousnesses aren't even present anymore. It feels like I've upset them enough that they've walked out and left the front door open. And rather than apologizing, like a coward I head for the door. I need to find another place to think, and then I remember I hadn't had my shower yet. *Get clean and then get out.* I think at myself. I'm near the top of the stairs when I hear Blue speak.

"Persephone found."

Chapter 11

The weight of my long-life hits me all at once, and I need to sit on the stairs for a moment to catch my breath. I wanted a shower, but right now, I'm not sure if I want to sleep or head back to the bar for several drinks. I'm worn down; I'm beaten. First Alan, now this. I assume their discovery has something to do with the ethereal collective they coexist in. I don't know what effort it took to uncover this or how much time, but both, I gather, are different in that realm. However, the thought of genuinely alienating them by rejecting their generosity outweighs my better judgment to keep them safe.

I shiver at the thought if I had given up in the presence of Alan. I'll accept their information, even though, as I get up from the stairs, an image of scorched earth flashes before me. I take each step down into the chamber with the slow deliberation of a felon walking the long mile. "Are you sure?" I ask, giving them a last chance.

"Yes. Like you."

I've never heard Blue speak with such joy and pride. I can't bring myself any further down the stairs and sit with three steps to go. "Where?" My words are barely audible as my hand rubs across my mouth. But my communication with Red, Green, and Blue is only partially verbal, so the stalling attempt has little impact.

"Not here," Blue says with an equal amount of delight.

Green's laugh cuts him off. "Not here, not there, but both and in between."

Even though translating it into words diminishes its beauty, I recognize one of my favorite tree poems. "Nothing, nothing, nothing, rock." I recite the next line.

"This is hardly the time."

Red's curt tone never fails to make me feel like a child, but before I can respond, Green chimes in again.

"Rock is not sky," she doesn't say this lyrically, but instead with that tone that makes me think of her rolling her eyes.

I try to hide my chuckle. I know this poem too. It's part of their mythos. It's about an angry, stubborn sapling who ignores the forest and grows along the ground instead of skyward. The sapling later becomes a vine. Red and Green begin to argue, and I wonder if I should slip away when Blue speaks up as if he's been quietly waiting for his chance.

"To the cold, across the wasteland where you visit the sadness."

That would be how they recognize Cassy, wouldn't it? I'm not sure how to tell Blue that it doesn't narrow down Persephone's location.

"By the fire, just show him!" Red bellows.

Green says almost immediately, "Oh, I don't think that's a good idea. I mean, he is very small."

"Show me?"

"The Consciousness," Red says.

"It will probably kill you," Green says in a disconcerting sing-songy way.

"That is a chance he must take. The situation is dire."

I've never been offered the option of seeing The Consciousness – though I usually refer to it as The Collective as they've never named it before today. Frankly, the idea of visiting The Collective Consciousness has always frightened me. I've heard them describe it a few times, and it sounds vast, like space, and when you sit and try to contemplate the enormity and timelessness of space, it's crushing. As I understand it, The Consciousness is even more so. But, right then, there was a tone to Red's voice, and something is telling me that he – no, probably all of them, suddenly know more about what is going on than I do. And they're troubled by it.

However, I think of a compromise that will hopefully save my life. "If I may," I say as I stand and go to the shelves behind my desk. I pull an out of date atlas from its place among other maps. I open to the pages of New York State and lay the book out on my desk.

"Ugh!" Green says in disgust. "No texture. So flat."

I ignore her and place a finger on New York City. "North of the city," I start to draw my finger along the page up the Hudson River.

"There," Green says.

"No, not there," Red says.

"Almost there," Blue says.

My finger is near the Canadian border. I move it a little to the right toward the Atlantic.

"No. No," Red says.

"Too far," Green says.

"I think the other way," Blue says.

My finger drags along the map to the left.

"Almost," Green says.

"Not quite," Red says.

"Nearly, though," Blue says.

I slow my finger's pace, but it travels nearly to Lake Ontario, and they don't say anything. "Further?"

"It's so hard to say," Green says apologetically.

"How does your kind find anything?" Red growls.

Blue's voice does not follow his companions. In fact, more than a minute passes before he says anything. "Few forests. Green and yellow. Flat. Your metal stabs at rock…"

His voice is straining as if he's trying to read the bottom line of an eye chart. I think he's describing farmland. I pull my finger back along the Saint Lawrence.

"Near there," Green says.

"Nearly, anyway," Red says.

I wait for Blue. My finger is hardly moving at this point, and it catches the page and jumps. I sigh, thinking we'll have to start over, but then Blue speaks.

"There."

I lift my finger, *somewhere near Canton.*

Chapter 12

Flying at night is a beautiful thing. Stars below. Stars above. Vast seas of blue-black surrounded by shores of light. After a few hours in the air, however, I'm drained and wishing I'd been to Canton at least once in the last two thousand or so years. I spot a good place to land and come down on a lonely two-lane country round not far outside of town. Everything is covered in snow. The road is walled on both sides by the plowing of the recent heavy snowfall.

I wait and listen. No one is about. The customary flash accompanies my change. I become part of the still night and allow my mind to reach out. The tingle in my mind tells me she's away from town in this direction. I'm not sure how long of a walk that will be, but it will give me time to come up with a plan. I'd rather observe her than confront her. I need to find out if she's on a side or neutral. I caught her speaking with Gregor. Which makes it sound underhanded; the truth is that everything we do is secretive but not necessarily illicit. And I was there for the same reason, after all. And it appeared as if we both left unhappy. "Oh, wait a minute," I say out loud to the night air. "How did she know where to find Gregor?" This line of thinking causes me to stop. "I only know by accident. Is that how she knows him too?" I start walking again. "Too much of a coincidence." I find myself expecting Red, Green, or Blue to chime in. But there are only a few trees around. Most of what I'm passing by is snow covered fields broken up by thin tree lines. Just then, a gust of chilly air blows over the open land and pulls at my hair and coat.

In a moment, all is calm again. When there's no wind, the cool night is pleasant. It helps me focus – the wind is a distraction. I fold my arms across my chest and pick up my pace. "And now Manna has been burned down. Or not – should check on that. Either way, how did those thugs know where to find me? Gregor would be the sort to use humans, but I'm sure he doesn't know where I live. Persephone? No, she wouldn't use humans." And then an unsettling thought bubbles to the forefront. I find it makes me angry. "Someone could have asked Cassy." *I don't like that. I don't like that at all.*

"Someone is handing out information, and they've better not have involved Cassy."

The empty road suddenly becomes a busy place as two cars drive by in quick succession. These are followed by a third car – a truck. It pulls to a stop just ahead of me. The owner of the brand-new blue Ford sticks his arm out his window and waves me forward.

"Chilly night for a walk. Going far?"

The driver appears to be about forty with a very handsome bone structure. "Not sure." I glance at the road reaching out into the darkness beyond the headlights.

"Town's that way, you know."

I chuckle. "I know. I'm looking for someone. An old friend. I think she lives down this road. Thought I'd surprise her."

He looks at me suspiciously. "Not much down this road but a few farms. Most people drive it."

Right, no car. I can see how that's odd – I hadn't thought of that. "I like to walk. Don't have a car. I got a ride into town, thought I'd hoof it the rest of the way. Didn't think it'd be this far." As this is the era of rideshare, I figure that would make for a good excuse. Thankfully he nods.

"Who you looking for?"

I hesitate with that question. *Would he know her as Persephone?* I scratch at the back of my head and try my most innocent of voices. "She was married a few years back, but that didn't end well. I'm not sure if she kept his name or changed it back."

"This is a friend of yours?" he asks skeptically.

"Yeah, we've lost touch. I'm going for a surprise and reconnect. Her name's Persephone."

The driver thinks for a second. "Name doesn't ring a bell, but hop in any way. There's a crossroad not far. She probably lives down one of those spurs."

I walk around and get in the passenger side, and he drives on. "I appreciate this." I lean my head back and close my eyes.

"Been traveling long?"

"Seems like forever."

"I don't want to tell you your business, but maybe a surprise visit wasn't the best idea then."

"Well, I'm hoping this is a surprise visit. There's a chance she may have knocked on my door, and I can't have that."

"Knocked on your door? You said you'd lost touch?"

"Maybe. She might be looking for me, or I've pinged too hard. She'll know I'm coming. Either way, I need to ask what side she's on or if she's under a different set of orders. You see, you never know. Well, she'll know, but for obvious reasons, I don't know. And then, more than just asking the question, what do I do about it?"

"You a spy or something?" He laughs nervously.

I think he's regretting his generosity. "Or something." The energy in the cab changes. I can feel his side glances. But, for me, this is nice. The truck has a comforting hum to it, which revs a bit as he steps on the gas. It's oddly soothing.

A few minutes pass, and the truck begins to slow down.

"I'll drop you here..."

The tone is polite, but I hear the subtext, which says, *get out of my car and please don't kill me.* "Here, let me give you something for the ride."

"Oh, that's not -"

Before he can finish that statement, I snap a small twig in his face. A pink smoke envelops his head. "Thanks for the ride," I say, even though I know he'll remember nothing of this. I step down onto the side of the road, and the tingle in my head points me towards the lane on the opposite side. I'm a few strides down the frozen trail when I hear the truck pull away. A little bit further down the road and I begin to get the impression that the road has turned into a driveway. Trees line the trail. The hawthorns, a couple of trunks deep on either side, press against the road, creating an effect of walking down a hallway. They're eerie and beautiful with the moonlight bouncing off the dusting of snow in the branches. Funny trees, hawthorns, associated with both life and death. Also - less funny - known hangouts for fairies.

Those pixie bastards and I have not had the best of relationships. Twice in the last hundred years, they've almost caused me to fail missions and - I'm pretty sure - had something to do with the death of Alan's parents. I've made damn sure not to have anything around my house that would grab their attention. They're not bad, but they're not very bright. They enjoy jokes and pranks. And I've never seen one turn down a sweet or something shiny. I wouldn't be able to see one unless it wanted me to. They can stay hidden from everyone, including each other – probably so they don't steal each other's hordes. But all the same, I keep to the center of the lane; somehow, it feels safer.

I soon come to a stout wooden gate, although in about fifty feet in either direction, the fence scales down, becoming posts and wire. Electrified too. "Hmm, not good." *The electricity will mess with my magic, and if she's smart, she's got this line of wood and wire configured in such a way to surround her place in a ward. If it comes to a fight – the odds will not be in my favor.* "Let's not panic," I tell myself. "First, we observe." And with that, I transform into a falcon and settle on one of the posts.

At a glance, there's little to be worried about. Everything seems simple and ordinary. The large yellow and white farmhouse is nestled up ahead in the saddle of two rises with the ground sloping down towards the gate and me. It's the odd landscaping that has me curious. There's a gravel path, about a car's width, from the gate to a circular drive off the front porch. To either side of this, running the length of the path, are untouched stripes of white where I'm guessing grass would be in the spring. The rest of the lawn and land around the house, for as far as I can see, is all torn up as if someone had been doing doughnuts with a motorcycle. My eyes shift back to the house. Several minutes pass, and I start to think no one's home. *It's going to be a long night.*

Chapter 13

As dusk of the following day approaches, I observe two things. I've become very bored, and Persephone is not home. The last sixteen hours or so have revealed little other than highlighting the peacefulness of this spot. Actually, I also know that the electrical fence never came on, and I'm pretty sure, despite my first impression, the fence is not doubling as a ward. Even in standby, wards glow faintly in the UV – or there's a vibration as it oscillates in and out of normal space. No such indicators appear along the fence.

I yawn and stretch my wings. I'm bored and hungry. I want a shower and my bed, but I can't have either because I'm supposed to be here. Well, not here precisely, but I'm expected to be working the mission. I reaffirmed a decision I had during the long night. I place the blame of this resolution on the frosty stakeout. I've decided I'm okay with this. I genuinely hope Seph has something to do with this. I have no problem taking a backseat to this mission. Let her take control. I'm done with it. She probably knows more than I do anyway. Hell, she knew where I lived before I had found her. *Or maybe not, still not sure about that.* She's got this. It's like we're two field agents from different organizations unknowingly working the same case. Or – she's my opposition, and we're about to have a big fight.

Either way.

Something on the wind causes my head to twitch. A familiar sound – tires on dirt, moving fast. No engine noise, just the crunch of dirt and pebbles. Suddenly the gate opens and closes. I wait. I'm struggling with my senses. I'm positive I heard a car, but at the same time, my eyes are telling me I didn't.

Thunk.

That was a car door. I think in a very I-told-you-so way to my eyes. With a flap of my wings, I'm airborne. As land falls behind, and I observe more of the surrounding area, almost immediately I feel distracted by a scurrying rodent far below, and it occurs to me that I've been a falcon for far too long. As I circle, my attention grabbed by the chipmunk, something dark and large – about the size of a bear cub – cuts its way across the chewed up yard and through the open barn doors. It's enough to bring my mind back to full consciousness.

Demon? I'm not sure. We've never been at odds before. I curse the gods, and I don't care who's listening. There's a small shed near the back porch where I land and change. The first thing I do is take in a deep breath. One hand presses gently against my unsettled stomach, and my other hand goes to my head. It's like coming up too quickly from a deep dive while low on oxygen. "Move, Aedan," I command myself. I'm not sure if I should prepare for a friendly conversation or a fight, but right now, surprise is my best advantage.

I step up the stairs to the porch, and of course, the board creaks. "Smart," I say, looking admonishingly at my feet. The back door is open, but there's a screen door. Nothing comes sailing at me, and I don't feel the tingle of any power. *Maybe she hadn't heard.* Through the kitchen is a narrow hallway of pale blue with a white chair rail. I peek into the dining room, living room, and a small sitting room – the warmth of the place strikes me. There are pictures on the wall, paintings, drawings, framed photographs, and a large fishbowl nearly full of bottle caps. I'm not sure if it's art or a knickknack. I come to the front hall and the stairs to the second floor.

I'm not getting caught by creaking floorboards this time. I risk the flash from a change and turn into a bat just long enough to get to the top landing - five doors in a mossy green hallway. *One of them must be a bathroom. One's probably a closet. That leaves three rooms.* From behind the nearest door, I hear the thunk of a drawer pushed shut. I focus on the door, my heart thumping. *I really don't want to fight her.* Too many questions and not nearly enough answers. *Is she part of this? Is she against me? Do I go in blazing? Just knock and say hello? And, oh by the way, do you want this task?* I remind myself that I'm not here for a fight – I just want to ask a few questions. Find out what she knows. I walk up to the door and into the room as if I'd come over for our usual cup of tea.

"Anant," she says sweetly. "nice of you to finally come in."

And then it occurs to me – I may not be here for a fight, but she may be. I slide my hands in my pockets, a twig in one fist, a stone in the other. I glance around the room. It's a nicely decorated study with a big window behind the desk where Persephone sits. "I go by Aedan these days." Her smile is disarming. "You knew I was coming?" She nods. There are probably a dozen ways she knew I was here, but one jumps right to the top of the list. "The fairies?" She nods again. "Of course."

"I've got a good relationship with them. They like my trees."

"Making friends with an easily distracted pickpocket who has a sweet-tooth sounds dangerous." She laughs at this.

"And yet, they've ruined your surprise." She eases back in her chair and stares at me like a psychiatrist waiting for me to speak.

The blouse she's wearing is stylish, with no shoulders, and I can see the muscles tensing, but I hold my ground. "We've never been at odds before," I say peaceably.

"But here you are, in my house. Let me see your hands."

Something in her tone as she said that makes me think I may have been wrong about her knocking on my door. "I just want to talk."

"We can... after you remove your hands from your pockets."

She has a no-nonsense tone and the body language of a crouching tiger. The problem is if she *is* the one I'm up against, not having my magic at the ready gives her a significant advantage. She's a better fighter, stronger than I am, and on her home turf. All I have for leverage are my spells.

"As you say, we've never been at odds. It is the only reason you are still standing. Now, let me see your hands."

I almost say, show me yours, as she's still hiding her hands on her lap, which is obscured by the desk. Then I noticed the two umbrella stands full of umbrellas on either side of her desk. I'm not sure how I had missed them, but then I remember Persephone's talents - weapons and altering perception. I slowly pull my hands out of my pockets. *There was a time when I was good at this*. I sigh and make a big deal of showing that my hands are empty.

"How did you find me?" she asks.

"You don't expect me to answer that, do you?"

She smirks. "No. Then how about telling me why you're here?"

I glance at the umbrella stands again. I can't be certain, but I'm pretty sure the only thing between me and six months of regenerating is what I say next. *Why am I here then?* We stare at each other. *The mission.* I sigh inwardly in frustration at suddenly feeling like I've been lead here like a dog.

"Someone's been summoning Sidhe and abducting hikers. Any new hobbies you want to tell me about?"

Her expression is placid. "We don't involve humans in our work."

"That's less a rule and more a guideline."

"Not to me." Her pale-blue eyes and steely gaze never waver.

Her tone is aggressive. Forceful. Angry even. And yet, something in those three words tells me all I need to know about where I stand with Persephone. The tension in my body eases, and as it does, I see the same in her. I smile. "How you been, Seph?" There's a pause. *Is that irritation at the informal use of her name, or is she still struggling with trusting me?*

"Busy. You?"

Her tone is even, revealing nothing to help me understand if she welcomes the unannounced visit or if she just wants me to lower my guard. "Until recently, feeling very normal," I say in the hopes of keeping the conversation going as she still hasn't revealed her hands.

She raises an eyebrow at that. "Normal?"

"Human."

A soft chortle escapes her lips as she slowly shakes her head. "Oh, An – Aedan, you were always the romantic. You can't have your cake and eat it, too."

"There's always hope."

"Hope is a lie we tell ourselves."

With that, Persephone produces a small crystal orb from her lap and sets it down on an empty wooden base next to the phone on her desk. The umbrella bins waver. I stare at the small but deadly looking ballistae with bolts of emerald points to either side of her desk. I almost jump as I also notice, out of the corner of my eyes, the two six-foot axes on either side of me as they slide back into the wall. It seems rude to sit without being invited, but I do in the chair opposite her desk anyway. "I meant what I asked. Any new hobbies?"

"Nothing worth mentioning."

My turn to cock an eyebrow.

With a shrug, she answers. "I've recently taken up needlepoint."

On the wall behind her, I see a framed square of canvas. The details are missing, but I can tell it's of a small rocky waterfall. For just a second, a smirk forms on my lips - she catches it and scowls. "Sorry, it's just – well, I've seen you behead a guy."

"I can do both."

I nod and lean forward. "Is that why the yard's all torn up? Been beheading guys? A little catch, release, and chase them down for fun?"

She leans forward. "You said something about hikers?"

Smalltalk never lasts very long with our kind. This time, it's my fault, though. "Three, maybe, and I've witnessed some very odd demon behavior."

"Odd, how?"

"Cambion working together. And I'm suspicious about how they got here – they may have hopped a fence. Or had help." Her face crinkles. At least she finds this as worrying as I do. And something else, something in her thoughtful expression. "There is something you want to tell me."

Her face changes. She's stern again. "What proof do you have?"

"Just the odd behavior – and my gut."

"They could just be demons, doing demon things. Are you sure this has anything to do with your hikers? People are abducted every day."

"I don't like coincidences."

"You never have. But, I assume your interest in this has more to do with being tasked. And that doesn't explain why you're here or how you found me."

I smirk. We never like knowing that we've been discovered. She's handling it with a bit better grace than Gregor. "I was in New York." The realization is instant.

"Ah, both the reason why you've looked me up and your uncertainty as to my side."

"Yes."

She leans back in her chair, and her whole expression changes again. A thin smile creases the corners of her mouth, and she eyes me quizzically. "Still finding your way into and out of places. Still that little mouse no one can find even when you know it's around."

I'm not sure whether she's talking to me or thinking out loud. "Yes," I say with a heavy hint of suspicion.

"You discovered my tranquil little hiding place. Now I must move it. I'd say you owe me," she says quickly, the curious tone gone.

"I do?"

"Yes." She abruptly gets up and leaves the room.

I follow. "But -"

"We can talk on the way."

"On the way?"

"New York," she says, leaving the house through the back door. She shuts and locks the door after I've passed by and leads the way around to the side of the house. She stops in front of the detached garage. "Hop in."

I look around. My eyes can't focus, and I find that I keep looking away from the garage. She gives a self-satisfied snort and places her hand on something made of thin air. A massive beast of a red truck fades into sight. She enjoys my expression of awe. "A little conspicuous?"

"No one will see us unless I want them to," she says in a return to her business tone. "Now get in," she orders and then whistles.

The morning's silence is broken by soft thunder as if a storm lay in the distance. Racing around the back of the house, at a startling speed, comes a black and brown mass. It cuts a fresh groove into the soil as it approaches, and I take a terrified step back. Without slowing down it comes to a complete stop just in front of Persephone. It's a boulder, a rough sphere of rock about three feet in circumference covered in mud, dirt, and moss. "Seph, you said you weren't raising demons."

"Hush," she says harshly and then strokes the boulder lovingly. "This is Mym."

"Where -"

With a snap of her fingers, she cuts me off. "In."

I'm not sure if she is speaking to me or the rock, but we both react. Mym rolls to the back of the truck, where Persephone waits with the tailgate down. There's a rumble, like a giant digesting something, and then a whoosh of what sounds like steam erupting from a broken pipe. The truck rocks, and I hear the tailgate close. Persephone joins me in the cab. Without a word, the truck starts up, and at full speed we race towards the gate – which slides open at the last second. "Shit!" I yell as we thread the needle with hardly a few inches to either side of the truck.

Chapter 14

Once I became used to the idea that the hellish speed we are traveling at isn't going to end with the two of us wrapped around a tree, I begin to relax. The interior was quite lovely with soft red leather, sat-nav, and huge cup holders. Persephone is intently watching the road as she shifts the car from one lane to the next with no irritated cry of a horn to be heard. "I could have opened a portal."

"I'm trying to concentrate," she says dismissively.

"You said we could – that's a car!" We swerve effortlessly around the small sedan.

"I don't remember you being this jumpy."

"When I'm going this fast, I'm usually in the sky." I grip the overhead handle as we cut across four lanes of traffic. "Seriously, we can pull over, and I can open a portal. We'll be in New York in seconds."

"We'll be there soon enough. I don't like to portal. Besides, they make too much noise. We have our missions, which means the other side is watching..." She's distracted for a moment and must jerk the wheel to avoid hitting another car.

"Seph, we're immortal, not indestructible!"

"Please don't call me that."

I cringe at another near miss. I think she's enjoying this. The last time we paired up, we had to make a quick escape down the side of a mountain – I recall facing the same cold amusement from her as I screamed most of the way down. And I hate to admit it, but the thrill awakens the part of me I keep asleep – the part of me that wants to stay asleep. The part of me that used to be good at this. The part of me that cared. There's a warmth that comes over my spirit as I allow myself to be in the moment. It's the same sense of self that I have when I'm in Cassy's presence. It's the self that can disarm, undermine, and provoke by applying pressure with the careful use of question after question. I hate to distract her, but I can't help myself. "I feel you wanted to tell me something back there. Something troubling you? Have you encountered something odd?"

"My mission, my burden."

"And yet, here I am."

She stretches her neck from one side to the other. "You talk too much."

I wait.

She skewers me with a daggerish side glance. "I have noticed..."

"Yes?"

"I have noticed an unusual bit of attention."

So as not to stifle the conversation, I admit the same. "My Patron seemed nervous when last we spoke. I assumed she was keeping an extra eye on me."

"I thought so as well, but..."

"But?"

"This is different. This is – I don't know, these eyes cast a much larger shadow."

As she says this, I realize how right she is. I've sensed the same thing. Eyes on me, but different from Brigit's presence. I decide not to tell Persephone about Father walking among us. At first, I had thought Lugh had told me to throw me off my game, but in her own way Brigit had said the same thing – and I feel she had chanced a lot more in letting me know. For her sake, I say nothing to Persephone.

There's a significant reduction in speed followed by an exponential acceleration as we detour off the highway to avoid a traffic pocket. When it's safe to speak – when my stomach drops from my throat back into its proper place - I continue. "Can I know why I've been kidnapped?"

She sighs. "I haven't missed the constant questions."

I feel this is meant as an insult, so I don't bother with much of a pause before my next question. "Late in the day to come home, where were you coming from? What were you up to?"

"Hunting," she says without pause.

"Is that why you were in New York?"

"I wasn't in New York."

Was that a lie or is she trying to distract me? "When you were visiting Gregor."

"Ugh," she grumbles, "Gregor."

She's definitely trying to distract me from my question. I decide to go with it. "He never changes." Which I chuckle at, not because it's funny, but at the irony, given the Sisyphean nature of all of our lives.

"More than you know," she adds quickly. "About seven years ago, I was in the city visiting a friend. I happen to see Gregor. I don't know how he's still there. His Patron is playing a long game. That's worrisome."

"By my count, he's been there at least fifty years." She gives me a side glance. I shrug. "Same story. I was in the city visiting a friend, and there he was." Persephone goes quiet after this. She's good at the quiet game. But this is different. She's in her head. I might as well not be in the car. I doubt she's even paying attention to the road anymore, which is worrying. I suppose there are lots of reason to be in a city like New York, but I can't help but wonder if she goes to New York for the same reason I go to New York. I can't help myself; I need to ask. "Were you visiting Cassy?" This does the trick, and I can see her attention return. She nods. We may have just answered a few lingering questions we've both had about each other. The silence isn't distant this time. It's mournful.

"She misses you."

Her words are almost too soft to be heard. I don't know why she told me this, but the phrase is a knife to my heart, and I have to look away.

After several minutes, she clears her throat. "Have you ever come across the Cult of Eleusis?" she asks.

It takes me a moment to answer. Not because I need to think about it, but I need the time to unclench my throat. "No. Not to my knowledge."

A weary sigh escapes her lips. "It seems like I'm always dealing with them. The last time – the last time it was big. They were trying to enact the Ritual of Solomon."

"*That* I've heard of."

"I'm not surprised. It's the only way that I'm aware to kill one of us."

"Or all of us."

"Or all of us. But it's a complicated spell. Precise timing. Precise words. Sacrifice. Seven cursed artifacts. Well, six. But it's all wrong this time. It's too early - besides I have three of the seven artifacts and I keep running into them as if they're still preparing."

"There's a lot to ask about there, but let's start with – is it six or seven?"

"I destroyed one. Which is why I don't understand how they're moving forward with this."

"And you're sure they are?"

"All the signs say yes."

Maybe I wasn't wrong to be uninterested in the kidnapping mission I've been tasked with handling. *I don't need to foist it off on Seph, because Brigit knew it would lead me to Persephone.* Something about that doesn't sit right, but the part of me that's happy to be rid of the responsibility is too loud to figure out what.

"The other thing is..."

I sense her reluctance. Not over telling me, I don't think. It's something else.

"They're powerful this time," she clenches her jaw. "Stronger, with magic they did not have access too last time. They're a cult of assassins. They worship the idea of reaping the world and re-growing it in their own image. This new power - it's like they can make darkness solid. My last one-on-one with a group of them... it didn't go well."

"You beat them, though, I mean, you're here, so..."

"Of course I defeated them," she says with indignation, more like herself. "But -"

She doesn't have to finish. I can see it. She was afraid.

She grips the wheel a little tighter. "I'm lost, Aedan, I can't figure this out, and it's really starting to piss me off."

"Misery loves company." She glances at me. "Never mind. So, you have three of the six artifacts – of which, there used to be seven, but you destroyed one long ago."

"Yes. Over the years most of them have been buried by time. I keep an eye on the Cult. We have our run-ins, but nothing earthshattering. As far as I knew they had lost track of the artifacts too. At least, that's what I thought. I only knew the location of one of them, and I checked on it regularly. But – I don't know. I don't know if they've always known about it or found it. Either way, about a year ago, they came for it. There was a fight, but they got away. I wasn't prepared for this new magic they are wielding. Afterwards, I came up with a plan. If I found the rest, they'd have nothing. I've been searching. Been lucky. I've managed to get there right before they have. Been some scuffles, but I've managed to keep the rest of the artifacts out of their hands.

"And the last two?"

"Gregor has one."

"Ah."

"I tried convincing him to give it to me. But he wouldn't."

"And the last?"

"At the moment, safe in the New York Museum of Natural History. While you were staking out my place, I was tracking the artifact. It's there. Safe, for the moment. I don't know if they know about it. Even if they do, they'll have a hard time stealing this one."

"Trapped?"

"When I ruined the Ritual of Solomon the last time, I had this idea on how to keep the artifacts out of their hands forever. If I could alter the perception around each of the artifacts, they'd be ignored. Forgotten."

"You should have destroyed them." She winces at my words.

"They are not easily destroyed."

I know the taste of a bad memory when I see one. The nerve seems too sensitive. I don't ask. Besides, I'm caught up on something else she had said, a "Huh?" escapes my lips.

She sighs. "What?"

"Sorry. You said they came after the one you knew about, and then just happen to be steps behind you when you found the others."

"Yes?"

I have never been able to tell if she doesn't bother to hide her irritation or if she's just no good at hiding her irritation. "Well, I don't like luck. I place it in the same basket as coincidence. Are you sure... I mean, you're watching *them*, is it possible *they're* watching you?" I can tell she doesn't like the question. She has a face remarkably similar to the one I made the first time I ate pickled herring.

"The last two artifacts are safe. Gergor has one. The Cult isn't going to go up against him. The other is lost among a sea of other artifacts at the museum. They're safe."

I'm good at reading people, and right now, her face lacks the confidence that would typically go with that statement. "You're sure?"

There's a pause, and then she says, "Mostly," we swerve right, speeding up an off-ramp, and then take a sharp left.

I waited for my organs to return to their proper places. "So you've kidnapped me for what? To show me how safe the artifacts are?"

"No."

Chapter 15

New York reminds me of that time I unknowingly fell asleep outside a bear den while traveling in the Yukon. I awoke to this tranquil, serene scene, which masked the danger quietly snoozing just out of sight – a danger that could wake up at any moment. The growl of Persephone's crimson monster reminds me of those bears. At the same time, her weaving in and out of traffic is very reminiscent of me stepping lightly around twigs trying to be inconspicuous. She makes a left, and I suddenly realize where she is taking me. But why?

She parks about a block away in among a few other trucks, construction equipment, and iron scaffolding. We exit her vehicle, and she stops to pat the boulder in the bed. "Wait here, please." Persephone takes the lead and walks away in the direction of Manna. "You can get in and out of places, right?"

"I don't like to brag -"

"Then don't."

I clear my throat, the smile dropping away. "Alright. But I think I know what you're asking, and this isn't going to work."

"We're going to pay Gregor a visit, and while I have him distracted, you're going to sneak into his office and find the Blade of Gabra. It's a small stone knife." She holds her hands apart about six inches.

Both her tone and plan smack of desperation. I do not say this, however, and instead, I just repeat my warning. "This isn't going to work."

As we approach from the direction of Madison Avenue an unforgiving blast of November wind gusts into our faces. Persephone doesn't even flinch. I, on the other hand, pause to zip up my jacket. She's ahead of me now, and I watch as a change comes over her. Even from this far up the block, yellow tape can be seen. Stalwort focus dissolves into confusion and disbelief. As I come alongside her the anger in her face is replaced by suspicion. She slows. "What?" Halfway to the restaurant, she stops. "I was just here," she says in disbelief. "When did this happen?"

"'bout two days ago. The same day you were here." A steely gaze fixates on me.

She rushes forward, lifts me about an inch off the pavement, and presses me into a brick wall. "You knew about this?"

"Yes."

"Did you do it?"

"No."

"Why didn't you tell me?"

"I was curious what your reaction would be." She lets out an annoyed grunt and drops me.

"Testing me?" she snaps, her words sharp with frustration.

"Yes," I say and pull down on my jacket and sweater. "You know how this works, Seph. Trust no one. You didn't kill me back at your house - which I'm thankful for - but I was still unsure if you knew about any of this. Maybe it was you who sent those goons to my door. I wanted to see an honest reaction." There's a moment of pain on her face, quickly replaced by resentment.

"And?"

I study her for a moment. "You didn't know about this." She shoves me against the wall and walks away.

I rush to catch up. "We came all this way, and we're not going to take a look around?"

"It was the Cult, must be. There won't be anything for us to find. And if they've managed to get this one..." she stops. "What goons?"

"Humans, if you can believe it."

She abruptly spins in place and storms over to me. "I don't use humans."

"I know, but," I shrug.

She resumes walking away. "How did they know where to find you?"

"Don't know. They weren't going to talk, and I didn't want to kill them, so I sent them away."

"Sounds like something Gregor would do."

"I know, but – his place. I think he'd sooner cut off a foot. No, it's someone else, and whoever I'm playing against has been way ahead of me from the very start." As I say this, I feel gnawing guilt in my gut – *ahead of me because I've been dragging my feet.*

"But it's not me, right?"

"I don't think so." Her laugh is sardonic. I feel bad now. "Seph -"

"Stop calling me that."

I don't press. She marches ahead of me on our way back to her truck.

"Get in," she orders.

I obey. "So, that's it?"

"No."

Chapter 16

No one notices as Persephone pulls up onto the sidewalk at the corner of seventy-seventh and Central Park West. She gets out of the car without a word and moves to the back of the truck while I try to orient myself. Night had settled in; traffic, of course, ignored this fact, and there were plenty of people around. I can see a wrought iron fence and an impressive nineteenth-century building through the gaps between a few well-established oaks. "The New York Museum of Natural History – why?" I felt the truck rock, and a few seconds later, Persephone is at my window.

"Come on."

She has Mym at her side and a black satchel over her shoulder. I exit the truck and feel the need to quietly close the door – as if shutting it naturally would draw more attention than the act of driving a two-ton red truck onto the sidewalk. "We're just going to park here, are we?"

Her look of impatience is back. "You're walking along, and there's a box, or a signpost, in your way. Do you walk into that box or signpost? No. You walk around them, never paying the motion any mind."

As she says this, a group of twenty-somethings approach and skirt around the back of the truck to wait their turn at the streetlight.

"This way." Persephone starts down seventy-seventh with Mym at her heels.

Within minutes, we come to a small plaza with a beautiful double stone staircase at the far end and a large balcony slightly above. The glass doors seem to be our obvious destination, so I take a step, but then a hand takes my shoulder.

"There's a staff door just to the other side of that tower."

We make our way around to the door. From here we're mostly hidden from the street and sidewalk. The door itself is also slightly disguised to match the stone of the building. There's a flat handle and a pad where those with the proper ID can unlock the door. I stare at the door and then at Persephone and shrug. "What's the plan?"

"Open the door."

"That's an action. What's the plan?"

"The plan is for you to open the door."

My hands rub at my face. "You've cased the place, right? You know the guards' routines. The alarm system. Cameras."

"I know the object is inside, somewhere."

"And it doesn't bother you that we'll be seen as soon as we enter?"

"Assuming you can get us in without a fuss, we will not be seen."

There's no arguing with her expression – a mixture of confidence and determination. I reach out to examine the door more closely when something occurs to me. "Wait. You said somewhere. I thought you knew where this thing is?"

"I said I had tracked it down. It's somewhere inside the museum."

I take a step back and hold my arms out wide. "It's a big building." She steps up to me; we're face to face.

"Get. On. With. It."

I feel Mym press against my leg – it's odd to be able to sense intent from something without a face, but then again, I do talk with trees. "I suppose asking to take a few days to watch the place is out of the question," I ask just to be irritating. I know the answer is no – not only because she'll say no, but because I'm aware time is ticking on how long it will before the Cult shows up. I slip by Persephone, who doesn't give an inch and examine the door.

The seal around the door is too tight. There's nothing I can change into to squeeze through. "Mesopotamia..."

"What was that?" Persephone asks.

"There was a guy, one of us, I remember, he could change himself into this gas. He'd be really useful right now."

"Concentrate on what we have, not what would be useful."

Thankfully, she can't see my smirk. Out of all my brothers and sisters, she's the one over the centuries I've had the pleasure of working with on a few occasions. I hadn't realized how much I'd missed this. She has this focus. This gets the job done attitude. Very kick-down-the-front-door. It juxtaposes my slow and steady mentality - and as I remember, not always amicably.

"Well?" She verbally pokes – her impatience showing again.

I've figured the door out, but I let the tension build for a minute more. I step back with an air of uncertainty and look at her with worried eyes. Which lasts all of a few seconds as I'm suddenly distracted by her change in outfit. Her modern casual look has been replaced by what can only be described as burglar chic. "When?"

She finishes zipping up her bag, stares at me for a moment, and then cocks an eyebrow. "The door?"

"I've run into this type before. It's magnetic, with a physical lock that engages if the power's cut. Easy enough to bypass." I step up to the door. I consider the anois spell – it had worked so well at the police precinct, but I'm afraid that type of disruption will alert the guards. My hand rustles through my pocket. I pull a twig, examine it, and then place it at the foot of the door. With my hand hovering over the twig, I whisper, "Dervo." And then I step back in a hurry. It's never easy to predict how magic and modern will interact. I perceive a slight tremble in the air, and then creepers of green mist begin to weave their way out of the twig. The tendrils sink into the ground and snake over the door. Within seconds the wisps consolidate into woody vines forming roots, a trunk, and branches. The solid tree – sapling really - partially forms in the space between the door and the wall, forcing the door open. Persephone presses forward, but I hold up a finger telling her to wait a moment. A second later, the sapling's vibrant greens and browns turn gray and crumble into ash.

"I didn't know you still spoke your old tongue," she says as we cautiously step over the threshold.

"I don't. But a lot of my power words are from the old language."

She nods and takes the lead into the museum.

It's dark. The only light comes through the partially opened door behind us, which I close. "Hold on a sec." I dig around in my pockets and pull out another twig. I snap it in two and set the ends in my empty palm. They begin to glow as if on fire. The light is better than candlelight, but not as good as a flashlight. I hold out the light and scan the room. The room appears to be under construction, nearly finished, by the looks, but not ready for the public. There are counters, a small kitchen – an eatery of some sort. There's a doorway ahead of us, and Persephone signals me to follow. We enter a pillared and darkly decorated foyer. There are a couple of choices as to which direction we go. "Which way?" I ask.

Persephone considers each hallway and passageway and then says, "Which way?"

"I asked you."

"Shhh. I wasn't talking to you."

I'm confused for a second and then realize she's speaking to Mym.

Mym rolls forward slowly but soon crosses the room at a quick walking pace and enters the next exhibit.

There's no pause to enjoy the dioramas showcasing flora and fauna. I do, however, lag behind when we eventually come to a large hall. It's dark - the only light comes from my palm and some dramatic lighting, but it's not hard to see the two skeletal figures commanding the room. The allosaurus, claws at the ready. The barosaurus rearing up. It's dramatic and worthy of the lighting effect, but also effortless; you can feel the movement and the scene's emotion as if witnessing it firsthand. Of course, it's not real. Real fossils are too heavy, too rare, to set up in such a pose. I feel a heavy tap on my shoulder. I look, and Persephone gives me a sharp hand gesture indicating to move and in which direction.

"Do you think we'll ever go extinct?" I whisper. I feel more than see her eye roll.

"We're immortal. Immortals don't go extinct," she says with this perfect tone that expresses "you idiot," and "we don't have time for this," simultaneously.

I don't bother getting into the whole us versus them, in-society-but-not-of-society, like-it-or-not-we-are-still-human conversation. I take up the rear with Mym in the lead. They seem to be taking me toward a tucked away hallway. The archway is large and prominent, but also beautiful and could be easily overlooked as just part of the overall decor. There's a small plaque which reads Security. There are three doors in this corridor; one at the back with a sign indicating this is for staff only, a large double door to the left, and another normal-sized door to the right. This one is slightly ajar, allowing the light from within to spill out into the hallway. Mym pulls to the side, allowing Persephone to take the lead. She has no weapon readied, but she doesn't need one to be deadly. "Let's not kill anyone. They're just doing their jobs," I whisper.

Persephone shoots me a glare. She signals me to stop and then peers around the edge of the door – I grip a small stone in one pocket and a twig in the other hand, one to restrain her and the other to restrain the guards.

But the tension suddenly diminishes as her shoulders relax. She swings the door open wide, and I enter in beside her. The room is small, but there are two desks, a table, a wall of flashlights and walky-talky chargers, several monitors - showing static or snow – and three dead guards. The one closest to the door has had his throat cut. The guy in the chair behind the desk is upright, his hands up in surrender – his face is ashen colored, his eyes sunken, his jaw hangs open in a silent scream. The third, a woman, is slumped on the ground against the back wall. I can't see her face, but her hands are the same green-gray as her friend's behind the desk. "Well, I see why you weren't worried about security."

"This isn't me. I didn't do this." There's a pause and then a sharp intake of air. "They're here. We're too late. We need to get into the catacombs -"

I catch her arm. "Wait, catacombs?"

"An expression. The maze of tunnels and storage areas under the museum. That's where the artifact will be. We need to get down there." She rushes from the room.

"Give me a sec," I say a little too loud. I slip the glowing twig pieces into a pocket.

"No time."

I don't bother asking again. I slip my coat out of my bag and begin to button up the waistcoat. I feel the change, which starts with the first button and ends with the last. I ready my staff by touching the appropriate runes. I step out into the hallway. I feel powerful. I feel ready now. This is me in the game.

"You're still wearing that?" Persephone smirks.

I'm momentarily taken aback. "As I recall, you wore that crimson armor into combat for a long time."

"Not in almost five hundred years."

"Still, I'm sure you miss it." I flash my own smirk and head for the door at the end of the hallway. The sign that reads staff only also has an icon indicating stairs.

"Not that way." She points at Mym.

I admit that I sometimes push through problems instead of figuring out how to get around them, but I don't deserve the sigh that very loudly says, "men." My pride is hurt enough that I say something. "I'm not used to taking

Mym's limitations into account." This seems to hit home for Mym as she rolls towards me. I square up to the boulder. Before anything can happen, there's a soft ding as the double-wide elevator doors slide open.

"Are you two coming?"

Mym and I both try to enter at the same time, she wins.

"Sublevel one or two?" Persephone asks Mym.

Rumble.

"Down doesn't make that completely clear." She examines the panel; her finger hovers over SL1. "Alright, alright, we'll start with one."

There's a moment of awkward silence – well, awkward for me at least. I nervously tap the side of my leg. "So," I hear the crunch of stone as Mym rolls slightly from side to side as if turning to look at me. "I'd just like to point out that you said this one was supposed to be especially hidden."

"I also said they'd never go after Gregor." Her brusque reply is followed by a be-quiet stare.

"This new power seems to have emboldened them." She doesn't respond to this. "Does this cult -"

"The Cult of Eleusis."

"Right. Do they also have," I glance at Mym, "a friend to track down these artifacts?"

"They would seem to have other means, yes." She glances away from the lights tracking our descent.

I know that expression. I see it every morning in the mirror. She's angry with herself. Disappointed. "Mym says it's in the building. There's still time."

She shrugs off my attempt at being supportive. "The perception imbalance I placed on it will slow them down. They obviously know it's here, but they'll have a hard time laying their hands on it. It's probably why they've waited until the last to go hunting for it."

"But once we get it, that's it; you've won." She doesn't respond. "You said you've been picking them up so the Cult couldn't get their hands on them. Even if we miss this, you still have others. They can't complete the ritual."

"They have two. The one they got to before I did and now the one Gregor was holding. I have the rest. Yes."

"And the ritual?"

An aggravated sigh puffs out her nose. "Even if they get them all," her words drift off. "I'm missing something."

I understand that feeling. You're looking at the puzzle, but none of the pieces seem to fit. I want to say something comforting, but the elevator comes to a halt, and the doors open. The ding of the door opening is uncomfortably loud. We may have lost our element of surprise. I don't need to look at Persephone to know she's thinking the same thing. The situation is made even less ideal by the narrow paths between stacks of crates and shelves, but the hallway up ahead does open up where a line of numbered doors begins. As we reach the first of the doors, Mym suddenly stops. "Has she found it?"

"No. I don't think so."

The words are hardly out of Persephone's mouth when Mym begins to roll away, picking up speed as well as a fiery glow, very quickly. The darkness at the end of the lane wavers. Like a cannonball, Mym slams into those shadows. Cries of pain fill the air. Crates tumble. Shelves give way. A large slab of sandstone with a partially excavated dinosaur femur cracks in two as it crashes into the ground. There's a pause as the thunderous crash of that assault is swallowed by the silence – and then murderous battle cries signal the counter-attack.

Several figures appear out of the darkness. All of them dressed in white linens with a tabard of red and gray tied at the waist with a dark leather belt. I drive my staff into the gut on the nearest one and then club her over the head. The second elbows me in the face and jabs at me with her dagger. Neither the elbow nor the blade does any lasting damage to my bark-like skin. I rotate my staff behind her back, trapping her, and squeeze the air from her lungs as my forehead comes down on her face. She drops away, dazed.

I turn to the sound of Persephone spewing curses at her opponent. She had drawn two short swords from somewhere and was trading parries with a cultist using a long curved dagger. There's a ballet to Persephone's skill in battle. I've seen her on many battlefields, against nightmarish demons, and there's never any wasted movement. A miss is fed into a dodge, is fed into another attack. There's an elegance to her viciousness, and seldom does it take more than a few swings and jabs before she's zeroed in on her enemy's flaw. And then I spot it, as does Persephone, and sure enough the cultist shifted too much of her weight to her left leg. In one quick motion, Persephone deflects the thrust, passes both of her blades to one hand, brings her free hand back, and punches the cultist in the kidney. In another motion, both hands are carrying a short sword again as blade points are driven into the robed enemy's back.

And then the ballet is over in an explosion of darkness. Persephone gets knocked to the ground – tendrils of black writhe and grasp for her. A cultist runs towards her, dagger at the ready. I pull a twig from a pocket. "Bhru," I say and toss it in Persephone's direction. There's no wind, no sign that anything has happened, except that the cultist stops dead in her tracks as if coming into contact with a wall – a second later, she rockets back, crashing into other red and gray tabards.

Persephone and I share a glance; it's not to silently thank me - we both feel it. Eyes are on us, and I can see in her face the thought in my mind, *why?* I look away at the sound of something shuffling towards me. Down the end of the lane, I see a figure. Well, see isn't the right word. I see darkness – and then the darkness rushes at me, hitting me like a fist of solid rock. It throws me against the wall, but I manage to keep my feet. I dig around in a pocket and retrieve the glowing twig pieces. I call upon my power and send them streaking down the lane. There is a figure. It's about halfway down, cowled in robes of black and dark blue. I can't see a face.

"Mym!" Persephone shouts.

I look to my left, past the five crushed cultists to a group of six more rushing the boulder; they surround her and pass a chain between them in an attempt to wrap it around the animated rock. Hands and bodies encapsulate Mym. Persephone charges, but even before she's halfway down the lane, the smell of burning flesh permeates the air. Almost in unison, the group surrounding Mym cries out and staggers back. Persephone stabs two of them, leaps up onto Mym, and launches herself into the air, coming down on a third trying to escape. Three others flee. My skin prickles, and then I hear the crackle of magic. "A portal," I look back towards the figure dressed in black, but it's gone. I weave my way through the lanes trying to cut them off, but I'm too late. I catch the eyes of the last one, the figure in the dark robes, as she glances over her shoulder, slipping into the portal. The face is long and angular and white as a ghost. There's no fear or any sense of defeat. What I see is amusement. I hear Persephone coming around the corner and hold my staff out to stop her.

"We must follow!"

I slide back against her strength. "We don't know where that goes." I grit my teeth and push back. "The artifact? Did they get the artifact?"

She eases back. "No..."

We watch as the portal spirals closed.

"No," she says again, "I don't think so." She turns sharply and marches away.

"You're welcome," I call after her and then follow. I catch up, gently rubbing the lump forming on the back of my head the result of being thrown at a wall. "That was the Cult of Eleusis?"

She stops and looks me up and down. "Hurt?"

I touch the swelling on the back of my head. There's pain, but not enough. I feel incomplete, a little emptier; that connection I feel with this world after such a fight is missing. I bring my hand to my eyes. No blood. I frown.

"Don't be so disappointed," she scoffs and begins walking again. "Yes, that was the Cult - some of them anyway..."

I can see it on her face; something is bothering her. "Did we miss something?"

"They're usually harder to scare off."

"You're welcome," I say, smirking. She doesn't respond. "Mym did squish a few of them," she answers with a thoughtful grunt. "We won, what's the problem?"

"They were waiting for us."

"Well, you said laying hands on it would be difficult for them."

We find Mym pacing back and forth in front of a door with a five painted on it. I try the handle. "It's locked." I fish around in one of my pockets. "I think I have something -"

"Mym!" Persephone yells, but it's too late.

Mym rams the door, and then a second time. The door comes down. She rolls up and over the downed door and into the room.

"Impatient, isn't she?"

"And a bit of a temper," Persephone says as she slides her short swords into sheaths strapped to her upper thighs like a western gunfighter. "She's gotten better." She shrugs and slips into the room.

Inside the room, I find a light switch and turn it on. It's a small area, maybe fifteen feet by fifteen feet. There are some shelves and counters as well as tools and small bottles of chemicals. The room doesn't look like it's been used in years. There's a small wooden box on one of the counters sitting there as if forgotten. Persephone approaches the box and reaches for it, but stops. "What's wrong?" I ask.

"Have you ever had the feeling that you were about to do something that would change everything? As if your action would set in motion a series of events – and you're pretty sure those events aren't going to be good."

I want to say yes. But instead, I say, "You're paranoid."

She nods and reaches into the small wooden box. She pulls out a blue metallic circlet with an eye-catching sapphire set in silver as a focal point. "Hello, again, my little friend." She smiles.

"Can we go now?"

"Yes."

Chapter 17

I realize now the brilliance of Persephone's driving. It took the trip down to the city and an hour of the return trip, but I get it now. Magic, even magic that is designed to hide you, leaves a trail - a scent. I'm particularly good at tracking those scents, and I'm not the only one. She's still driving ridiculously fast, but her actions are more controlled now. Almost calculated. The look on her face is bordering on strained. I feel her power. The ripple of her magic in conjunction with the spell already placed on the truck - she's making sure we're not followed, and if we are we go unseen. Because it's not about invisibility, but perception, with Persephone. Even though changing perception isn't as tricky or power-intensive as invisibility, it will leave a trail to those who know what to look for. But – then you add in the suicidal speeds and the cutting across traffic, and you get a trail that can't be tracked by anyone. All that metal and man-made products weaving in and out of the trail kills the magic, scatters it, much like the misty cloud I found curbside. Plus, she likes to drive fast, so I think she enjoys the excuse. "Smart," I nod.

"Picked up on that, did you?" She answers as if reading my thoughts.

I turn to say something else but stop at the look of concentration on her face. The furrowed brow and tight jaw speak to her covering our tracks, but her eyes – there's something in her eyes that says she worried, unsure, possibly afraid. This is unsettling, and it makes me think of what Gregor had said to me. I turn back to her, and this time, I don't hesitate. "What are you afraid of, Persephone?" She's instantly offended by this question. undaunted, I continue. "You're worried, and it reminded me of something Gregor said to me." Saying she reminded me of Gregor may have been a bad idea – seething replaces the fear in her eyes. I press on. "When I sat down with him in his office, he said - well he said a lot of things, but what really sticks out is what I thought at the moment was just a smartass, off the cuff, comment. He said everyone's afraid of something. I don't think he meant there's always something to be worried about. I think he meant actual fear. Knocking you down and not being able to get back up fear. The type of fear that sucks away your confidence, abilities and chills you to the bone. Fear -"

"I get it," she snaps.

"What are you afraid of, Persephone?" I let the question linger. At first, I watch as she dismisses my question but then, around the time that highway turned to two-lane roads, her shoulders relax. She's at least answering the question internally. She doesn't speak of it – still, even in silence, I feel the conversation has moved along, and it was my turn again. "I'm afraid of Them – which pisses me off. You shouldn't fear your gods," I say, both to say it - to feel that weight lifted - even for just a moment, off of my chest, and to see if she would agree. I hear her snort softly and then fall into silence. I return to my thoughts, which brings me even less comfort. I can't help but picture myself running in place, but it's more than that; I feel like I'm someone's comic relief. I'm running in place, but it's because this big brute has his hand on my forehead. We begin passing through the outskirts of her town. Even at this hour, I see homes with lights on and people on the streets. I sigh, my breath momentarily fogging up the passenger window. And then I hear Persephone sigh – which I think she was doing in response to my sigh.

"You want to be like them?"

"We are like them."

"We *were* like them." She makes a turn, and we're now on the road leading to her place. "They toil mindlessly through their short lives, masked in this air of superiority, with no sense of the big picture. They fear and hate being told what to do but scream at the darkness when there's no one telling them what to do."

"Are we that different? We're different because we are told we are. We're apart from them because we are told to stand apart from them."

"We are a part of something bigger and more powerful -"

I groan and rub at my eyes. "Stop. Please, stop. I'm sure your handler will be very proud of you regurgitating the company line."

The truck slows to an average speed as Persephone threads the gap of the barely open gate, and gravel kicks up as she brakes hard just outside the garage. "Come with me." She picks up the cloth-wrapped artifact and exits the truck. I follow her to the back of the vehicle and watch as she lowers the tailgate. Mym rolls out, plops onto the chewed-up ground, and heads towards the barn, though she does several doughnuts in the backyard before vanishing into the interior. Persephone leads the way into her house and up the stairs to the den where this had all begun. She lays her hand on the blank wall to the right of the desk. The air around her wavers like heat coming off a road in summer. A door appears. Well, it didn't appear, I tell myself. It's been there this whole time; I just didn't see it. She opens it.

There are a couple of shelves on the inside. On the shelves are various objects: a skeleton key, a simple wooden cup, an eye floating in what looks like an empty crystal jar. Persephone carefully unwraps the blue metallic diadem we'd liberated from the museum and places it on the shelf next to the skeleton key. "What do you see?" she asks.

"A yard sale."

"I see the world a little safer. I see a foiled plot. And because of that, the people of this planet have at least another day to figure out how to kill themselves. You asked me what I fear. I fear failing a mission. I fear what happens if we don't do what we're told to do." She steps back from the closet and turns to look at me. "We're not like them, Aedan, because we can't be like them. We serve a higher purpose."

"*Serve* being the operative word."

Her eyes narrow. The closet door slams shut.

"You don't want to lock that?"

"I don't need to."

The door wavers and vanishes. I can't even keep my eyes on the spot of the wall where the door had been. I know it's there, but my attention keeps drifting away. I pinch the bridge of my nose. "You're happy with things the way they are?"

"I like having a purpose. Would you give up what you are to be like, like, those guards?"

"Liking who I am and liking the life I have are two different things." I walk away. I want to slam something too, but it's her house; I don't know what's okay to smash. I feel her hand on my shoulder. It's a calming gesture.

"Let me show you one more thing."

I nod.

Persephone takes my hand, and we walk back down the stairs, over snow covered and mud ruts of the backyard, and into the barn. Mym sits at the center of the barn, and despite being a rock, I get a distinct impression that she is asleep. "Mym," Persephone says softly. Mym rocks slightly back and forth and then rolls about a foot toward us. "What we do, Aedan, our missions, they're important. Someone needs to do them. If not for us, this world would not be here because the gods would have destroyed it long ago. We're necessary, and a lot of what we do, the people of this planet could not understand or handle. Look how jumpy and jittery they are."

I raise a hand and begin to argue, but she waves me quiet.

"Even with our knowledge and power, there are things we don't understand – and yes, fear. Show him," she says to Mym. The boulder rolls in place, sliding what had been her bottom to the top. "Look," she says to me.

I step closer. At first, I see only the uneven surface, but then I notice a jagged gash, and near that gash there's a small indent with symbols or writing. I lean in closer, but as I do, Mym puffs out some steam and rolls away.

"I've seen her shake off a lightning bolt, roll through knights, and battle against maces and hammers pounding against her. I've seen her whacked like a croquet ball. In all of that, I've never known her to lose more than a few flakes of stone or some moss."

"So, what was that?"

"That was a failure. A failure, despite all sanity, that seems to be returning."

I'm frozen at the sight of a tear in Persephone's eye.

"That is what happens when we fail at what we do. It brings her pain, you know. She's in constant pain, like a burn that never heals. I was fighting the Cult. They'd overpowered me and had managed to chain Mym to the floor. They'd finished the ritual. This fountain of energy was springing forth out of the circle of objects they'd collected. They dipped a sword into that fountain; it came out glowing this sickly green. They approached me with that sword. I was finished. And Mym -" the emotion of the memory brings her to a stop. She clears her throat. "Mym - Mym leaped into the fountain, smashing their circle and destroying one of the artifacts. It was a ring; she landed on it. It burned into her."

"I," I try to speak.

She continued, shaking her head in sorrow. "If not for me, they would have that power. If not for my failure, Mym would not have needed to have made that sacrifice. What we do - what we do, normal people can't do, Aedan."

I take a few steps in Mym's direction, giving Persephone a moment to wipe away her tears. "She made that choice. I don't know what she did before you found her, but she chose to join you. She chose to fight alongside you. And she chose to sacrifice herself. What we've been made into - I don't deny that we're necessary. There are things in this world that need to be opposed." I turn back to Persephone. "What I'm asking for is to be allowed to make that choice for myself. To be my own person, not a tool in the shed." As we stare at each other, I see an understanding pass between us. She disagrees with me, but she understands.

"Tea?"

"No, thank you." I smile and then puff out, "I have my mission after all." We hug, and I lead the way out. I fish around in my pocket for a portal stone – noise be damned, we made a whole lot of noise tonight.

I hear Persephone clear her throat. "I was thinking about that..."

"Yes," I say absently as I begin the ritual to cast the portal.

"Your mission - this person was kidnapped. Stolen. I don't know if it helps any, but it's probably not the only thing stolen. I'd look for other missing people or objects, probably taken around the same time."

I stand up from drawing the portal circle, and as the magic begins to swirl, I can't help but think about the folder Alan had put together for me. I nod. "See'ya around, Seph." I step into the portal.

Chapter 18

The portal opens into my backyard. The night air is crisp. The rumble of the portal closing disturbs the serenity. It's not a rock concert, but the sound is appreciable in the quiet of the evening. I glance to my left and right - *nothing to worry about*. "Things to do," I mutter to myself and begin what feels like a very long walk to my backdoor. *Research? No, rest first.*

It was nice to see Persephone, but the trip was a waste. *Another dead end. More wasted time. Two failed attempts to push this off my plate. I'm looking for that one and done battle and I'm starting to think I'm going to be made to walk there instead of run.* It was beginning to feel purposeful at this point.

I feel like I'm in a spaghetti western, and the bad guy is firing bullets at my feet, making me dance. But if I'm going to be made to walk to the end game, I'm going to take a nap first. *No.* "Cookies first," I stop at the kitchen counter and peel back the cellophane. Tasty, but nearly at the point of being stale. "One more, then bed." I add in case anyone is listening. "And then research."

My eyes open. I roll over to look at the clock on the wall - nearly noon. I think about calling Alan or texting him, so he knows I'm still around – I really don't want to have *that* fight again. *Right, melted my cellphone.*

Several minutes tick by. "I know," I growl at myself. It's not my lack of direction or the feeling of defeat that's weighing me down; it's the image of Alan's face. That look of fear and disappointment is haunting. Parents are supposed to be disappointed in their children, not the other way round. A voice reminds me that I'm not his parent. I throw the covers off and stomp into the bathroom where I find my bag, my staff, and my coat – *need to put this away.*

I shower first. The water on my skin is soothing - last night's dirty work washing away. *If only failure was as transitory.* I try to blank my mind, to lose myself in the waterfall of my multi-nozzle showerhead, but I hear Persephone in my mind – *'what we do matters.'*

I try to shake it off. I turn and put my back to the water spray. I consider breakfast. In the middle of deciding on eggs or alcohol my attention drifts, and I find myself thinking about those poor security guards. Seph's words echo in my mind - '*I fear what happens if we don't do what we're told to do.*'

I turn to face the water again. "Fine," I growl – I'm the kid who's been told to eat one more brussel sprout before he can leave the table. I focus on Brigit's visit - saying so much and so little, as usual. "Three," I say with water cascading down my face. "Why tell me three?" She didn't give me any other information. "Because she couldn't, or because she didn't need to?" It occurs to me that I've been chasing my tail rather than focusing on what bit me. *You know this game, Aedan.* We all have rules. Rules you follow. Rules you bend. Rules you break – when no one's watching.

I turn off the water and step out of the shower. As I stare at myself in the mirror, anger grows within me. I picture Cassy, and then I picture Persephone – the image says nothing, but I can read the facial expression. "You let your miserable, jaded ass fog your senses. Your lack of focus has endangered the mission." That's the conditioning talking. I feel shame – and I hate that I feel shame.

I scramble to get dressed – putting on my favorite green sweater – and then gather up my discarded gear from the bathroom.

I catch myself in the hallway and stop. I feel the bubbling frustration. The struggle between that part of me who knows Persephone is right and that part of me who is eager to just have this over with. I sigh. *Know thy self.* I'm not running to the ritual room. I'm running away from a problem. I'll get down there. Put my things away. Allow myself to get distracted by the trees. And then go for a drink.

Focus.

"She would have given me all that I needed." I walk calmly to the living room and pull *A Tale* from the shelf and enter the ritual room. I don't bother with the robe, though I do tap the notch in passing; a small prayer that I never have to use it slipping over my lips. The folder I had stolen from Detective Darren is on my desk where I had left it. Suddenly the three begin speaking at once.

"You should tell him."

"No, you."

"I'll tell him."

"No..."

"Better if it were one of us."

The rapid-fire comments end abruptly. I give it a moment. "Tell me what?" I ask as I put away my gear in the armoire.

"You're looking very sturdy today," Green purrs.

"We've been talking -" Red cuts in.

"Hush." Green admonishes.

Silence follows. I get the impression they're discussing something behind my back. Something in the way Red had said "We've" makes me think he's referring to more than just the three of them. I step over to my desk.

"We want you to know that, despite your lack of roots, we do see you for the sapling you are." Green again, her tone guarded. "We've talked and -"

"You can't help what sits in your branches," Red states with his usually bristled tone.

"Yes. Of course. But we want you to know that we have been talking and, well, locusts are coming, my dear -"

"They're here," Blue's nervous squeak raises my eyebrow.

"What we're trying to say is, careful where you grow," Green says.

What the hell? All of the alarms in my head are going off. Green's caginess. Red – well, Red seemed normal. But, Blue speaking in over the other two - something wasn't right. They sound like Brigit. The warning alarms in my head come together into one melancholy tone from a heavy iron bell. *Are they playing the game? Has someone gotten to them?*

As I pick up the police file, something occurs to me. *Have I put them in danger? Have they put themselves in danger?* I think of the folder upstairs - the folder resting on my couch like the one ring on Bilbo's floor. I go out of my way to keep Alan safe – selfishly ignoring the one thing that would probably end any threat to him. Red, Green, Blue – I've worried that they might get drawn into my mess, and I feel as if that concern now has proof. "I'm always careful." Across the room, Green's charm glows as if she's about to speak, but then it fades. "I -"

I don't finish that thought. But, if things are getting serious, there is something I should do. "Thank you for the warning. Perhaps it is time I at least move the civilians out of the way." On the bookshelf behind my desk are two envelopes; I pull them down and take a seat in my stone circle. Ever since the death of Alan's parents, I've always felt better having a way to get the innocent out of the way. It took some trial and error, but I've found that winning a free trip is a good way to motivate people into being someplace else.

I set the envelopes before me and begin to chant, "Credsin agus bi sabhalt." As I repeat the words, my hands begin to glow. I reach out and touch the paper. The glow transfers, the envelopes shine brightly, letters of fire etch the addresses of my neighbors onto the paper – there's a flash. I stare at the spot on the ground where the envelopes had been. "There - safe from locusts." As for me, it's past time for me to run headfirst into locusts. I return to my desk and stare down at the police folder. Oddly, I think Detective Darren is the key to what I need to do next – what I should have done from the beginning. But I didn't want the brussel sprouts, so I ignored it. I ignored it and tried to get my brother and sister to eat it. Suddenly, I'm worried that the trees can read my thoughts – read my shame. I know what I need to do now.

Time to do it.

I retreat upstairs.

I don't particularly appreciate how any of this is feeling. It's all taking on a personal note, and I've never felt that during a mission. Get it, get it done, move on. But this time? It's me. I've made it personal. I've gotten too comfortable this time. Made friends. And then there's always Alan. Something else Persephone had said rings in my head – "Hope is a lie we tell ourselves." I close the trapdoor and focus on my work. "You would have given me all I needed to know," I mutter as I read the note Brigit had given me, now stuck to the outside of Alan's folder which is sitting on my couch like a house guest who won't go home. "I have all I need." I tuck the police folder under my arm and walk into the kitchen. I reach for the plate of cookies. "Apparently, I had more than a snack last night." It's empty but for some crumbs. *Cookies are for closers.*

I have a plan. A plan that will hopefully lead to cookies. *What we do matters.* "Time to tack into the wind," I say, heading for my backyard. My next steps are as a cat. I climb Red, leap off his upper branches as a hawk, and fly east towards the city.

I drift on the breeze as I come to the edge of the city. It had snowed during the night, and everything is painted in white. The trees of the park where Becca Trent had been abducted are especially beautiful. I wonder if I should have another look around. I'm missing a lot - or is that just the feeling of playing catch up?

I can't shake the nagging notion that now that I'm looking, that I'm missing the forest for the trees. *Stick to the plan.* I move on and come to a nice neighborhood not far from the abduction site. Trees and fresh lawns line the streets. It looks like one of the neighborhoods built during the nineteen eighties – large homes, big square-pillared porches, overhangs. The transition between one holiday and the next has begun for some. I find a hidden spot and shift. Becca's address rolls around in my memory. It takes a moment to get my bearings. A short walk up the street and I find a blue and white house with a double garage and a single tree in the middle of the front yard. I ring the bell.

A small woman with cascading brown hair answers the door. "Yes?"

"Miss Trent?"

"Yes?"

I hold up the police folder – *I need to make myself a fake badge.* "I'm Detective Garret. I've been given the case involving the disappearance of your daughter. I was hoping to ask you some questions, maybe have a look around."

She steps back, a sad scowl on her face. "I thought Detective Darren was handling this."

"He's been reassigned." I step into her living room. It's splashed in yellow and blue with a large comfy couch in front of a fireplace over top of which is a flat-screen. Family pictures hang on the walls, alongside some excellent art. "Did you paint these?"

"Yes – and that one, over there, was done by Becca." She points to a framed piece next to the window.

"Two artists in the family."

"Three, actually. Her father, too..."

I glance around. A bearded man appears in several of the pictures, but not since Becca was about ten years old. "She was into hats," I note.

She chuckles. "Oh, yes. That multicolored octopus was her favorite. There was a time Kevin and I forgot she had hair."

"Miss Trent -"

"Meredith, please."

"Meredith, was Becca out in the woods that day for a hike or inspiration? Maybe to meet someone?"

"Meet? No, I don't think so. At least she didn't mention it. But a hike? Inspiration? Both." Meredith smiles. "She loves trees."

"Was she looking at art as her major?"

"No. Painting was a hobby. She wanted to be an archaeologist."

I nod. "Did you speak with her that day?"

"No. Well, kind of. I sent her a text that morning. Nothing important."

"Did she ever mention being afraid of anyone? A boyfriend? Her roommate?"

"No. Her roommate, um, Sarah, they got along fine. Becca didn't have a boyfriend that I knew about."

"An old boyfriend?"

"A couple. Oh, I don't think any of them - her first boyfriend," she smirks when she says this, "Tomas. She was thirteen. They dated for about a week, fought, and that was it. It was adorable – though she was devastated."

"Anyone more recent?"

"She dated Andrew for almost two years, junior and senior year. But she told me that ended as best it could. He got accepted at a school in California."

I didn't feel any of this was helping me. "Thank you, Meredith. I'll check in with Sarah and Andrew, just in case. This will help." I lie to her as I reach out and touch her arm. "Do you mind if I have a look at her room?"

"Upstairs, end of the hallway."

"Thank you." Stairs creak as I head upstairs. I can't help but think about young – younger – Becca trying to sneak down these. *To sneak out? To sneak a snack?* There are more pictures on the wall here – more art. It's all very good, compelling; I don't recognize the style and assume it's more family creations. But there's something more, a feeling I can't shake. Perhaps it's my imagination or Meredith's sorrow, but there's an odd – something - to the house. Like picking up a box and expecting it to be heavy, but it's not.

I open Becca's door. *So, Becca, were you a risk-taker or a homebody?* Her room is neat, with lots of blue. No trophies. Some ribbons from art contests. A small bookcase with some youth and teen novels. I begin to consider

Becca. She lived in the dorms. She kept in touch with her mom, probably better than most college students. Liked art. Loved trees. This is not the room of a cavalier person. *Maybe college changed her.* But she'd only been at college for a short time – time enough to move on from this? I don't think so. *Why her?* "Maybe I do need to speak with Sarah and Andrew." I step over to a small vanity. There are pictures stuck to the mirror, more recent than what's on display downstairs. "Red hair..."

I take one last look around and then return to the living room. "Miss - Meredith, did Becca have red or black hair? The report says black, but I noticed some pictures with red hair."

"Oh, red - like her father, but in high school, she started to dye it black on occasion. Is that important?"

"I don't know," I say out loud and then smile, trying to play it off. "Thank you for your time." She walks me to the door, and as I step out onto the porch, I turn, "Meredith, I don't want to give you any false hope -" She holds up her hand.

"I've done my research, Detective Garret. I know the odds. Just find her, please."

I nod, and the door closes.

Chapter 19

Returning to my backyard, I find myself once again halted in thought, standing in the relative quiet of my little slice of nature. *Red hair? Is that significant?* I could ask the spriggans if I could find them. My feet begin to move before I'm completely aware of it. "The stones have been cast," I mutter. "Don't ask the stones why they broke the window. Speak with the parents of the brat kid who threw the stones." A terrifying addendum to my plan begins to form. "Are you really thinking about doing this?" I ask myself. I don't need to answer.

I stop at my backdoor – my hand halfway to the handle. I stare at my small abode, afraid to take a step because this is mostly a terrible idea. As I stare, that sense of oddity returns. There's something off about my house. Nothing is different; I feel as if I've seen a crack in the wall that's been there for months. There was something about the Trent house that's poking at me. At first, I assumed it was Meredith's evident sadness, but I recall now that I had had the same sense while visiting Persephone. The house, their houses, felt like homes. At Persephone's place, it was a comfortableness, a – for lack of a better word – happiness. At the Trent house, it was as if that happiness was gilded. Like a large chocolate Easter bunny, just a shell. Persephone, despite all that is asked of us and all we are denied, had made a home out of that house. *How?* And the Trent house – a place where Becca had grown up, where Kevin and Meredith enjoyed their time together – the warmth is all the more noticeable in its absence. I recognize this now because my house is only a house, and that feeling of home isn't here. It's like looking at a picture – flat. *Then why am I afraid of what I'm about to do?* I've got nothing here. Nothing worth missing. I try telling myself, at least.

As I finish reaching for the handle I glance over my shoulder, a shred of guilt hitting me. *Best not to lament the lack of hominess around Red, Green, or Blue - especially as I'm going to be needing them shortly.*

I'm through the kitchen and into the living room in a few large strides, pull the book, and step down into my ritual room. My second thoughts are stomped out under the weight of my mission; I need to be certain. Mrs. Trent said something that has sparked a hunch. But getting that hunch verified will be difficult and dangerous. I remove my sweater and pants and don the robe and bunny slippers.

In my arrogance, indolence, and petty pouting, I picked Gregor to speak with because that was the easy choice. Easy answers. Quick answers. Maybe someone I could pass this off to and then forget about it. A quick end so I can get back to pretending to be me. *What we do matters.* I shake my head at myself.

My flight back from the Trent house was full of self-admonishment. *There's a time for protest, and there's a time for getting the work done. If I'd taken this task seriously from the start – if I'd thought about doing this sooner – time might not seem like it's slipping away. I might not feel rushed.*

I can't decide if I'm doing this because of guilt or is this really a good idea?

On my desk is a nondescript narrow wooden box. I gently lift the lid and stare at the long, slender blade within. The white opal blade is seven inches long and set into a handle of elk bone. There's a faint glow that intensifies as I slip my fingers around the bone and bring the blade to eye level. "Are you there?"

"Always, honey," Green's smiling tone embraces me from every angle.

"I need your vigilance."

"Leaves we are not." Red's tone is indignant.

"Yes, of course," I say as I move to the stone circle at the center of the room. I make myself comfortable on my back. "I need to go somewhere," my words tremble. Their consciousnesses hover around me. Silent – a knowing silence.

"Rest in our shadow, dear."

With that, I take the opal blade and place the tip at my heart – I gasp as the full length of the blade of white stone presses into my flesh. Icy cold tendrils snake through my chest, down along my arms and legs, and up into my skull. The ritual room darkens and is gone.

Chapter 20

I've never liked summoning. It's messy, or can be. It's like fishing for sharks; much safer to get a shark cage and step into their world. I was brought up with a concept of heaven and hell – Albios and Dubnos. But in my many years, I've come to know that the Otherworld is more like Annwn. Good or bad, the spirits of the dead come here. Bad people are influenced by trickster gods, and the good by tutelary gods. This Otherworld, the world of the Sidhe, a world of clownfish and sharks, is a construct, a dreamland, not unlike swimming over a coral reef. And like a dream, like a coral reef, beauty is everywhere, but dangers lurk in the dark places.

Shadows and disparate voices swirl around me in a ghostly mist. As I become aware of my surroundings, as the darkness fades and light gives shape to shadow, I find myself in a roadside bar. It's empty, but for the bartender and me. He has intelligent eyes and is heavily muscled in the upper body.

"Just you?" His words are a lyrical rumble like a taiko drum.

I glance around. "Just me." He waves me to the bar.

"You seem uncomfortable."

Which I'm sure is a statement in response to my nervous looks around. I've only been to this side twice before – once by destiny, the other by choice, and neither visit was fun. Although, come to think of it, I suppose most people only visit the one time. All the same, this was not what I was expecting.

"Not what you were expecting? Would you prefer something else?" He says as if reading my mind – probably reading my mind. "I feel this might be more to your liking."

The bar vanishes in a dazzle of soft light. I now stand on familiar grassy hills; purple flowers are all around me, rocks and boulders break up the landscapes, gray snow-covered mountains lay in the distance.

"I know you," he says, tapping at his bottom lip.

The longer I stay in this place, the more he will know about me, and the harder it will be to leave. "I don't think you do."

"No, I do. Yes. Your presence is very familiar." He closes his eyes, his head tilting slightly back and forth as if listening to music.

I assumed I would be meeting with Ogmios - I didn't want to, but I assumed I would because that's how my luck runs. Part of my apprehension over this trek had been the likelihood that Ogmios would be my psychopomp. My other forays into this realm had all brought me face-to-face with him. I don't know the logic behind what gate you arrive at when you pass – especially if you willingly cast yourself over the waterfall - but each other time I've met with Ogmios. Although, at one of those times, I was following the silver thread of another.

"Yes. It's coming back to me. You were stolen the first time. And the next..." there's a pause as his eyes open, and he looks directly at me, "the next time *you* stole from me."

In many ways, I'm more afraid of Ogmios than Lugh. I've never faced Lugh on his home territory, and although as powerful as any god, being in the mortal realm has put limitations on his abilities. Here, in this place, Ogmios is supreme and could conceivably cast me into the void. I open my mouth to try and smooth this over, but he continues to speak.

"Can I tempt you with a drink?" He holds out his hand, and there, clasped gently between the fingers of his very large hand, is a tumbler of amber liquid. "This is an apple whiskey." He sniffs at the rim of the glass and smiles.

I know this about the Otherworld: the living can visit the dreamlands – in fact, many walk this place in our sleep - but should never eat nor drink of this place. "No. Thank you," I say as politely as I can. The chilling pain at the center of my chest slips a little further into me as I say this. A firm reminder that there's an hourglass and the sands are running out. "Fair Ogmios, please allow me to ask you a question."

"Fair," he chuckles. His hand drops away from the glass, which remains suspended in the air. He walks a few steps away, his hands on his hips, appearing to take in the serenity of the hills. "Well, I guess that is how this is supposed to work. But it's usually I who asks the questions. Questions to ease your passage. Questions to judge you. Questions to settle that which is unsettled. My words will ease your mind as they have so many others."

I'd say he was purposefully wasting my time, but I know he's telling the truth. In ancient times he could bind even the unwilling with an eloquent phrase. Personally, I think he just likes listening to himself talk. My hand suddenly flies to my chest as the pain spikes. I feel beads of sweat forming on my forehead. I catch his smile as he cocks his head over his shoulder.

"Something not agreeing with you? This may help," with a slight nod, the tumbler drifts about a foot closer to me.

"You watch the gateway," I spit out, but catch myself – and grit my teeth against the pain. "You watch the gateway. Spirits don't move between the planes without you knowing about it."

"I'm not the only gatekeeper," his smug smile is irritating.

"I know how this works. It's like a pond. Things create ripples as they enter and leave -"

"I'm not the only gatekeeper." He turns to me, adding a head shake with that smug smile.

"Fine!" I shout. "It's more like a pool with lifeguards. You're in charge of this bit of the water, but you see what the other guards see and vice versa." I grit my teeth. The pain is making it hard to breathe – and for a place without air, that's saying a lot.

"Ah, there they are."

I'm confused for a moment and then see the shadows.

He laughs. A deep guttural chuckle that I feel vibrate through me. "So many - are you sure you wouldn't like that drink now?"

The glass doesn't move, but I do step away. The shadows are those that have come before, those that know me, those that I've sent here. Every mistake. Every decision. They're my tattletales. They get to say their piece. The gatekeeper is supposed to take what I have to say into account, and then it's decided if I move onto the Dreamlands or if I get special attention. "I've got a long past," I say.

"So you do," and then his eyes brighten, "Aedan."

Shit – the naming of the beast. "I'm on a mission."

"I'm sure you are." His frown is deep. "But this is my place, and you have transgressed. And. Not. For. The. First. Time."

"I was on a mission then, and I'm on a mission now." He doesn't say anything. His slow, steady approach is enough to get me to take a step back. As I do, the wind kicks up as a chilling breeze comes down from the mountains – helped by the shadows creeping closer. "It wasn't her time."

"She was here. It was her time. She was mine."

The rumble of his voice is like a thunderstorm approaching. "She wasn't yours." I can't stop myself from saying. I watch as Ogmios leaps into the air and comes crashing down, fists pounding into the earth. A wave of rocks and soil wash over me, and I lose my footing and tumble down the hill. Before I can get to my feet, I feel hands come down on my neck and lift me into the air.

"I have only to speak the words..."

My mind is racing – words, as much as muscles, are his weapons. I need a word. Thinking becomes increasingly tricky as his fingers squeeze around my throat.

"Any last words before I help you cross over?"

"Fomorians," I gasp, my hands feebly trying to remove his. It's not just his hand, however, that I'm feeling. There is almost nothing left of the picturesque view. It has nearly been wholly washed over in gaseous forms of black. I can feel their icy touch on my legs and arms. The cacophony of whispers is pierced occasionally by a single unfriendly voice – "ours," it says. But Ogmios isn't moving. He's waiting or considering. As my essence blends with this place, he slowly comes to learn everything about me. He either knows I'm telling the truth or will very shortly – but whether that will sway him or not is anyone's guess.

And then he drops me.

"Speak," he commands.

I don't feel he's referring to my immediate situation. "They were trying to destroy the veil. The girl -"

"Orlene,"

"Yes, Orlene. She was the key to stopping it, but the Fomorians found out and had her mugged. Killed her. It wasn't her time, or if it was, it wasn't fair."

"Fair," Ogmios scoffs.

The stabbing pain in my chest goes straight through to my back now. I lose the ability to stand. "Yes, and It wasn't," I bark. "She was human. We're not supposed to use humans. But They did. To be used by both sides. To be tossed away by both sides. To have no choice in the matter. She lives in Provence now. Has grandkids, great-grandkids." I feel tiny under his intense gaze and mountainous frame. But even a mouse can stand up to an elephant. He hasn't destroyed me yet, and that is filling me with confidence.

Humans have a word – paladin. It sums up who I am and my relationship with the Gods very well. Champion of justice. Protector of the weak. Destroyer of evil. Empowered by divinity. I don't usually wear the face of my status. Frankly, I've come to see the celestial armor as a shackle, which is why I came up with my own persona, but in this case, it's time to flash the badge. From my prone position, I put on my most serious face. "I have the authority to be here. I have the right to ask question. Of Anyone. Now! Have you seen, or do you know of, any unusual passings into the mortal realm?"

He steps away as he speaks – and as he does, the shadows push away. "Beings come, and beings go."

"Beings that wouldn't normally enter that realm, or are the type to do so, but they ended up someplace unusual?" I get to my feet.

"The entities of the here rarely make their minds known, and once they're on the other side rarely choose to return, unless forced. That's your job, though, isn't it?"

"You've also fought your share of intruders." My knees give out and I drop to the ground.

"Yes, I have, and still do in my own way. How about that drink?"

The glass reappears and drifts closer. I shift onto my knees and put my back to the glass. The pain in my chest is almost unbearable. "I just want to know if a spriggan, possibly two, has passed by."

He smiles and stifles a laugh. He stares at me for a few seconds. His eyes, bright and lively now – the look of someone who has been keeping a secret and is happy to be rid of it. "There was a time when I'd see many of those spirits sneaking into the mortal lands." He snorts, "Well, they thought they were sneaking."

"And recently?"

"Not many."

"But some -"

"Oh, yes," he steps over to me. "But that is to be expected when gods travel between the realms – especially as frequently as some. You see, undesirables can hide in the wake of the crossing. And sometimes, the door can be held open. Oh, they say it was an accident, but I know. I know." He sits down next to me. We gaze out over the hills, which had begun to manifest again. "I had the ears of many, once. They couldn't help but listen. They'd follow me into battle. Great deeds would be done. Mighty feats. Walls would crumble under my strength. Enemies would fall." He kicks at a football-sized rock. It comes free of the ground and tumbles further down the hill. "I had a picnic with a lovely young lady not that long ago. We got to talking. I told her some of my stories. She described me as retired. She said it as if it were a compliment, something to celebrate. I wanted to smite her. Didn't, of course - she was a good soul. We worked through some of her issues, and I sent her on her way."

"You're still mighty, and you're still important. You guard the gateway. You help souls. Yours is the last word on what happens to that soul." There's a long pause, during which the voices that had been pressed back to the edge of my hearing begin to gain my attention once more. The shadows, still at a distance, start to become more distinct. I can see eyes now - eyes that stand out against the contrast of their otherwise dark exterior. My hand presses against my chest. I'm dizzy and begin to sway on my knees. For his part, Ogmios does take my elbow and help ease me into a sitting position on the grass. "The spriggans, Ogmios. Please..."

I'm not sure he will answer me, but then he smiles – it's warm. "You're sure it's a spriggan?"

Despite the smile, his tone suggests one last spar.

"I read the signs. I'm sure." *I'm not.*

He sighs; it's heavy, forced - he's putting on a show of reluctance for some reason. "There are rules, Aedan. We all answer to someone."

"Ogmios -"

He holds up a stiff hand and looks at me with a deep frown. "Three."

"Can you tell me where they were going?"

"As long as they behave themselves, I don't ask questions." His voice is loud and painful to my ears – but he speaks out over us, not to me.

"You might not ask, but you like to know, don't you? You watched? Ogmios, you watched. You watched because you're a gatekeeper, and a guide, but also a warrior. You watched them because even though it's not your job to stop them, it might be your job to fight them." You think of the Gods as being absolute. Always sure. Always with purpose. In a word, happy. It's a horrible thing to see one turn sad.

"Not with you and your brothers and sisters around. That is no longer my job," he says bitterly. "I keep the border. The task of defending it falls to others – or so *my* brothers and sisters insist." He sighs again and then suddenly laughs. The sound is hardy and echoes off the landscape. "That's not to say I haven't cheated. That's not to say there haven't been times - while their backs were turned - that I bent the rules. Something, I gather, you know a lot about."

His head sinks a little. He begins idly plucking grass blades. I wait because I don't know what else to say to him and because the pain is all I can concentrate on. I want to lie down. I want that whiskey.

"Those three did end up in places that were not typical for their kind. Public places. Two along busy trails and the third to a large home surrounded by trees." He speaks without looking up, his voice almost a mutter. There's no reluctance but his words are guarded.

"'Those three?'"

"You only asked about spriggans." He smirks.

I lean my head against his burly frame. I want to ask more but I barely manage to say, "Thank you,"

Several seconds pass. We watch the last of the scenery vanish into darkness. Eventually I hear him whisper, "Do you hear that?"

I don't have the strength to answer.

"Someone's calling for you. Here."

He presses a finger to my temple. I do hear a voice. A single, calm soprano in the chorus of angry and covetous wailing rising all around me. It's faint but slowly rises above the chatter of whispers. A young voice. Familiar. A color comes to mind – no, not a color. A name.

Blue.

Chapter 21

The first thing I become aware of is Blue speaking. "The cold has melted, Aedan. Turn your leaves to the sun. Aedan -"

I gasp and cough as I roll onto my side. The act of pulling the opal blade from my chest is agony. It clatters to the floor. I continue to gasp for air – this is not the type of pain I find satisfaction in. Even with the knife out, I still feel its presence. The weight of it on my chest. The stinging, searing pain stabbing through me. I groan and curl into a ball. They begin to talk all at once. "I'm back. I'm back," I say weakly. There's a tremor to my arms as I push myself into a seated position. "I'm back." I feel paper-thin. *No time*. I get to my feet and fall forward but manage to stay upright. Panting, I crash into the chair behind my desk. When the dizziness passes, I open drawers until I find the silver mirror. It's not magical - I just like it. I don't like what stares back at me, however. I touch my cheek. My skin is waxy and gray. My eyes are bloodshot. I look like I've been drinking nonstop for a week – and feel like it.

"It's been two days," Green says before I can ask.

"You've got rot, my son."

"Thanks, Red." I set the mirror aside and am distracted by a pain in my head. It feels like a hot poker is trying to push its way into my skull through my temple. "It was worth it, I think." It feels good to lay my head down on my desk. "Confirmation at least. There are three of them. But they're not hiding. They came here looking for something – someone. Why? Ugh, my head." Sitting back up was a bad idea. "I'm going to throw up -"

"Good for the roots."

Red's harrumph is almost good-natured. "I need," I say almost without thinking.

"Maybe lay down?" Green squeaks nervously.

"No, stand up," Red orders.

"I need..." I try to stand up but crash back into my chair. "I need..." grabbing the sides of my head isn't helping. "I need..." my hands leave my head and slam down on the armrests as my workroom vanishes, and I'm pulled forward as my mind vomits imagery. The world blurs around me and then suddenly stops. I can still feel the chair beneath me, I hear the faint worried cries of Red, Green, and Blue. I can smell the damp earth of my workroom. But my workroom is not what I'm seeing. I'm at Becca Trent's abduction site. I see the spriggan. It looks like it's just arrived. It glances around, a wicked smirk on its face, before taking up a position next to a sycamore. Several people go by as I'm watching, including a number of students with Drexel logoed hoodies. He's tempted, but he waits.

I'm whisked away again. The world blurs. I come to a stop in an unfamiliar spot. It's another trail. Again, the spriggan sniffs at the air as it looks around and picks a hidden place near a narrow footbridge to wait. As before, there are hikers and joggers – several college logos are represented, but I see many for Carnegie Mellon.

I'm pulled away. A tunnel of distorted images streams by me. I come to a stop. It's a dark street. I see a signpost. Cars on the street. A large American colonial house. Trees all around it. Beautiful stonework and a wrought iron fence. And then I see the spriggan. It's climbing the wall to an open window on the second floor. It stops, its head cocking to one side as if listening to something. It nods and then leaps from the wall to a thick oak branch hanging near to the house, where it hunkers down.

I don't move, but I have this sensation of being dropped back into my chair. My ears are ringing. Slowly, I became aware again of the voices of my companions.

"Where's a breeze when you need one?" Green's voice is almost frantic.

"He's back." Blue's voice, child-like as usual, is full of relief.

They all begin speaking at once, and I hold up my hand in the hopes of quiet. Thankfully, they oblige. "I was – it was like I was, but I wasn't," I get that feeling I always do when I suspect they're chatting behind my back, and then I hear Green make a polite throat-clearing sound.

"Rest, dear, you need rest."

"Yes, yes – a good, ah, sleep."

"No, I need -" but I don't know what I need.

"What do you need, honey?"

"He needs rest, as you say -"

"Shush. Go on, Aedan, what do you need?"

"I don't know. It's like... it's like, it's like my brain is working with too much information."

"Do you need to vomit?" Red asks.

"Don't they – oh, what was it, pee when they're full?" Green whispers.

"He said head, that means vomit."

"I don't think that's right."

"Speak," Blue says with some urgency.

"I, I -" I try to describe my visions, but it's too much.

"Speak," Blue says slowly and calmly.

Blue's voice is tranquil, and I let it carry me. "I saw the spriggans. It was like I was there. It felt real – but at the same time, distant. It was almost like a memory, but – real. It was real, like I lived it, was living it. Did I see through time?"

"Ooh, ooh, that sounds like -" Green says with chipper excitement.

"Yes. Shhh," Red orders.

"In a manner of speaking," Blue says, his voice sounding like a child who is also a doctor. "You were experiencing time through the eyes of another."

"So, like a memory?" I ask.

"Like..." Blue goes away before completing that thought.

The others go with him, and I again have the impression they're in one of their private conclaves. I feel my eyes starting to close, and I catch myself and try to stand, with a little more success. I get to my feet, but my legs tremble.

"Sit, please, Aedan. You've been through a storm," Green coos.

"I've done too much sitting around on this one. Too much self-pity." I close my eyes against the spinning room. "I have a solid lead. I can't." I say with resolve.

"Sit."

I almost give into Red's command. "Guys -"

"You sometimes call it The Collective," Blue says.

I sit. "What?"

"That place where we exist when we're not here. You call it The Collective."

"I was in your Collective?"

"No," Red grumbles.

"Ours is much more fun," Green twitters.

"I believe it was a limited link."

"A limited -" And then I think, *Ogmios*. "I was given these memories -"

"Not memories," Red admonishes.

"Right. Not memories. I was -"

"You were allowed to experience those moments as they happened because, in The Collective, there is no time," Blue says in a matter-of-fact tone similar to that of a child explaining to a parent that of course Captain Buttons can fly his pirate ship to the couch because he has the magical amulet from the Cave of Dreams.

"Okay, okay, okay, let me think." I close my eyes – this time a mistake, but as tired as my body is, my mind is currently a race car coming into the checkered flag. "They were allowed to cross, and then coerced or bribed, lured into making abductions. They looked for students, specific students, and grabbed one from one end of the state and another from the other. Why? And why was the third at a house." My mind drifts back over the vision, now an actual memory and fading. "Virginia plates. 30th Street," I whisper.

"What's he saying?" Green asks.

"I don't know. Speak up!" Red shouts.

My eyes flash open. "I need to go." I shamble over to the armoire and pull open the doors.

"Aedan, dear -"

"I need to go." I begin pulling on my augmented duster. "It's still in my head. It's like I've been there. And if I've been there, I can go there again." I feel the change come over me. I load up with a boleen and my collapsible staff. I pull some twigs and stones from my bowls and head for the stone circle. I draw my circle, lay my hand in the center, speak the magic, and watch as the floor begins to swirl as a portal forms.

Chapter 22

The crackle of the portal echoes down the street. A few of the nearby houses may hear a few of their pipes rattling as the energy dissipates. It's dark. I need to move, but I'm afraid to take a step. I feel the quiver in my knees. I'm tired. I've never been this tired. *Move, Aedan.* A flicker of a movement catches my attention. "Move, Aedan!" I throw myself against the stonewall and crouch. The problem is that now I can't see if the person on the second floor is still at the window. Footsteps now, moving this way from the right. I dash along the wall and hide in the dense cluster of trees separating the properties. A man in a dark suit comes to the gate. He listens. He's frustratingly patient. He nods as if listening to someone and lifts his wrist to his mouth.

"Clear. But that was definitely something. It sounded like a truck. I *know* it wasn't a truck. Check on the old lady, and I recommend a full sweep. I'll walk the perimeter." With that, he starts coming my way. Even though he scans the trees, he doesn't see me. He continues along a narrow trail between the trees and the wall heading towards the back of the property.

I don't think I've thought this through. Actually, I know I haven't. I need a plan. I like having a plan, and right now, I'm moving on instinct. I don't even know why I'm here. Girls are missing, and I don't know why. Spriggans are showing up in unusual places. *Why?* I breathe in slowly and seek calmness in my thoughts. *I'm here for a reason. Let's find that reason. The suit mentioned the "old lady" and the spriggan was very interested in that corner window on the second floor. Let's see what the spriggan was interested in.*

The wall is more decorative than functional and easy to overcome. On the other side, I land in a flower patch. There's a garden path between lines of near leafless trees. The house is about sixty feet away. The moon is high and half-full, and I use the tree shadows to make my way to the back of the house. Whoever lives here has a park for a backyard - a park currently being patrolled by several suits. I take a stone from one of my pockets; I know it's the right one. I've never reached into one of my pockets and drawn the wrong glyph. I throw the stone as far away from me as I can. It's far enough that I lose sight of it in the night but hear it land among the undergrowth along the wall. There are no immediate motions from the guards to investigate, but then I think the power word, and suddenly there's a lot of noise as unseen vines begin to grow and lengthen. The noise is similar to someone, or maybe several someones, moving quickly along the wall. It's enough to draw the attention of most of the guards.

The moment the guards start rushing across the lawn, I begin making my way up the wall. The stonework on the side of the house creates several handholds – something the guards should probably think about changing. I make my way to the small balcony, where I rest. The exhaustion is dizzying. It's like being sick and suffering from working out too much at the same time. When my breath is back, I try the glass door. It opens up into a hallway with two doors. I take a few careful steps, testing the floor for creaks. The hallway leads to a sizeable four-way intersection. Two comfortable-looking benches sit against the walls, and portraits of stern-looking aristocrats hang above them. I make an educated guess on which corridor to search for the room I seek.

I try a door. It opens without argument or protest. Inside I find a four-poster bed surrounded by a color scheme of blue and pink. The bed is tussled – the covers either yanked back or pulled down. However, the room is clean, but for a small pile of dirty clothes near the closet. The posters on the wall suggest a girl. Posters of female superheroes, pink fluffy creatures, and attractive looking young guys in various stages of undress hang on the walls. The top of the dresser has a bag of dice partially spilled out and some sketchbooks. I glance out the window; this is the correct room. I investigate the desk. There's a picture here of a young girl and her friends smiling for the camera – she has red hair. There are several fresh scratches on the floor leading from the bed up to the desk. And more here on the desk. *A struggle? But why at the desk?* I take a step back, and something on the floor under the desk catches my attention. A pen. I leave it. As I turn, I see a bookshelf behind the door. From top-down, I witness a change in this young lady. Filled coloring books give way to young adventure stories, which change to mystery and romance novels, and on the bottom shelf are a stack of history and psychology books.

I venture back into the hallway, make my way to the stairs at the end of one of the other corridors. I hear voices but keep moving down. The agents are to my left. There are no lights on in the large hall I step into. I'm worried about the front door but make my way over to the grand piano in the corner without being seen. I pause to listen.

"Yes, ma'am." A door shuts. "She refuses to leave. I'm going to check upstairs. You two don't move from this spot."

A man in a suit passes me and heads up the stairs. There's not a lot to check upstairs, so I make my move. I pull a twig, snap it, and toss it into the hallway with the two guards. A green smoke begins to billow into the hallway. I rush forward. The light from the hallway plays off the smoke, making it hard to distinguish shapes; I know I appear to these two to be at least twice my normal size. They balk. My palm strike forces the first back against the wall with a thud, and my elbow to his temple sends him to the floor. The further one reaches for her weapon but doesn't pull it in time. I swing around her and clamp my arm around her neck and my hand over her nose and mouth. She struggles, the gun drops. Her strength is almost enough to break herself free, but she succumbs to my hold. I lay her down easy and check to make sure she's still breathing. I lift her hair out of her face and turn my attention to the door. The smoke will linger for another ten minutes; the confusion should hopefully give me time to get some information out of "the old lady."

The door opens and closes with a slight squeak. There are no lights on in this room, but the shaft of moonlight piercing the window gives me enough to see by. It's a handsome room. Wood paneling. Lots of shelves. A beautiful parquet floor. A couch opposite a fireplace. A desk at the far end of the room. A woman is sitting in the chair behind that desk.

"Are you here for me now?" She asks with calm authority.

"No."

"Will you return my daughter then? If not, if I go with you, will you return her?"

"I don't have your daughter."

She's momentarily confused by this. "I don't understand."

"I don't have your daughter. I'm not here for you. I'm here to help."

"But how? I mean, I was told – the note said not to..."

I hear voices and footsteps. I reach into my pocket and pull out a stone. I place it against the handle and whisper, "Spreach." The stone glows as I press it to the brass handle, where rock and glow transfer into the handle. I turn back to her. "I would like to ask you a few questions while we still have some privacy." The voices outside are now shouts.

"Can you step closer, please?" she asks politely.

I move to the edge of the moonlight. "You were given a note?"

"A note was left. I have it here." She picks up a plastic bag with the note in it. She comes around the desk, but her footfalls become much more cautious as she heads in my direction. I see her stare. I see her mind working. She's desperate – but she can't decide if that desperation is enough to make her trust me. She reaches me and still hasn't made up her mind. She continues to stare.

Someone tries the handle, and there's a shout of pain. I hear someone shout, "Break it down! Senator? Are you okay? Senator Fitzcairn?"

"Joseph!" The Senator directs her attention to the door, "Stand down. Give me a few minutes."

There's no response, at least none that I can hear. I doubt we'll get a few minutes. "Ma'am, I haven't much time. I have no wish to hurt your staff. Please tell me -" but she cuts me off.

"It's you."

Her tone of recognition is confusing. As far as I know we've never met. There are stories, I suppose. You can't leap between buildings and battle in alleyways without creating a few rumors. I don't know what she's heard. I've never hunted in this form in this area before. "I," I try but can't finish.

"Or perhaps I should say, you fit the description of a person others are greatly interested in. You're a bit far from Philadelphia." She tries to make eye contact, but my visage, I know, is off-putting – on purpose. I can only assume the moonlight is adding to the ominousness. Yet she persists.

As she steps closer, it's my turn to look at her. She's in her mid-fifties. White blonde hair. Blue eyes. Fit. And she is currently dressed in dark slacks and a billowy blouse. She's been crying, but other than some puffy eyes, she has a very wise and determined face. Her scrutiny is unsettling, so I reach my hand out for the note. It's one line. "For Your Own Good, Tell No One." There's also a small smear of red-brown. "Was any other blood found?"

"No. And the note - the handwriting is shaky, like Alyson was trying to disguise it, or maybe terrified while writing it, but it is her handwriting.

Joseph thinks I'm overreacting. He says it's a joke gone too far. That she's skipped out to see a boyfriend or to get away from the detail."

"And?"

"Alyson has never liked her shadows, that's true, but her boyfriend has called here looking for her. In fact, several of her friends have called the house looking for her. And somehow you know about this. I don't know how much longer I can keep it secret. What are they waiting for? I assumed they'd call with demands. I've hardly left this room. No calls. No more notes. Nothing."

Spriggans have a woody texture. If it forced Alyson to write a note by holding her hand tightly, that might account for the blood. *But why? Leaving a note, a spriggan has never done that - more odd behavior. And the note doesn't seem to be threatening harm to Alyson, but the Senator. They wanted to delay the abduction becoming news. Why? Are they waiting to be discovered?* My eyes linger on the page. *They're waiting – why?*

My eyes catch movement outside the window. It's the woman I put in the sleeper hold. She's speaking into her wrist – and then, seconds later, nearly simultaneously, shots come through the door as the windowpane is broken. I take half a step, placing the Senator more between me and the window. I'm being ordered to step away. The Senator is being ordered to get down. We both ignore it. More bullets penetrate the door. "How long?" I ask as I bend to start drawing the portal circle.

"A week."

I do a rough count of the days in my head. I got the call about the same time Alyson was *forced to write the note.* "The people who took Alyson aren't the type to make demands, Senator. Do what you think is necessary, but don't wait up. I can't make any promises." I place my hand at the center of my circle as the door behind me comes down.

Chapter 23

I drop into my workroom and my head rings as it impacts the stone floor. I don't rush to get up, and when I do try, I quickly choose to lie back down. From my position, I see the room is a bit of a mess. Purple lightning is still arcing around the room, jumping from gnarled root to gnarled root, knocking dirt loose as it dissipates into the earth. Books have been shaken from the shelves. I see the shattered remains of one of my bowls – the one with the twigs – its glass form strewn on the floor by the desk. The room has a ransacked look to it. *Confined spaces don't handle portals entirely well,* which is why, as a general rule, I remind myself, I don't portal into the workroom. But I'm fatigued. Not thinking straight. Not thinking much at all. I should have planned that better. Acted too quickly. "Well, I needed to act quickly, didn't I?" I growl at the judgmental voice in my head. "That wasn't a time to linger," I say and try again to get to my knees, this time with success. It's too quiet. I don't get the sense they're huddled - they're present, but they're just watching. I shuffle to the armoire and unbutton my coat – I don't even empty the pockets. *I'll tidy later.* The act of disrobing saps a lot of my strength. The wood creaks as I lean against the closet.

"Someone is here," Blue's quiet, child-like voice creeps into the room.

I nod and drag myself over to my discarded clothing. I let the ceremonial robe I had been wearing under the duster fall to the floor as I struggle with passing the sweater over my head. The climb upstairs is just as arduous. I can already hear the thumping at the front door. I ease the floor back into position, listening for the click of it locking. More thumping at my door – *or that could be my head.* "This better not be more police," I moan as I open the door.

A fist greets me.

I awake in a shaft of light. I hear the clink of a cup against a plate. My nose and skull throb. My chair has been moved to the window, and Persephone is sitting there. *I need to have a talk with my wards on what constitutes a threat.* "Make yourself at home," I grouse.

She finishes a sip from the teacup. "You look terrible." She sets the cup down on a saucer and tosses a newspaper at me.

Usually, I find her muddled French accent soothing, but not today. "You punched me. My nose is the size of a bowling ball." I snap.

"You can't blame all of this on me."

She indicates all of me – although her bemused eyes seem to linger on my sweater. I ignore the insult. "What's this?" I ask, only half caring.

"Page two."

I open the paper to page two. I see the story about the break-in at the museum right away - no mention of people in robes or the stolen artifact. There was, however, mention of the dead security guards and missing meteorite fragments. "This wasn't us."

"Wasn't it?" Her sharp eyes dart over top of the pages she's reading.

"Meteorite fragments?" And then it hits me – she's reading the pages from Alan's folder. "Hey!" I shout and lumber onto my knees. I crawl, and half fall forward, trying to slap the pages from her hands. She easily reels back and casts a disgusted look at me.

"Rude." She pushes me away with the bottom of her stylish boot.

I collapse into a seated fetal position and cradle my face for a moment. "What have you done?"

"What have *I* done? What have *you* done?" She stands up and slams the pages down on the coffee table. "I came here to kill you in a very slow and painful way – and when you reconstituted, I was going to kill you again."

I don't know what reaction she's going for, but my face remains in my hands.

"But, but I've decided to stay my hand - for the moment."

"Why?" I sigh and look up at her.

"Because I choose to. Explain yourself."

"What do you want, Persephone?" I shrug and decide not to say more, but Persephone's hands are suddenly on me. I'm pulled up and roughly forced to sit on the couch. I flop like a rag doll.

"I'm losing patience."

I wait for the room to stop spinning. "I'm on a mission. I'm looking into the disappearance of a couple of college girls. And after -" I wave away the admission of self-pity. "I have some traction now. Thanks for stopping by." With that, I close my eyes and lean my head back. I hear her pacing.

"Not good enough!" she shouts. "Where are they?"

"Who?" I can't gauge her state of mind. I've seen her in action – directed rage. She's poetic with a blade. This, this is just anger.

"The Cult. I know you're working for them. I need to know where they're at right now."

I stay as non-threatening as I can be. My arms are motionless beside me. My head tilted back, eyes closed. "Don't get mad at me because you've lost track of them. Besides, I thought they'd been muted. You have all the knick-knacks now." She grabs my sweater - I hear it tear - and pulls me up. I open my eyes to hers.

"Where are they?"

"I will help you find them, but at the moment, I'm kind of busy with my own shit. How's tomorrow?" She pushes me back against the couch, her fist heavy on my chest, and then she lets go. She's pacing again.

After a minute she stops, lifts her arms, and lets them flop at her sides. "No wonder you hate your life. Look at this place." Her voice has less of an edge to it.

"I don't hate my life," I say meekly. "Alright, the idea of walking alone on a cold dead world millions of years in the future is a little terrifying, but I'll cross that bridge when I come to it. It's not my life I hate. It's my job."

"You don't."

"I just said I -"

"Or, if you do, you certainly put a lot of work into something that you hate." She points at the pages on the coffee table and then flops down on the couch next to me.

I glance sideways at her – she has apparently made up her mind not to kill me. *I wonder what it was that I said?* "I hate not having a choice. I hate being used. I hate living at arm's length from life," I mumble.

"I feel like I've told you this before. What we do is important -"

"I've never argued otherwise -"

"And," she continues sternly, "we need to learn," she pauses, "we *all* need to learn - that attachments make that important work even more difficult."

I wait. I see the words on her lips as she fights for control.

"Maybe it should be more like this? A fortress of solitude." She gives a mirthless laugh. There's a pause. "Do yourself a favor, Aedan, build yourself an oasis. Make a calm place you can return to, no matter where you are in the world, no matter what happens. A place where you can rejuvenate. But," she pauses again, "keep it like this. Solitary."

The vulnerability in those words frightens me. "What's happened?"

"What always happens when an oasis is discovered."

"What's happened, Persephone?" I roll to my side.

"My home was attacked -"

"Seph -"

"Mym is gone. They took her. They took everything. Well, almost everything." She rolls to face me. "I was examining the artifacts, hoping to get an idea of where The Cult is holed up, and I saw that the diadem we collected was missing. I assumed it was you."

"Seph -"

She shakes her head. "The attack was swift..." she squeezes her eyes shut and shakes her head. "I spent two days looking for you."

"How did you find me?"

"How did you find me?" she smirks.

"So, two days looking for me - that must have been fun."

"I expected more of a fight, Mr. Wards."

"I don't usually lock my door to friends."

"Yeah, that was my first clue." She adjusts to face forward again.

"First clue for what?"

"Covus," she calls out.

One, and then two, fairies drift into the living room from the kitchen. The first has a faint blue glow, and the second a soft yellow glow. "Ugh, Seph, I don't mind you bringing pets over, but a heads up would be nice."

"They're not pets." She gives an angry sigh as she gets off the couch. "I was about to begin the torture I'd spent two days dreaming up when Covus spotted Lith," Persephone points to the yellow fairy. "Been missing things lately? Shiny things? Sweets?"

I knew I hadn't eaten all of those cookies. "Pixie bastards." I stare at Lith, who hides behind Covus.

"This fairy saved your life."

"One of yours?"

"No."

Persephone lays a hand on me, pushing me back onto the couch as I try to get up. She bends and whispers in my ear. "She's terrified."

The fire within me returns to a simmer. "What? Of me?" I whisper back.

Persephone shakes her head. "Lith says she's been your shadow for several days, although she won't say who she's been reporting to. She's also been collecting." Persephone pulls one of my pots out from under the coffee table and sets it on top.

I lean forward. I see one of the snickerdoodles, a silver flip lighter, a ring, a small glass frog, and the diadem we took from the museum. "I have no idea how this got here."

"I suspected."

"And yet you continued to shout at me." I see her shrug out of the corner of my eye.

"As you would say, there were unanswered questions."

"And now?"

"Still unanswered, but I'm willing to move forward."

"Good for me."

"Indeed."

She moves off to speak with the fairies. *Maybe if I don't see any of it* - but I give in and reluctantly move the pot. Spread out over the coffee table are the packets of information Alan had put together for me. There's a lot of it. More, it seems than there should be. *I only asked about spriggans.*

I grab a packet and glance at it. The top page is a 'have you seen' poster. Adaline Crumb - the picture on the poster shows a girl with long red hair, a small round face, about twenty years old, wearing a Dickinson College sweatshirt. I flip to the next page, which is a police report. My foggy mind skims the report, taking away that it's dated last year and it's for a missing person, possible abduction. "Hmm," I utter and set the stack aside. I pick up another. Stephany Miller - she went to Penn State. Also a redhead.

"All from Pennsylvanian schools. You've done a lot of research," Persephone says as she comes back over to the couch.

"Not me," I groan as I sit back. "I really wish you hadn't opened that folder."

"Why?"

I rub my face and begin mentally laying out what I know, my mental imagery overlapping the pages scattered on the table. "Is it too much to ask that we share what we know? Because I'm sensing that our paths have converged." And then I laugh. I see the quizzical look from Persephone. *You're all-in now, you stupid sod, but this was the excuse you were hoping for so you could pass this off.* I laugh at myself again – at irony, at coincidence.

Persephone ignores the outburst. "I don't know that I have more to add. In recent months, almost a year now, The Cult has become openly active again. We had a couple of close calls before I decided to start beating them to the artifacts. You were there for the last one."

"They found you somehow." I look over my shoulder but the fairies are gone.

"Yes, I have a feeling now that Lith had something to do with that."

"And yet you still sent her away with that other one – no supervision. You can't trust a fairy."

"Your racism aside, I have asked Covus to keep an eye on her. They have ways of protecting their own kind, even ones who have been summoned and bound."

"The guy she's terrified of?" Persephone nods. *Whatever, still hate them.* I clear my throat trying to clear the pang of guilt I now feel. I stare at Alan's pages. At the newspaper. And then something occurs to me. "And Mym?"

"Gone."

"I'm sorry,"

"I'm getting her back," she growls and stands up.

"Yes, of course, but listen - her and not you?"

"I don't want to talk about this anymore."

"Why would they *take* her, not destroy her. Take *her*, and not you?"

"I said I don't want to talk about this anymore."

I can tell she's now thinking about that, but I don't press. I switch tracks. "I was told -" I mentally curse Brigit, "I was under the assumption that three women had been abducted. For some reason, Summerland creatures had come through, possibly forced or coerced -"

"Like Lith."

"Yes," I grumble, "like Lith. Summoned here to go after these college girls. Now it looks like there's been a whole bunch more than what I was originally told about - from schools all over PA. Oh, and the police came to my door. We fought."

"You fought the police? Wait, what? Humans?"

"I'm pretty sure they were human, and yes, most definitely police. Not the good ones, though." I waggle a finger at her, and as I do, I connect a possible dot. "Oh, hey, would these cult guys -"

"It's an all-female cult. Sexist."

"Okay, could they have sent the goons to my place?"

"I don't see how The Cult would have known where you live. Besides, they wouldn't use men."

"Who said they were men?"

"You said goons, I assumed -"

"A goon could be a girl. Now who's being sexist?"

"Lith!" Persephone says in an a-ha tone.

"Lith?"

"She pointed The Cult in my direction. She probably did the same to you."

"But you said they wouldn't work with men."

"As a general rule – but they may be working with someone who would -"

She cuts off suddenly, and I know why. We both feel it. There's a feeling of a presence in the room. More than one. The gods can hide themselves. They can make it so they aren't sensed, or only sensed a little, depending on their mood. But I – we've – been sensing them on and off for days. Even for gods, masking strong emotion is difficult – excitement, worry, they tend to bleed through even the sternest composures. They've been paying particular attention to this mission. More eyes, more emotion, much harder to stay hidden. Right now there are a lot of eyes on us. This passes quickly, pushed aside by a greater shadow. Persephone stares at me. I shrug.

And then we both turn to the window at the same time. The world has changed. The sun is shining, but the light has dulled. There's air, but it is very still. There's sound, but it is muffled as if at a distance. I slowly get up and approach the window. A line of dark shapes stands between my house and the park, with more arriving. "Friends of yours?"

Persephone steps up behind me and pulls the curtain further aside. "We brushed against a few acolytes at the museum, nothing too difficult. This, however... Aedan, allow me to introduce The Cult of Eleusis."

Chapter 24

"I know what to do," I say. "This always works," I flip off my porch light. There are a few seconds of quiet, and then the house rocks as something massive hits my wards. There are two more in quick succession; both Persephone and I fall to our knees. "Not your typical trick-or-treaters," we get back to the window in time to see a cluster of about ten cultists raise their hands. A black orb forms over the top of them and then streaks towards the house, striking the ward wall. "This is new, you say?"

"They've always been deadly assassins, skilled in combat, able to do some manipulation, but this – nothing like this."

The house shakes again. "Do you think they're here for you or me?"

"I think they are here for the diadem."

"Not pulling any punches anymore, I see. They've cut out that whole secret part of their secret society."

"It would appear so," she growls and rushes to the door. Her hand is on the handle before I can stop her.

"Wait!" I shout, but it's too late. The door opens as another explosion ripples along the energy barrier. The concussive blast of this one shatters the window and sends both of us to the floor. My ears are ringing, and I feel the trickles of blood from glass exploding into my face. Persephone is on her back several feet from the door; she's not moving. I glance out the hole in my living room wall. Cult members are clustering together in larger groups. One of about twenty-five raises their hands, a black orb forms. I slide next to her and cover Persephone just in time as the orb strikes the barrier showering ceiling sections down on the two of us. This time there's a flicker of blue lightning that arcs around the protective bubble my wards create. *Not much longer.* She startles me when her eyes suddenly spring open.

"How long will your wards hold?"

I point. "See that fence? Every picket is spelled. It all overlaps. I could invite an army of vampires into my house, and not one of them is going to get through that barrier. We've got hours," I gather from her raised eyebrow that I may have oversold it. She stands up, her face smudged. Her yellow dress is less than perfect. She lifts the hem and pulls a six-inch slender dagger from her boot. I stand and pat down my pockets, hoping that I had left a twig or a stone in them – nope, everything is in my other coat.

We stand at the front door threshold and watch as beings, much like the one I had seen at the museum, begin laying hands on the ward wall. They're human in shape only. Skin as white as paper and just as thin. Arms, legs, much too long. Their black and blue robes hang from them like flags in the wind, like the edges of a wraith. Shadow, like smoke, gently falls around them. As they press forward, small tendrils of green energy reach out from where their hands contact the blue barrier, infecting it and causing it to falter. They should have been sent reeling back as if yanked by a movie prop ripcord in its fully powered state. But they knew they'd done too much damage - apparently, the flicker had not gone unnoticed by them. Persephone stands ready at my side.

"Tell me when," she orders, her eyes on the cultists.

Mine are on the barrier. *Not long now. One – two – three...* In a flash very reminiscent of someone placing both hands on one of those plasma ball lights, blue lightning snakes and wavers over my house and then is gone. I feel Persephone tense as she readies her charge. "Not yet," I whisper as the shriek of a hundred voices all at once cry out in victory. Black-robed forms, some with curved daggers at the ready, others with staves, some with hands glowing green, all run at the house. "Wait," I say. Green globules blast away portions of my fence, letting some charge unimpeded while others vault the pickets.

The first one to step into my yard vanishes in a burst of light. I count as a second, and then a third and a fourth vanish. By the time the eighth is gone, I hear the screams of the first few as their bodies come crashing back down to earth. As the tenth one goes up, I take a step; on my second, there's a flash and a small crack of sound as my form billows out into a Kodiak bear. I charge forward, a brown muscled bowling ball, and plow through the first dozen, making my stand in a thicket of about fifteen dagger ready cultists. My claw tears away the face of the first. My jaws crush the skull of another. I feel the sting of a dagger in my side and lash out, gutting the wielder. There's the bite of two more blades into my flank as a burst of energy strikes my shoulder burning away fur and flesh.

I swing my claw in a wide arc catching three of them, and bring my jaws down onto the shoulders of a fourth, but it's not enough. For every one I cut down, two more take her place. I'm being pushed back towards the house. I glance over and see Persephone in even more dire straits. Even still, she's a blur of precise strikes. She uses a flying side kick to launch herself up into a round kick, which she turns into a leg sweep, all the while her own dagger is jabbing and slashing. But it's not enough. She's surrounded, and the space she's created for herself is shrinking fast.

I bellow, causing those around me to flinch, and I take that opening to charge free of the cluster surrounding me. I continue to roar and swipe as I cut a path towards Persephone. I don't stop as I come upon her. She grabs a handful of my fur and pulls herself up and over onto my back. As we flee, I catch sight of Persephone flinging her dagger into the forehead of a cultist who had leapt in an attempt to body slam her off of my back. As we reach my small porch, she slides off my back. There's another flash of light as I'm back to me again. My momentum carries me into the living room; I stumble and fall onto the couch.

"Any more tricks?" she calls over her shoulder as she takes up a defensive stance in the doorway.

I barely hear her. Blackness is creeping into the edges of my sight. My body is heavy. I look down at my hands. I hadn't shifted back to me on purpose – the power had left me. Stepping into the beyond has left me weak, but there's more to it. There's a weight on my ability like a cup has been placed over a candle. I close my eyes and reach out for Brigit. "I need you," I mutter. But instead of her, I feel a tickle in the back of my mind – a tickle which strangely comes across as a familiar and unsettling crazy laugh. "You son of a bitch," I whisper. I hear the grunts of Persephone fighting someone at the door. I glance over my shoulder and see a jam of dark robes, some now clambering through the broken window. In two steps, I've scooped up the diadem, and I'm at the bookshelf pulling on *A Tale of Two Cities*. The floor unlatches and opens. "Seph!" I call and rush down the stairs. *I've got one more trick.*

I grab the small vial from its notch at the bottom of the stairs and rush over to the thick roots where the runes that help me speak with Red, Green, and Blue hang. I kneel. I'm panting and can hardly lift my hand. Sweat drips from me. There's little left of me. I can feel it. "Move, Aedan," I say, and as I'm reaching for Red, I hear,

"Reach high, my son." With a small whimper, I gently pull his rune free.

I hear Green, "Dig deep," and I hesitate to pull hers, but manage.

No last words from Blue. I close my eyes as I pull his and as I do, a strange sensation comes over me. I've never felt anything like it before. There are no arms to be found, but nonetheless, I feel two tiny arms press around me, and suddenly the weight lifts from my mind, and an energy I've never felt before courses through me. I place my hand on my shoulder and even though nothing's there, for just a moment, it feels as if my hand passes through something.

"Aedan!"

Persephone's shout returns me to the workroom. I stand up quickly and rush to her side as the two of us struggle to pull the trapdoor closed. I hear the lock latch but am reluctant to let go of the handle – there's a strange comfort in that Persephone doesn't immediately move either. "We need to retreat. Is that going to be a problem?" Neither of us flinches as a hammer or an ax begins coming down on the door.

"I fled my home; I don't think I have a problem abandoning your hovel." She peers at me for a long moment, "Tears?" Her face isn't judgmental but quizzical.

"Don't worry about it. Here," I press the diadem into her free hand and lead her to the stone circle. I tap the raven, and the passageway opens. "This will take you to the creek at the back of the yard. The crawl might be a little tight, but you shouldn't have any problem."

"And you?" We both look up as cultists begin breaking through the trapdoor.

"I'm right behind you," I say as wood snaps and metal cries out against being bent back. "Go!" I almost push her down into the passage. As the door is ripped up, I grab my gear and bunny slippers. I'm tackled before I can get back to the passage. A dagger slips into my shoulder, but I ignore the pain and clock the blonde acolyte in the side of the head. She rolls off me as another, and another, start coming down the stairs. I quickly crawl to the passage, but before going in, I lift the small vial to eye level, speak "Ro," and snap the glass shell and twig within.

Over the shouts of the cultists, I hear a rumble and a crack and wait no longer. I fall into the passageway and crawl away as quickly as I can. There's more snapping, and then the sound of a massive crunch is carried up the tunnel on a gust of air as the section of earth I had displaced into the void to create the space for my workroom phases back into reality – crushing the five or six cultists who remained behind. I quicken my pace even more as the tunnel I'm in begins to collapse. My feet get caught as I get to the creek exit, but Persephone is there to pull me free. "This way, hurry." I try to lead the way, but my legs give out as the world around me swirls. The energy boost Blue had given me has helped, but I still lack my usual greatness.

"You're burning up," she says as she keeps me from falling.

"Just some jet lag. This way," I try to pull away from her, but she holds firm.

"Point," Persephone commands as she pulls my arm over her shoulder, and her hand tightens around my waist.

I gesture over the creek and up the embankment further into the trees - the yard of the house that backs up to mine is about a hundred feet away. We've moved only a few steps in that direction when we hear a whoosh and feel the heat of my house exploding into a fireball.

"Your neighbors are going to hate you."

"Not home. Miraculously, one set won tickets to Disneyland and the other an Alaskan cruise." Persephone carries me a little further, and then I indicate to set me down at the edge of the trees before they give way to the brown and snow patched grass. "Here,"

"They will follow," she stresses as she sets me down.

I fish around in my coat pockets, pull out a travel rune, and begin making a circle around us. I glance up as I'm finishing. Smoldering ash and smoke, but thankfully the spell had worked as intended, and nothing else had caught fire.

"Where are you taking us?"

By way of an answer, I say, "In for a penny," and place the hand holding the rune at the center of my circle.

Chapter 25

Blue's hug gives me enough energy to properly direct the portal this time, and we don't come crashing down onto the floor. We do, however, stumble a little stepping through the portal into Alan's apartment and bump into his dining table. There's a rattle of pictures, the small potted plants on the windowsill, and various metal objects from the kitchen as the portal swirls closed behind us. Jagged purple energy lines streak across the wall like snakes scattering from a field and knock a holiday wreath of hand-turkeys from the wall. Alan's studio apartment is bathed in the light of the morning sun streaming through the two windows at the front of his living room. We glance up at the sound of footsteps rushing towards us.

"What happened? What's going on?" he asks in quick succession, taking two steps at a time down from the upper loft area where his bedroom is located. He takes my arm, and my weight shifts from the table to him. He leads me to his couch. "This doesn't look like a win."

"It was not." Persephone's tone is deadpan. She follows us to the couch and gives a head bow to Alan. "I am Persephone."

"Alan," he says, offering his hand, "Let me get you some water – and then I want an explanation."

As I place my coat on the arm of the couch and my slippers – which are now holding Red, Green, and Blue's rune stones – at my feet, I catch Persephone's eyes lingering on him as he walks away. He's only dressed in boxer-briefs and a t-shirt. "Don't get any ideas."

"Who is this?" she asks, but I notice she's still ogling him.

"Alan," at this, she looks at me with a particularly icy stare. I'm not sure what she's assuming, but I can guess it has something to do with possibly betraying the love of another. "You can trust him. He knows all about us,"

"Aedan -" she begins to say, but Alan returns with two glasses of water.

"What happened?"

The adrenaline is wearing off; I can hear the worry in his voice now. "Thank you," I take the water and sip slowly. I'm amused by Persephone, who is unsure of what to do and has decided to copy me. "She punched me," I say as I stretch to put the empty glass on the coffee table. Neither of them thinks this amusing. "Laundry day?" I ask.

He looks down, and I see the little flush in his cheeks. "It's ten in the morning; I wasn't expecting company." He pulls down on his t-shirt in an attempt to cover his boxer-briefs. "Don't deflect. What happened?"

I sink back into Alan's couch. "I really wish you'd left that folder alone."

"What?"

"I think he's talking to me." Persephone sets her glass next to mine. "I still don't understand why this upsets you."

"Folder? Oh," Alan says with a smile of pride, "you read it."

He's looking at me. I don't need to lift my head from the back of the couch to see this. I close my eyes as I shake my head and point to Persephone.

"Did it help?"

I hear his attention shift to Persephone. Let them talk it out. I need time to think.

"I didn't get to read much before we were attacked."

"Attacked? There's a lot to unpack here. Um, over here..."

I watch through slitted eyes as Persephone sets the diadem on top of my coat. Wisps of a new plan form. I remain still, no reason to draw attention to myself. In a moment, Persephone joins Alan at the dining table, where he's setting a box he pulled out of a closet.

"I made a copy. He likes to talk about always having a plan, but I also know he just as often has a knee-jerk reaction to things. I had a feeling the folder might end up in a fireplace."

"Yes. Very thorough," Persephone turns over a few of the pages, "I said as much to Aedan."

They begin trading comments on the abductions – I catch the occasional word out of the air like swatting flies. It's information I've already covered with myself. Redheads. Why all women? They don't see a purpose, but I think I do - now at least. I won't tell Alan this, but seeing just how many abductions there have been was the final piece. *I think it's a message – otherwise, why wait to take Alyson last? They were trying to get someone's attention – is it narcissistic to think it was me?*

"So, are you human?" Persephone suddenly asks as politely as one would for someone to pass the salt.

Alan's laugh breaks a moment of uncomfortable silence. "Yes."

"And you know Aedan... what he is?"

"He would say he doesn't know what he is."

"Yes."

"I'm right here." They continue to ignore me. *Good.*

"I met Aedan in New York when I was fourteen. He – he saved me..."

They were ignoring me, but now I couldn't ignore them.

"He was on a mission?"

"Yes. My parents worked for a university – archaeologists. We were in New York to do something, I don't know what, with something they had found while on a dig. We got mugged. The only thing taken was the case the artifact was in. Mom and dad were, well, worldly. They'd been in some pretty bad places. Both were competent martial artists. They could take care of themselves. So they went after the guy. I think they forgot I was there – they often did."

"Your parents loved you very much," I say solemnly from the couch. I hear Domonic's final words again - not so much the words, but the sad, regretful tone behind them.

"Anyway, I don't know what they thought they'd find when they tracked the guy down, but I doubt it was a ritual in a subbasement. We ran into Aedan – his first words still make me laugh. 'This is all a dream. Now go away.' We didn't, or more to the point, they didn't, and when he realized it would take more effort to get rid of my parents than to let them help, he gave in. I didn't do much, lots of shouting to look out, as I recall."

From somewhere within me, a need arises to reach out and comfort him. I want to tell him he had done a good job, and his job as a lookout had made things go a lot smoother than they could have. I want to, but don't.

"Things went sideways, as I'm guessing these things tend to. Aedan got caught up. Dad managed to get the artifact away from this... I have no idea what it was -"

"A leinth," I say.

"Yes. There were two of them, a man and a woman, human in shape, both naked - their features were distorted like they were made of smoke. They hit Dad with this beam of dark light, if that makes sense. When he went down, my mom rushed in to protect him – fought off a few minions, but she didn't make it. Aedan eventually won the day. Couldn't save Dad, though. Aedan said it was like radiation poisoning. Afterward, Aedan kind of adopted me."

"And now has you researching for him?"

"No. I've always been after him to let me in, but he's always kept that world away from me. I kind of went against orders this time."

"Ah," Persephone says.

I think I hear her set down the pages she's holding – *perhaps she understands now.*

"But I think I uncovered something big. I saw his note, the one he had that set him on this mission. It only had the number three on it. But look at these. I went rogue and looked into it myself. When I started ignoring, you know, human limitations, I found this pattern of abductions going back almost two years. All in PA. Redheads. All at or near a college. All women."

"I see," she says, but I can see her raised eyebrow in my mind's eye.

"It's a pattern. One from one side of the state, and then another at the other side of the state. One from the northern part, and then another from the southern. Each time at the same time or within a day, usually within an hour of each other. And then, after a pause, which seems to vary, the pattern repeats. East, west, north, south, each time a different school, each time a different college, each time moving a little closer towards the center."

I hear the shuffling of pages. But I don't need to look. I can picture it in my mind. They, the spriggans, or maybe other Sidhe, Ogmios kept stressing he wasn't the only gateway. Whoever. Whatever - they were looking for something. I make my decision - *sometimes, the best way to get around the trap is to spring it.*

"I think they were looking for something, or maybe waiting for something to happen," Persephone says mostly to herself.

"And kept going when it didn't happen," Alan pulls out a chair and sits.

"Is this the last one?"

"The last one I was able to get any information on at least - Becca Trent."

But she wasn't the last one – *do I tell them that?* My better judgment wins out. "There's one more. Alyson Fitzcairn. A senator's daughter. A bit higher profile than the others, but otherwise, the M.O. hits."

We all delve deep into our cerebrums.

Alan speaks, "Was she the focus? Persephone, you'd said they might have been waiting for something. Were they waiting for her?"

"Hard to say. Was this Alyson doing something in the last year that made her unattainable? Why abduct the other women?"

"Bored?" Alan asks.

"Spriggans don't get bored. They hunker down in an out of the way place, and when a wayward traveler happens upon them, they pounce." She's quiet and then calls out to me. "Aedan, are you sure it was spriggans? Most of these abductions are along hiking trails," Persephone says.

"Pretty sure. And Alyson was abducted at her house and forced to write a note – 'don't call the police.'" I say in ominous mockery.

"I don't think this is funny, Aedan. That is strange, however – very."

My mind drifts away from their conversation. *She was the only one they drew attention to. I had told the Senator, these weren't the type to make demands – I should listen to myself. It's not a demand. It's the period at the end of a very long sentence.*

"Are these spriggans the ones that attacked you?" I hear Alan ask.

"No," both Persephone and I say at the same time.

Persephone continues, "Our paths have crossed. A cult came looking for something that I was protecting. I thought Aedan had something to do with it, so I dropped by."

"Why would you -"

"Because our Patrons," I snap but catch myself.

Persephone picks up where I left off, "The Patrons don't always agree with each other. Sometimes they have plans that conflict with something else another Patron is doing,"

"And you guys get called up to defend the plan," Alan says. "So you never know who your friends are. That's sad."

"It is what it is," Persephone says. "What -"

This time I finish her thought, "What we do is important." However, my reiteration had less sanctimony.

"If you're going to keep commenting, why don't you come and join us?" she derides.

"You guys are doing fine." *Besides, I'm trying to figure out how the Cult ties in. I'm trying not to sound self-important here, but I don't believe in coincidences, not while on a mission. That fairy? I don't think the Cult set her on me, but who? It must have been Gregor.* The thought is unsettling – *who is he working for?*

"So, the Cult attacked you guys. Is that why Aedan is -"

"Aedan is just fine, thank you."

"No. He was – not well before I got to his house."

"So what happened before Persephone showed up?"

I can tell they're both looking in my direction. "I took a trip – to the other side..."

"Uninvited?" Persephone's tone is heavy with dismay.

There's definitely judgment in her tone this time. "I was in a rush."

"Can one of you explain what you're talking about?"

"Aedan died."

"Shit, Persephone, terrify the kid, why don't you?" I rouse myself from my cushion and look at them from over the edge of the couch. "I did die, but I got better. See," I wave at him and then settle back into the sofa - this time laying out. "Your soul, Alan, is like a battery. When it's away from your body, and you run the charge too low, it takes time to power back up. I'm just recharging."

"Is that true?"

I'm a little annoyed that he felt the need to get confirmation from Persephone.

"Close enough. The Cult attack hasn't helped."

"Are you guys safe now?"

I hear her about to answer – but that is not a question you answer with the truth. "We're fine. The type of trail we left fades fast, and they were preoccupied with fire." Absolutely not the truth, but I have a plan – I think. Thankfully, Persephone doesn't contradict me.

"What's the next step?" Alan asks.

I know what *I* need to do. I just need an opening – and before they put too many other things together. *I shouldn't have told them about Alyson.*

"We need to find the Cult. I don't know how they fit into the abductions Aedan was tracking, but I'm certain they're at the center of all of this. If nothing else, they have most of the pieces of a great weapon. I'd say they're more important than a few missing humans."

Ouch. I can hear Alan reel from that. He's polite enough not to say anything and instead asks, "Weapon?"

"A ritual. They have all the parts but one."

"And if they get that last piece?"

"It's impossible. It's destroyed. I have no idea how they think they're going to move forward."

"But if they do?"

"They can destroy those like Aedan and myself. They can destroy a great many things, but our kind would be the first to go."

"Like for real, like dead dead? Because Aedan has mentioned, um..."

"Reconstituting. With this ritual, they'd be able to banish us permanently. The thing is..."

She's getting too close. "How about a drink, Alan? The good stuff." I shout from my relaxed position.

"I'll have to go downstairs. Persephone, would you mind getting some glasses?"

I hear the door open and close. The next thing I know, Persephone is leaning on the back of the couch, looking down on me with a wicked smirk. "What?"

She leans in a little closer. "All your bluster, I honestly thought it was selfishness. I believe what I said to you was that you should find a place you can retreat to, no matter what happens. I didn't realize you already had one. Huh," as she measures my reaction, her smirk becomes a genuine smile, "That's funny."

"What?" I grumble.

"You didn't even know you had such a place." She feigns disappointment. "I get why you didn't want me looking at that folder, and I'm sorry." She nods a further apology and heads towards the kitchen.

As soon as she's out of eyesight, I sit up. A pad of paper and a pen are on the coffee table. I write a quick note: I'll get her back. I underline for emphasis.

Final nail in the coffin. My mission. My burden. No one else is getting hurt. I take a deep breath. Teleporting is a lot like deep diving. If you don't take a deep enough breath, you're not going to get very far. I grab the diadem

and my coat, take another deep breath, and teleport as I think at Persephone
- *Keep him safe.*

Chapter 26

Crisp midmorning air whips by my face – and then metal trashcans and hard pavement. A light snow is falling, and I take a moment to enjoy this and to get my bearings. "I hate teleporting." It's a quicker travel option, harder to trace, but dangerous as for a moment you're everywhere at the same time. I aimed for the docks, didn't get any further than the side alley. *How is it possible for everything to hurt?* I make almost as much noise standing as I did landing. I dropped my coat in the fall. I check to make sure the diadem is still in one of the pockets – everything is where it should be, including the handful of runes and twigs I had never cleared out. I hear two car doors slam and look up. Two familiar shapes approach me from the street. "You're out of uniform, Detective Darren," I say. They stop at the curb.

"Could you come with us?" the leaner one asks.

"I'm sorry I've forgotten your name." I smile, and lean, arms crossed, against a dumpster.

"Get in the damn car," Darren growls.

He takes a step, but the lean man puts his arm out. "Let's not make this difficult," he glances up at Alan's building.

Do they know about the wards? "Come and get me." I hold out my wrists.

The lean man laughs. "We're both short on time, sir. Do you really want to play this game?" This time he doesn't stop Darren from stepping onto the sidewalk.

Darren pulls his Glock.

"Not too far, Darren," he does warn.

Darren does stop, but not before throwing irritation over his shoulder.

The lean guy unquestionably knows about the wards I've placed. He's right; I don't have time to play. Persephone and Alan will be looking for me. Someone's gone to a lot of trouble to send me an invitation. Time I RSVP. I step away from the dumpster, smile at Darren as I walk by, and say to the lean man, "I've got shotgun, um,"

"Dave."

"Right, Dave," Darren's meaty hand clamps down on my shoulder as he swings his fist into my gut. It drops me to my knees. They scoop up my coat and toss it in the backseat, and me into the trunk.

Alan was right when he said that these things tend to go sideways, but this is all way above average. It's felt like that since the beginning. Brigit's caginess set the tone. *No. Lugh's surprise visit and insistence that I stay in my lane set the tone.* But I've literally been in tighter spots before. I feel around in the dark. The trunk is empty. I sigh. Just me and my wits - some of my confidence deflates. "Smells like fish back here. That's going to hurt your resell value." I shout. A few seconds later, I hit my head as the car hits a pothole. I wish I could say I have them right where I want them, but the best I can tell myself is that this saves me the time of trying to find them. Some big questions remain, and as Persephone says, I ask a lot of questions. But first, patience.

The drive is agonizingly long. If Dave and Darren listened to music during the ride, none of it filters into the trunk. If they talk about their crazy Saturday night, I can't overhear any of it. Something tells me they don't hang out when off the clock, and I get the impression that they barely tolerate each other during business hours. Darren's obviously on the take, but the lean guy - he works for a boss. *Maybe it's an "I'm the favorite. No, I am" thing.* I finally hear something other than road-noise: a chain-link fence being unlocked and opened, and then the unmistakable sound of a jet engine – very nearby. This time the drive is very short, during which I hear several planes landing and taking off. I hear another gate, big by the sound of it. We're in a building. The car stops.

I'm pulled from the trunk and thrown into a cage. It's too small to stand up. Thick bars, it's not comfortable sitting on metal bars. I examine the lock and bars. I could probably get out if I'm left alone for a few minutes. Dave and Darren huddle together for a moment near the table and chairs – we're the only things in the room. It's freezing. A ring of high windows - all broken - lets in plenty of light, so it's not hard to see where I'm at. It's a large abandoned airplane hangar with an office at the opposite end of the hangar doors. The broken door to that office has my attention. I sense - not energy exactly, more like shadows of energy, like faint echoes. I close my eyes. My senses reach out. The hangar isn't warded and bathed in nothing more than background energy, but there's an odd concentration at that back doorway – not magic though. Something else, something old, something feeding on magic.

"I'll make the call," Dave says; he steps away.

Darren drops my coat on the table and plops into one of the chairs.

Time for some magic. "Can I have my coat? It's chilly in here."

Darren ignores me.

"You don't even have to get up; I'm fine if you want to toss it at me."

He ignores me.

"Still a cop?"

His eye twitches. "Do you have a closet of other uniforms, or did you just steal the local guy's uniform I saw you in last?"

"Shut. Up."

Got'im. "Have you always been on the take, or is this a recent choice?"

This time he glances in the direction of the lean man, who is still on the phone. Darren gets up and reaches in – I let him get a grip on my sweater and pull me into the bars. "I'm not telling you again. Shut. Up."

I cock my head right and left. "Your nose looks awful." He roughly lets go and returns to his seat.

I let him get comfortable. "How long were you stuck in the holding cell I dropped you in?" He adjusts his chair so he's facing the table. He digs around in his coat pocket and pulls out a deck of cards. I've never seen angry shuffling before. "I find it hard to believe you came up with a brilliant lie to explain how you ended up in a holding cell in another unit's uniform. Did you luck out and have another dirty cop find you?"

His cards scatter as he kicks back his chair. "Say another word -"

I can't help myself, "Word."

He fumbles pulling his gun free, and before he can point it at me, Dave returns and stops him.

"Easy. Easy."

"I wasn't going to kill him -"

"No damage. Just containment."

There's a moment, I'm not sure Darren's going to listen, but then he lowers his weapon.

"What's the word?" Darren asks as he picks up his chair.

Before Dave can answer, I ask, "Can I have my coat? It's chill."

Darren spins, but Dave steps in between the both of us. It's enough to get Darren to back down. Dave turns and squats down in front of me. "Now you listen here. I've got limited pull with him, so if you have any interest in living, I'd shut up."

"Okay, but I've got to know, please, before the end," I lean out and look around the guy's shoulder. "Is he still a cop?" Curiously, he smirks. I think he wants to tell me.

"I've seen the Boss do things I can't begin to understand, but that little trick you pulled off – smoke and mirrors?"

"Something like that," I mirror his smirk.

"Anyway, it got Darren put on administrative leave and the two of us chewed out by the Boss." He leans in a little further. "I get to kill him if he steps out of line." He puts a finger to his lips and steps away.

Dave picks up the cards. I let him get comfortable. I even let him shuffle the cards and deal out five to each of them. "Can I have my coat – please?"

Darren thumps the table and stands.

I watch as Dave's hand very slowly slides down to, but doesn't grab, his gun.

Darren grabs my coat.

"What are you doing?" Dave asks as Darren begins to go through the pockets roughly.

"He wants the coat. Why?"

"Because it's pissing you off."

Darren begins dropping twigs and stones onto the table. "It's garbage -"

"I told you," Dave says.

And then he finds the diadem. "What's this?"

I shrug.

"Leave it for the Boss. He said he'd be a few minutes."

Darren looks at the lean man and then drops the diadem onto the table. He continues to pat and dig. "Ah," he says as he pulls out a wooden cylinder. "What's this?"

I don't answer.

"Whatever it is, you're not getting it." He sets it on the table.

"Can I have my coat now?" He does another pass through my pockets. "My coat, can I have it?" He shakes it out like a picnic blanket at the end of the day. "It's chilly. Come on - can I have my coat now?"

"You want your coat?!" Darren scoops up some of the twigs and stones and begins throwing them at me – one of the rocks nails me in the forehead.

"Well, you throw a little better than you detect. You should have been a ballplayer instead of a cop. I mean, come on, Darren, your desk was full of missing persons. I thought for a time that they all had to do with this, but they don't, do they? You're just terrible at your job."

"I've spent twenty years putting shits like you behind bars!"

What the hell does that mean – and, man, is this guy easily triggered. I reach my hand out through the bars. "The coat, you're already holding it..."

Darren balls it up and is ready to throw it at me when Dave clears his throat.

"How about we don't. He's playing you, man. The Boss will be here in another minute. Why don't you go sit in the car until then?"

Darren drops my coat and steps on it as he walks away.

The lean man gathers up the cards, and then, not looking at me, says, "I see you, man. I see you. You're not getting your coat. The Boss said to watch out for booby traps at your place. I don't know what you've done to your coat, but it ain't happenin'." He deals himself solitaire.

Without drawing attention to myself, I'm able to pick up two stones and a twig. *I can work with this.* "How did you know where to find me?"

"After our last meeting, the Boss said to wait at that address, that he'd make sure you'd show up, and to grab you when you did." He lays down a seven of diamonds on an eight of diamonds and flips the next card.

"Is your boss the forgiving type?"

He shrugs. "He's practical. He'll deal with it until it's more trouble than it's worth. Why?"

I look down at the rune in my hand - the stone of Uruz. "Just making conversation." Before I can activate it, a side door opens. I glimpse a black car, and then the door shuts. Two, a man and a woman, enter the hangar. She walks with fierceness, and with such presence, I'm surprised the ground doesn't part before her. And him, rounded features, nice suit, an inexplicable smile – the Boss.

Chapter 27

"My boy. My dear, Anant, it is always good to see you." Gregor greets me as warmly as if I'd come to his door for Thanksgiving. He continues to move towards me, but the woman who came in with him, Aela, sidelines to stand near the faded green sedan the goons had arrived in. She effortlessly, unnaturally, is able to find the few shadows not driven away by the light pouring in from the windows of the hangar. Her clothing - and I'm annoyed that her black coat is very reminiscent of my own duster – the blacks and dark blues blend with the darkness so well that she's practically camouflaged as she stands near the vehicle. I'm concerned looking away will cause me to miss her moving. "So undignified," Gregor tsks and snaps his fingers. "Join us, and you, let him out," he orders. Darren exits the car and approaches the table while, without question, Dave slides a key from his pocket and opens the cage.

I manage to grab one more stone and add it to my limited arsenal, slipping all of them into the cuff of my sweater as I'm getting up. "Gregor," I nod. All the questions in my mind find answers. "This is all you? You and your Patron."

He begins to laugh and claps me on the back. "No. No. As usual, Anant, leading with your heart, not your mind." He taps his temple and then comes in for a bear hug – he lifts me from the ground.

I'm even more confused. "Gregor," I puff out, "Gregor, damnit -"

He puts me down. "Confused, yes. I see," he smiles a gleeful smile as he waggles a finger at me. "You must be hungry. Thirsty?"

"Gregor!"

"Yes, my friend?" His Greek accent flows from him like a sparkling spring.

I try to begin, but I can't find the words. There's too much.

He laughs, puts his arm around me, and leads me to one of the chairs. "Sit. Sit." His joyfully bellowing voice echoes around the hangar.

"No coincidences," I mutter, my eyes downcast.

"What was that?"

"You were dormant for years, many years, and then I decide to come to see you. You set the fairy on me, didn't you?"

His smile, boyish, mischievous, is rather irritating. "Let's not dwell on the past. I'm here to speak to you about the future – oh, but first," he steps over to Darren. "Give me your hand," Darren hesitates for a moment and then raises his left hand. Gregor places a small white stone into Darren's palm – I recognize it as the truth stone I had given him. Darren starts to pull away, but Gregor fixes his eyes on him. "Don't," he snaps and places his hand on top of Darren's. With a smile, Gregor turns to me. "This has already been so much help. Again, thank you." He clears his throat and turns back to Darren. "Anant, my friend, would you kill this man here?"

"No."

"Yes, always a decent fellow, my friend. You are a good person. Now, you Detective, if I told you to kill Anant, would you do it?"

"Absolutely."

"Such purity, such pure hatred. This is why I like you. If I told you to kill our friend Mr. Kane, would you kill him?"

This time Darren takes a second to answer. "Yes."

"Diligent, commendable – if a little sloppy, huh?" Gregor smiles a wide grin. "Huh?" He pokes Darren gently in the gut. "Now," he speaks with authority, clearing all friendliness from the air. "If you were told to kill me, would you?"

"No."

Darren's eyes widen and he tries to pull away but Gregor is too strong for him. His face unflinching, Gregor asks, "Did you feel that?" he tsks.

Darren doesn't answer, but we all see the angry scared expression on his face.

"Is that one of those artifacts I see on the table?" Gregor asks, turning his back on Darren and moving to the table.

I see a shadow move. Darren suddenly stiffens and grunts. Aela slips around him, a gimlet knife between her fingers. She takes Darren's palm and pulls him close as she stabs him another four times – finishing with a jab to his throat. She steps back. Darren coughs, stumbles back, and drops to the ground. Aela sheaths the knife, steps up to Gregor and places the white stone into his waiting hand. My eyes linger on Darren. "I think you know it is." I say.

Gregor stares at the diadem. "As I said, I'm here to speak to you about the future." He holds Dave in an intimidating stare and gestures at him with the stone between his index finger and thumb. Gregor raises an eyebrow. The sweat on Dave's forehead is not hard to miss. Gregor smiles. "Mr. Kane, take the day. Ditch the car. Who knows what the Detective has stashed in there, and I can't be bothered to look," Gregor pauses and then adds. "I'm tempted to humiliate you postmortem, but no." He smiles at Darren's body. "Drop the body off in the usual place." He says and waves Dave away. "Anant, walk with me. I want to show you the temple." Gregor heads in the direction of the back office. Aela picks up the diadem but ignores my gear, so I grab my coat and cylinder.

I slip on my coat as I walk, but don't button up. "I didn't like the guy, but that wasn't necessary."

"Taking out the trash is always necessary. Besides, I seem to recall a story about a young vigilante storming a camp and killing ten knights."

"They had just raped and pillaged a village so they could pay for passage to Jerusalem so they could rape and pillage."

"So, you felt justified?"

"Yes."

"So do I."

As we enter the office, I feel a change in the air. It's like stepping from an air-conditioned house into a Georgian summer. It is also hard to miss that most of the floor of the office has been torn up. I lean forward and glance down a long staircase descending into the earth. It appears to have been repaired in the last few years. Even so, this modern stonework was not the entrance I would have expected. Standing at the top of the stairs, I can't discern the noise, but there is a faint sound drifting up towards us.

"They tell me this temple was built by a lost expedition which set out from Pylos around one thousand B.C. - and before you ask, just before my time." He starts down the stairs. Torches on the walls light our way as the light from the outside begins to fade the deeper we go. "A storm brought them to these shores, and the survivors built what was probably the first permanent settlement in the area. Friends were made and of course enemies too. Eventually this temple was built to honor, if not their bad luck at being castaways, then their ability to survive and flourish."

"Home is where the heart is," I interject.

"Indeed, well, as long as no one else wants it, or in this case, doesn't want you to have it -"

"Their bad luck continued?"

"Yes." He answers as we come to the bottom of the stairs.

This was the stonework of an ancient temple that I had been expecting. Simple by my recollection of what the ancient Greeks were capable of in those days, but then again, they were far from home. The mezzanine's gray-blue stone where we stand overlooks a large open area, at the center of which is a sun symbol with rays stretching out in all directions. Acolytes and cultists, dozens of them, move about, with several of them kneeling at the center of the sun symbol chanting. I hear the clang of metalwork and the sound of chisel on stone – and crying. What I can see is only a little bigger than one of the lecture halls at the college, but a colonnade is blocking a perfect assessment. "You were saying..."

"The day after dedicating this temple to Demeter, a hurricane sank the temple and their village into the marsh."

"Poseidon is an asshole." We both look up, which is stupid because the ethereal is all around us, not in any one direction. We exchange looks; he was thinking the same thing.

"Most of the temple was made of wood; this room is all that remains. It was rediscovered in the modern age by Anastasia Markos. She's a member of a sect that has fallen on hard times -"

"The Cult of Eleusis."

"You've had the pleasure -"

"You've been helping the Cult of Eleusis?"

"We do as we are told," He says, but I catch a hint of amusement.

"Why this place? Why this temple? There are dozens of lost temples. Why this one?"

"You don't see it?"

I look around. It's a temple. I look along the mezzanine. I see stairs leading down into the main chamber. I see archways leading away from the mezzanine, now blocked by masonry – the stone wet from the water seeping through the mortar. I look behind me. I almost do a double-take when I finally spot the line of darkly dressed cultists standing at attention along the wall like a line of ghosts waiting for the order to haunt something. Given the Greek use of symmetry, there should have been another archway. Instead, the stairs up are framed by an elongated doorway that they're still in the midst of trying to blend with the rest of the temple aesthetic. "No, I don't see it."

"Allow me," with that, Gregor slaps and rubs his hands together, purple-tinted energy collects around his hands, and then he touches me on the shoulder.

Instantly the temple changes. The room pulses with a green-white light, like a heartbeat. At the center of the room, where the cultists kneel and chant, red tendrils extend from their chests, licking the air and drawing in the green-white energy each time it pulses. The energy passes along the tendrils into the bodies of the cultists, and for a moment, their skeletons are visible before the energy flows into the rock of the temple. *They've tapped a ley line.* "This is monstrous."

"Anant," Gregor tsks, "such short-sightedness. Beauty is in the eye of the beholder." He claps me on the back, and the temple returns to normal. "Come," he leads the way down the stairs to the main floor. "Let me tell you a story -"

"Didn't you already tell me one?" It's hard to miss the collapsed tunnel on the main floor under where the modern stairs come in – the original temple entrance? The enormous columns that have been toppled and make up the majority of the debris at this location suggest yes. I now notice that beyond the colonnade, the walls are lined with smaller rooms. One has a furnace, others are being used for storage, and many have been converted into cells, behind which are the faces of young women – some angry, some sad, others catatonic. "Gregor," the heat behind his name makes him jump as I cut away from him and approach the nearest cell. Seemingly for the first time since entering the temple, one of the darkly dressed cultists notices me and approaches. She says nothing but lifts her hands in a "Stop!" gesture.

"They don't speak to me either. Their leader does, but she owes me a lot."

I try to press forward, but the cultist doesn't budge – I half expect to pass right through her. My eyes linger on the crying woman, and eventually, I drift away to my obstacle. Her features are cloaked in shadow as if the flickering torchlight is afraid of her. I can see the hair falling out of the cowl appears to be blonde, but the color is dull, washed out. "Gregor, do something."

"I am. I'm walking away." He takes several steps but stops when he sees that I don't follow. "My dear, Anant, they are very busy right now. Why don't we leave them to it? Which reminds me," he waves over Aela. "Deliver our gift."

She moves away towards the other side of the temple. I lose track of her as she enters the colonnade. "Gregor, what is going on here?"

He looks over my shoulder with a grimace of near disgust. "They're probably the ones they haven't converted yet - or the ones that refused conversion."

"You can't do this."

"I'm not. And besides, they're only humans. There are seven billion of them; I don't think they'll miss a few."

"We're human!"

"Oh, Anant -"

I begin counting bodies and noting weapons.

"Anant," Gregor places his hands on my shoulders. "I see your mind working. Wait; let me tell you a story."

As he's about to speak, there's a commotion on the other side of the temple. Several cultists come running from the direction I saw Aela vanish. Others run towards that side of the temple. As I watch an impossibly old woman, robes of black and purple, make her way slowly towards the center of the chamber, she raises the diadem above her head.

"The day," she says, and her voice carries with unnatural strength, "The day has come. We have come through the mountains. We have come home. We have failed, been punished, and have now been given a second chance."

The cultists are in awe of both the artifact and the High Priestess. I take a step, but Gregor stops me.

"Oh, Anant, let them have their moment. Look how happy they are -"

"This isn't good, Gregor, not for any of us. The Ritual of Solomon,"

"Oh, it's worse than you think."

His impish grin is back. "Tell me." I force his hand from my arm.

"The temple," he gestures, "it will allow them to bend some rules -"

"No time date stamp on the ritual." He nods. "And their new talents? Wait, don't tell me. Parasites."

"Aren't all humans?"

We're interrupted by a cheer.

"Have the ore made ready. It is time!" She and the small crowd that has formed around her move back into the colonnade. I run to catch up. Gregor tries to stop me, but I'm too quick for him this time. I reach the outer cluster of cultists. They try to stop me, but I don't let them – their attempts become more aggressive the further I push through. I hear a weapon unsheathe.

"Let him through!" Gregor's voice booms.

The hands around me freeze. All heads turn to the old woman.

She looks out over the crowd, looks past me, and then nods.

The hands drop away, and the crowd parts slightly. Gregor steps up beside me and ushers me towards the front but off to the side. The room is open to the temple and about twenty feet deep and wide. Great chains hang on the walls, along with hooks, hammers, and shackles. At the center of the room is Mym. Some of those great chains secure her; four have been driven into her surface. She pulls against them but doesn't move more than an inch in any direction. I take a step, but Gregor clamps a hand down on my shoulder and then slides around to face me. His grip is iron – he's much stronger than I am and holds me to the spot.

"Reforge The Ring of Mitra!" the High Priestess cries out.

"Hail the High Priestess!" the crowd responds. They repeat, in unison, "Eleusis. Eleusis."

Several minutes pass, and then the crowd pushes back as two acolytes approach through the colonnade handling a glowing red-orange ladle.

The crowd begins to chant, "Nizael estarnas tantarez. Nizael estarnas tantarez."

Each of their voices becomes a green ribbon of energy that enters the crucible held above Mym. Just as they're about to pour, I recall Persephone's story about how Mym had acquired her scar. "No!" I call out, but it is all I can do. The molten metal is dumped onto Mym. She vibrates, and then from cracks, steam shrieks out – a scream by any other name.

The chorus of chanting intensifies.

The High Priestess hands the diadem to another and pulls from a deep pocket a silver band. She approaches Mym, holds the silver ring high, "Nizael estarnas tantarez." Like the others, her voice becomes a ribbon of green energy that loops around her hand and is absorbed by the silver. She holds back the sleeve of her robe and slowly presses the ring into the spot of molten metal. The intense glow of the molten metal softens into a gentle radiance almost instantly, which shines all the brighter as the High Priestess pulls the now completed ring from Mym's body. Her eyes, a mixture of crazed jubilation and maniacal insanity, remain on the ring as she steps away. The crowd parts before her and then begins to fan out along the colonnade.

I fight and press against Gregor's hold. For a second, I'm free, but he is able to grab hold again and, this time, presses me against the stone wall. He leans in close; I can feel his breath as he speaks. "Listen to me. Listen to me; we haven't much time now. Listen, please."

Chapter 28

I'm not listening to Gregor. I'm watching and listening to the hag as she makes her way to the center of the room. The kneeling cultists haven't moved, did not move during any of this. She comes to stand beside them. "Open the vault," she orders, eyes still on the ring – and she begins to laugh. "Open the vault."

Within minutes, a parade of artifacts begins showing up, carried in by fresh-faced acolytes. I see the skeleton key carved from bone, the simple wooden cup, and the eye in the crystal jar from Persephone's closet; added to these are a small bone, possibly a finger bone, and a stone knife – the Blade of Gabra that Persephone tried to get from Gregor. "I'm stopping this," I declare.

"Yes, maybe. But first, I need you to listen -"

There is a strain in his voice, impatience mixed with fear – no, panic. It's the panic that catches my attention. "What?" I snap.

Despite his insistence, he is silent for a moment. He has the face of someone who has been planning for something but never actually thought he'd see it happen. His mouth falters like a fish gasping for air, but manages to find his words. "Do you remember what I said to you when you visited me at my restaurant?"

"I remember not getting any answers."

He sighs and lowers his head in frustration.

I take the opportunity to try to free myself, but he's got my arms pinned – I can't reach any of my pockets.

"I told you everything is afraid of something. Have you ever asked yourself what it is that a god is afraid of?"

I have, actually. "No. Now let me go." Acolytes begin placing artifacts along the rays of the sun as directed. "Rules, Anant. The universe pivots on rules. Some we know, some we understand, some are to be discovered, but everything and everyone is subject to those rules. And gods, with their great power, are subject to even greater rules. Who keeps that tally sheet?"

"I don't know," I truthfully answer, actually captured by the question.

"No. I don't know either. But the gods do, and I'm certain they are as afraid of that answer as we are of them."

It's unsettling to hear Gregor speak of fear. I've seen both him and Persephone – on opposite sides – dive into the maws of ancient monstrosities. I refocus on the cultists. The High Priestess has come out of her enthralled stupor. Her face has become tight. She's straining with effort as more artifacts are placed, requiring more of her focus and attention. It's a moment before I see the wavering energy around her. She stands at the center of fractured space – as if she is a stone freeze-framed in the process of smashing a window. Gregor shakes me to regain my attention.

"I tell you this because – because we don't know all the rules. Because They haven't told us all the rules. They guard these rules, Anant, and it was no small effort to discover just one of these," a wicked smile curves his lips. "How many times have you been threatened with destruction? How many times have you been told, 'this is your last warning', and then been punished in some demeaning, painful, and inconvenient way?"

His grip on me becomes very painful.

"They aren't allowed to destroy us. They can, but they're not allowed to – can you imagine the punishment they must fear? What would stay the hands of such powerful beasts? If we know this, we could fight back. We could refuse their demands. We could live our own fate. Now," and because he can't help but talk with his hands, he removes one and gestures with his finger like a teacher emphasizing for his students. "I'm not saying that they aren't powerful, but a lot of that power, a lot of that hold over us, comes from our belief that they are all powerful. Just imagine, just for a moment, that they are no more powerful than water is to fire. Strong, yes, but not undefeatable. I have used this information to gain my freedom. True freedom,"

"And yet," I nod to what's going on around us.

"I take the odd contract on the side – for fun, and sometimes because I see opportunities." He leans in close and whispers in my ear. "This is an opportunity." He pulls away – and then I try to pull myself away. "Listen! Listen." He shakes me again. "I defied my god, but together we can defy all of them."

I stop struggling.

"I know you are unhappy, Anant." He pauses and smiles warmly. "My dear friend, Aodhan Anant. You are like me – like I was. You are tired of servitude. You serve because you are told. You serve because you have no choice. They play with this world like a toy, and we are merely puppets. We are nothing to Them – a tool to be used and then hung back on the wall. I tell you true; it doesn't need to be that way. It is that way because They will it. It is that way because we believe it to be."

I'm lost in thought – lost to his words. I feel his hands loosen and then pull away. I'm vaguely aware of an acolyte placing the diadem at the tip of a ray near me.

"Lugh came to me years ago, raving, but with an idea – with a purpose. He wanted to embarrass Brigit by breaking her favorite toy."

"You mean kill -"

"I mean destroy."

"But you said -"

"And here is where I began to pick the lock on my own manacles. I began asking the question: if we are nothing, if we are meaningless, if we can be used and discarded with such ease, why this elaborate plan? It's one thing for us to do battle in their names, us with such a smaller presence. But, wanting to destroy one of us - why not just snap his fingers and be done with it?

I came to realize that he couldn't. My research more or less confirms this. I was tasked with setting up these, ah, dominos, not because he would not but because he could not. Rules. He was bound by rules. When to act. When not to act. How to interact. Rules, my friend.

Eventually, I confronted Lugh, and he made me pay for the knowledge I had gained. It was not an easy fight, but I endured, and in the end, the chains were broken. We came to an arrangement. I promised to finish my task and to keep what I knew a secret, and he promised to leave me alone. So, I continued to direct the task, assuming it had something to do with building up the ranks of the Eleusinian. Oh, but I was wrong. So wrong. It wasn't until you walked into my restaurant that I realized it was you that I had been tasked with trying to smoke out. And I want you to know that I forgive you."

"Forgive me?"

"I kept what we talked about a secret," he sees my confusion. "You were asking about fey creatures and abductions. Reasonable as that's what I'd been put in charge of setting up. Lugh came to me shortly after you had left and demanded to know what you knew. I told him nothing – and he burnt my restaurant down."

"You mean he didn't already know?"

"The gods can't see everything, can't be everywhere at once, and there are places where their eyes cannot penetrate - and there are places you can make to be a place where their eyes cannot penetrate. Besides, their observations, we both know, draws attention. If he had kept too close an eye on you, this would have been noticed. Yes. So, this is why They have us." He laughs.

"I see -"

"I think you may. You feel it. You feel what I felt when you sat in that chair opposite me. I realized my purpose. New greatness formed in my mind, a new ambition."

"I want nothing to do with your ambition." I brush by him and reach into my coat to ready my staff. I stop when I see a struggling girl being brought into the middle of the room. She has red hair and is dressed in a soft rose colored night shirt. "Alyson," I try to take a step, but an arm pulls me back. I spin and push Gregor away.

He raises his hands in peace. We stare at each other for a moment and then he nods to what is happening over my shoulder. "And here is where I tell you – you can't. You can't save her, and you can't save yourself. The last domino."

"What? Why!?"

"After Lugh destroyed my place, I began looking into things, aspects of his great plan that before I was happy to ignore. It took some time, a lot of money, cashing in several favors, but I am very good at these things, so please believe me when I say she is of your blood."

I turn to look at her. I feel him come up behind me. He rests a hand on my shoulder.

"You know this rule. You know we are forbidden from making any contact or helping in any way with our kin. She will be killed. They will use her blood to banish you. There will then be nothing to stop them from using this temple to do," he takes in a deep breath and releases it as he says, "wonderful things..."

I'm sickened by his appreciation.

"There is more. I don't know if he ever intended you to find out all of this, or if this web was for Brigit to suffer with alone, but there's something more."

I run my hands through my hair; I don't know how much more I can take.

"She is the last of your line. Yes - the very last of your blood -"

"I don't even understand how this is possible."

"Aideen."

"But she wasn't -"

"She was – I assume she never had the chance to give you the news. The Romans were a very disruptive force, were they not?" He sighs. He lifts his arm and points at Alyson. "That young woman there is the last representation of that union. She is all you have left to link you to these humans."

I take a step; my conflict prevents another.

"If not from the start, Brigit must know by now. If nothing else, I am sure Lugh has delighted in shining a light on it by now. She has abandoned you. At the very least, She can do nothing for you. You will be destroyed because you save that girl, or you will be destroyed because you allow her to die. Either way, it will be because They play games to outdo and embarrass each other." Gregor steps around and faces me.

"I thought you said that They couldn't destroy us," the half-hearted attempt at a joke falls dead in my heart as well as on his ears.

"Punished in ways that I cannot even begin to picture then – or maybe this is that line that may not be crossed. Maybe, if you break this rule, They can destroy you. And if you don't, then the ritual will be your undoing. Either way, you are abandoned." He shakes his head. "But I have not abandoned you." He rests his hands on my shoulders. "I have looked out for you. Helped you. It did not work out as I had planned; I had hoped to have you here sooner. So we'd have more time to discuss this. Nonetheless, I have brought you here to free you. Join me, Anant. Join me, and I will save that human. Stand by my side, and we will bring down the gods. We will stop Their games. We will be a beacon for our brothers and sisters. I know you want this. You have always wanted this. Your life returned to you. This is my gift to you."

"Join you," I take a step away from him. I start to button my coat, reveling in the spell as it begins to take hold. "Freedom, my freedom..."

Chapter 29

A scream cuts over the sound of chanting and the orders of the High Priestess. It's Alyson. She's elbowed one of the cultists holding her, but another has rushed in to carry her forward. "There," the High Priestess points to a short sunray near her.

"There's no time left. This is your fate. Embrace it." Gregor steps up next to me. His voice isn't stern – he knows there's no denying fate. It is. To him, I've already said yes.

"I can't deny my fate," I whisper. "It is what it is..." I glance up, as does Gregor. The faint sound of a bird, an angry bird, is drifting down the stairs that lead up to the hangar.

There's a crash, followed soon after by another, and the angry bird becomes the long blare of a car horn. The tunnel fills with light and the grinding of metal against stone. The rev of an engine mixes with the sound of the horn that has now brought all action to a halt, but for the chanting at the center of the room. The mezzanine's stone wall explodes as a black SUV – the one I think Gregor had arrived in - rockets out of the tunnel, sails over the main chamber, and crashes into the colonnade not far from where Gregor and I are standing. We both duck. The engine screams as gears lock up from the damage; the horn continues to blare before ending in a sad squeak. The line of cultists on the mezzanine is unchanged, but several, including the High Priestess, have been knocked over by the rocky debris. I don't see Alyson. I do see, stepping down through the damaged tunnel, a figure in crimson armor carrying a morning star. "Persephone."

"I told them bringing that rock here was a bad idea," Gregor takes a step forward. I watch as he places a fingertip on his forehead. His helmet, as if it's been there this whole time, shimmers into existence, as does a bronze breastplate, and a spear of polished dark-brown wood, with a silvered blade.

The seven cultists lining the mezzanine wall draw daggers in unison and charge around the corner into the tunnel. The red warrior uppercuts one with the morning star. Persephone spins around a jab and embeds her weapon in the back of another of the cultists' head. She dodges out of the way of a swipe, grabbing a cultist as she does and using her as a shield against a jab.

Her armor moves with her deadly dance. It's as if she's wearing silk. There's no clinking, no sense of weight or encumbrance, her victims unknowingly playing their part in her thanatotic tango. In moments she stands alone at the break in the mezzanine.

A group of acolytes has gathered themselves together and are ready to charge the red warrior, while a second group of cultists has formed and was readying one of those black orbs. "Nope," I say and pull the twig out from my sleeve. "Bhfostu," I command as I toss the twig ahead of the acolytes. Vines erupt from the stone floor, shooting up and across the temple, capturing several acolytes and tripping others. I slide a stone from my sleeve and say, "Bhru," as I throw it at the cultists in dark robes. An invisible force yanks them from where they stand and sends them crashing into the colonnade. I hear the crack of bones; the vaporous dark robes flicker out of existence, and they are left covered in soot. I feel the pride of a job well done. I savor my smug smile as I move my last stones into a pocket and rush away from Gregor, who has shifted his focus from me to Persephone.

I ready my spear by passing my thumb over a few runes. It expands to six-feet, and then as I touch a few more runes, the top end curves and flattens into a blade. I swing as I enter the room cutting through one of the thick chains immobilizing Mym. I spin, bringing my glaive down on a second and a third; an uppercut severs the last one. I'm not sure how or from where the sound comes, but there's a rumble, very growl like, that emanates from Mym as she rolls away – the remnants of the chains still hanging from her clanging against the stone floor. I step through the colonnade and out into the main chamber, searching for the High Priestess, but Mym has found her first and is moving towards her like a cannonball. I witness the initial impact before being body-checked from behind.

The glaive is knocked from my hand as I hit the ground. I recognize the sound of an arrow whizzing past me overhead and striking the column I'm lying at the base of. A foot kicks into my guy and shoves me into the column. If not for my disguise, that would have meant several broken ribs - as it is I'm having trouble getting air. Another arrow hits the floor near me and skids away. I catch a glimpse of my enemy as I'm lifted over her head and thrown back into the chain room.

It's Aela – she seems very unhappy. I hit the ground, and this time there's a crack from within me. She charges me. I pull one of the runes from my pocket, "Isa," and slap the small stone onto the ground in front of me as I roll away. Instantly crystals begin to form in the air and settle on the ground, growing into an ice sheet that expands to fill the whole room. Aela loses her footing, slips, and slides into the wall. In an act that proves nothing should be taken seriously, the hammer, chains, and other tools on the wall rattle and fall one by one onto her head and shoulders. Ice is not an obstacle for me in this form, and I stand sure-footed. My coat holds my sides tightly, and I can already feel the magic seeping into my body; much of the pain has subsided. I hear the sounds of fighting, of Mym rolling around, of Persephone's grunts and battle shouts. I'm feeling very confident. "This will not end well, Aela."

"No, it won't," she says as she tosses a chain from her lap. The pupils of her eyes become slits. The black of her clothing pulses with dark energy, and I feel a ripple through the air across the room. As she stands, white streaks form in her dark hair. She looks at me with the fierceness of a wild animal. And then she leans into a step and roars at me – as she does so, black wings rip from the back of her coat. They are as dark as night with ash-colored veins; a choking smoke hangs on them where feathers should be.

"Shit," I mutter. She's one of the Wakeful, a Watcher, a Fallen – her kind has many names. I know her as a Fomorian. There's a rush of wind – she's moved so fast that there's still a ghost image of her across the room. A clawed hand comes down on my face, another rakes across my chest. I take a swing at her, but she's too fast. I drop low, spin away from her reach, and try a hook kick. I rip through air. With a gust of wind, her wings have lifted her off the ground. She knee drops onto me, knocking me to the floor. She plunges her fingers into me like ten icy daggers, lifts me, and slams me back down. I cough up blood and need to use a pillar to help me get to my feet. "This is your last chance," I cough again. I draw the power within my coat away from healing me and into my extremities. When she attacks, I move fast enough to catch her first swing, and then the second, and then I hit her with a palm strike that knocks her back. She rushes forward, and gut shots me hard enough that I crack the pillar as I'm pushed back into it. I stumble away into the colonnade. I need some distance – *I need to find my staff.* My eyes dart around frantically. I spot it, but it's too late. I feel a fist club me in the back of the head and talons jabbing into my back and shoulder. She swings me into a column and then kicks me into the main chamber.

She pursues at a walking pace. *Cocky piece of shit.* I think rather than say. I have time to get back to my feet. Most of the fighting has stopped. The room is mostly empty. Persephone is no longer wearing her helmet, and there's blood on the side of her face. She's favoring her left side, and her battered crimson armor is evidence of the battle between Gregor and her. Gregor is holding his right arm loosely at his side; blood drips from his fingertips. His breastplate is bent inward, and his spear now more resembles an iklwa. They're circling each other. I don't see Mym at the moment, but I do see the flattened remains of the chanters as well as what I think used to be the High Priestess. Aela strides up to me. I do what I can to match her height. A moment passes between us. I imagine a similar moment passing between a gazelle and a lion just before the lion pounces.

A crossbow bolt appears in Aela's shoulder near her neck. The impact forces her a step back. She howls in pain. With creatures not of this world, it's less about hitting vital organs and more about doing enough damage that they can no longer maintain their physical form – this goes for me as well. Her eyes scan the mezzanine. I slip my last stone from my pocket and squeeze Uruz in my hand. For a few heartbeats, I'm awash in an orange glow. The pain is still there, but I don't care. I feel ten times bigger. I step up to her, her eyes come back to me, and I punch her in the face. I knock her off her feet, but she rolls and bounces back up. She flaps her wings, and in a gust of stone dust, she dives through the air at me. She hits me. I bring my hands together and slam them down on her back as her momentum carries the two of us over the chamber and into the collapsed debris of the main entrance.

She rears back and tries to stab me again with her talons, but I catch her arms and flip her up and over. I grab a large rock as I get up and hurl it at her. It smacks into her shoulder. I seize another, bigger rock and throw it. This time it knocks her back down. I grab a mid-size boulder with both hands and chuck it. This time she bats it away with her arm, but I can see on her face the amount of effort it took to do that. Before I can grab another rock, I'm hit by one she has thrown. I lose my footing and slide down the rubble pile. I glance up in time to see her leaping at me. I can't react in time. Boots land on my chest, clawed hands bite into the sides of my head, and then I slam into the ground. We grapple, roll, and fall away from each other – both scrambling to our feet. I don't wait; she falls to my leg sweep. As I swing around, I take hold of the base of one of her wings, lift, and repeatedly beat her into the stone floor. I stop once there's no more resistance and drop her.

Aela lays motionless for a few breaths, but, broken wing and all, she begins to move again. "Come on," and I'm not sorry about how whiny that sounds.

"Yours still moving?" Persephone says as she comes up behind me.

"Yes," I say, pained. Uruz is wearing off.

Without waiting, Persephone takes a step and slams her morning star down on Aela's head. There's a wet crunch. The smoke around her wings evaporates as Aela's body turns to ash. "Fin."

"Gregor?"

"Gone."

"You finished him?"

"No. He teleported away while you were using the floor to pummel this creature."

I know better than to ask how she's doing even though that head wound looks terrible. "Did we win?"

"I think so..."

I scan the temple. The battlefield is a cluttered mess of discarded weapons, chunks of stone, and car debris. None of the artifacts remain in their ceremonial placements. I see a few skeletal hands clutching the relics. They died - a few of them by a crossbow bolt - trying to escape with or protecting the artifacts. In fact, the only cultists I see are dead. Ashen mounds of desiccated bodies, some nothing more than the phantom robes they wore, lay scattered about the hall.

Drifting on the stale air of the mortuary atmosphere are terrified whispers. Persephone taps my shoulder and points. There's a huddle of acolytes in the back corner – the will to do harm seems to have evaporated.

Nothing remains moving. At least nothing deemed a threat. The heartbeat's worth of calm suddenly dissolves as we are both alerted to a new sound at the same time. Movement - to the left and right of us - we hear the scrapes of footsteps and instinctively press back-to-back.

Chapter 30

A face appears over the side of the mezzanine. "Did we win?"

I recognize the voice instantly. I turn sharply on Persephone. "You brought him here?!"

"He insisted," she quietly moves away.

Alan makes his way down the stairs to ground level. He's carrying a broken crossbow, and Mym is rolling alongside him.

"Aedan," Persephone calls my name softly.

I step through the colonnade and move to her side. There, standing between two cells and brandishing a cultist dagger is Alyson. I'm too paranoid to speak with her – I nervously look to Persephone, who sighs.

"You don't need that anymore," her voice is surprisingly soothing.

Alyson begins to shake and drops the dagger. She backs up against the wall, her hands rising to her face as she slides down, tucking her knees into her chest. "I – I killed one..."

Both Persephone and I glance in the direction of the head nod. We see feet sticking out around one of the columns – I'm relieved to see the sooty remains of a black and gray robe, not a red tabard. "Well done." Persephone nods in approval.

Mym and Alan join us. He's hurt. His eye is swelling. There's a cut on his forehead. There's a gash along his upper arm. He holds out the broken crossbow for Persephone. "Sorry."

She takes it from him, examines it, and then tosses it away. "I have others."

Alan and I look at each other. "You look terrible," we say at the same time. I can feel the magic of the coat working on me – he'll be sore for weeks. "I'm sorry."

"You told me not to; I did it anyway. This is on me."

Actually, I blame Persephone, I think, but am careful not to say. He's looking at me strangely. I realize he's never seen me in uniform. I unbutton the coat, feeling the magic slip away as I do. The bark-skin fades, so too the moss hair and beard – and the healing. It's like coming off of pain killers, but your broken leg still hurts. The familiar and welcome sense of euphoria isn't there. I stagger under the weight of the pain as if someone had kicked my cane out from under me. In the span of a second, I have an entire argument with myself – I feel like a drug addict saying no to a hit for the very first time. Alan reaches for me, but I gently wave him off. "Is this better?"

"Sorry, I've never seen you -"

"Hey," a soft voice calls.

I look over to the cells. I recognize the face – it's Becca Trent.

"Can we, can we – can you, get us out of here?"

"Alan," I gesture towards Alyson and the cells.

"Aid and comfort?"

"Please. We'll see if we can find a key."

Persephone offers as we walk away, "We could just pull the cell doors down."

"It's an old building that's just taken a lot of damage. I'd rather not add to that damage unless we must."

She nods, "Mym, keep watch."

The boulder, which had been following, rolls away. I notice a few more cracks, and one of the chain ends has pulled loose. I wonder about the pain she must be feeling. And then I think of the stone and cement patchwork used to repair and shore up the temple. I make a note to mention this to Persephone. We survey the temple as we move along the colonnade. I stop when we come to two lifeless acolytes. I kneel and brush back their hoods. I recognize one of them from Alan's packets - Stephany Miller. My teeth grind and I want to look away, but I don't.

"Do not mourn those creatures."

"They're acolytes."

"And?"

"I'm pretty sure that at least some of the acolytes are the abducted women." I stand and look at her. "Abducted to smoke me out of hiding so Lugh could embarrass Brigit. The one with the dagger over there is of my blood – the last of my blood. This was all a trick - a trap - to draw me out and force me to watch and be able to do nothing to stop her death or my own." I look back down at the bodies. "They didn't need to be here. They shouldn't have been here." She spares me her usual defense of what we do – maybe at that moment, she doesn't believe it either. She lays a comforting hand on my shoulder, and we continue our search. We pass a forge, supply rooms, the room where Mym had been held captive, eventually coming to a huddled mass of acolytes.

"Interesting," Persephone whispers.

"What?"

"They did not run with the rest of them."

They cower as we step up to them.

"Make no trouble. Stay put," she orders. Many nod; some hide their faces. Over their shoulders, I see a door. "What's in there?"

The group exchanges glances, a mixture of fear and reluctance to speak with me.

"Answer him!" Persephone snaps.

"The High Priestess' chamber," a weak voice speaks up.

"Is the key to those cells in there?" I ask.

They look at Persephone before answering me. "I think so," the same one says.

"Get it. Unlock those cells. And for Gods' sake, take off those tabards." Her tone is very reminiscent of an irritated drill sergeant.

She marches away, and I follow. We come to the remains of the High Priestess. She bends and picks the ring out of the mush. "I'm going to collect the rest," she steps away. I make my way back over to Alan and wave him to me. "Are they alright?"

"No. But, they're alive."

"Tell them they'll be out soon and that authorities are on the way."

"Really?"

"As soon as I can find a phone. Mine had an accident, remember?" Alan nods and goes to deliver the message. I see Alyson; she's back on her feet. I approach cautiously but stop when she looks my way. "You are very brave. Your mother would be proud," I say, but picture Aideen, not the Senator. "We will need to go soon, and they'll need your strength. Others will come to take you all home." I want to ask her questions she probably has no idea how to answer. We stare at each other, which becomes awkward. She steps away and goes to stand next to Alan – who's holding the hand of a particularly battered woman through the bars of the cell.

I feel a nudge on my leg. I look down and see Mym. She rolls away. I watch and see Persephone approaching with her arms full of artifacts. "We need to go," she says.

"Alan," I call out. I hear him say goodbye to Alyson. I can't bring myself to turn around. Persephone is already headed for the stairs. Alan comes up beside me, and we walk side by side to the stairs. We're silent for most of the way. "You shot at me," I say when we're more than halfway up the stairs.

"I was aiming for her - that winged woman. I only had three shots left..."

"You missed."

"Persephone gave me about a five-minute lesson on point and shoot. God," he laughs, "that car made a hell of a racket. I'm glad I didn't talk her out of that."

"You tried?"

"I was worried it would hit you."

"And she wasn't?"

"She said -"

"I said, 'the car is going to make a lot of noise. If it hits Aedan, it's his own fault,'" Persephone says over her shoulder.

"Well, that aside, thank you – the both of you. That last shot, that was enough. It gave me an opening, time enough to act. Saved me." His head droops. "What?"

"I wish I could take credit."

"What do you mean?"

"That last shot. I was panicking. I'd already missed twice, almost hit you instead of her. and then, I don't know, there was this... presence. It didn't take me over, but it was like... like those Just Dance games where you have to match the movement. And then afterward, this feeling of joy, separate from my own – and laughter, a faint, but deep laugh, like rolling thunder."

Always watching. I smirk. As we reach the top of the stairs, all of us but Mym, who was lagging, and move out into the hangar. We stop to look around. Alan, too, senses it. Which speaks to how many are around. Nothing has changed, except the large hole in the side of the hangar. The table. The chairs. The cage. Some of the playing cards had been picked up by the wind and scatter to the ground. But beyond all of this, there's a weight to the air. Eyes are upon us. Many. It struck me as similar to a line of fans standing in anticipation at the side door, waiting for the band to exit. Only there's no cheering.

We walk through the hangar in silence. As we emerge from the building, we see that a light snow has fallen. For something as industrious as an airport, the occasional twinkling of the fresh white snow from the scattered rays of lights shining through the overcast made the metal and concrete seem magical. "Alan, do you have your phone?"

He checks for service. "Yes."

"Call the police. Don't give them your name; say where you are and that you've found what looks like a whole bunch of abducted women." As he steps away to do this, I lean in and whisper to Persephone. "I feel the need to flip Them off."

"I really wish you wouldn't."

"I'm pretty sure it was Gregor who told the Eleusinians how to reforge that artifact using Mym. And I'm pretty sure Gregor was working for Lugh —"

"Yes. Thank you, Aedan."

"Well, I'm not sure if they think I'm a crackpot or for real, but they say they're sending a patrol over," Alan says as he ends his call.

"Time to go," Persephone says.

Alan leads the way back to his car, which is parked near a shed about a hundred yards away. "How did you guys find me?" I ask.

"We heard a crash, looked outside and saw you being forced into a car. Alan was out the door before I was actually. You really should talk with that boy; his driving is very erratic. We snuck in, and when I saw Gregor get out of that SUV, I knew you were in trouble, so I teleported home to get a few things before commencing the assault."

"You look good. I've missed this look on you." There's barely a twitch, but it is a smile.

"I don't suppose now you'll teach me how to turn people into frogs?" Alan asks.

I don't answer, and I'm pretty sure he doesn't expect me to.

Alan gets into his car, with Persephone, after helping Mym into the ample roominess of the hatchback, sitting in the passenger side. I happily stretch out in the backseat. As we drive by the chain-link fence, I see the gate ripped down – and I smile at Persephone telling me that they had "snuck" in. The feeling of being watched passes as we leave the area of the airport. The drive home is done in silence, other than me suggesting a way to patch up Mym – Persephone does become thoughtful after this. It's late afternoon by the time we get back to Alan's. He pulls into the small garage he shares with the hardware store next door and the pizza place next to that. "What will you do now?" I ask Persephone.

"I need to decide what to do with these. The Eleusinians will eventually want them back. Destroying them will be tricky. Hiding them doesn't seem to have worked. And then, of course, await my next mission."

I want to criticize her. I want to ask her how she can still be so accepting. But I don't. I gather from her raised eyebrow that that is precisely what she's waiting for me to do. Instead, I give her an awkward hug, which she isn't expecting, and wish her well. Mym drops out of the back of the car and rolls up next to Persephone. In a flash and a swirl of wind, they're gone. "Are you sure you wouldn't rather go to a hospital? We can say you were mugged."

"I was hoping you would do a little magic," he smiles.

"It's not the answer to everything." He's still smiling. "I'm not a street performer," I grouse and start walking away. As he comes up next to me, I say, "So, Alan, um, my place sort of burnt down -"

"The spare room is always yours."

We head down the alleyway - the same one I had dropped into a few hours earlier - make our way inside, and up the stairs to his place. As he shuts the door, I wave him to me. "This may sting a little," I place a hand on his arm wound and over his eye. I channel some of me, some of that extra energy the coat provides my own healing abilities, into him. He'll still have a black eye, and that arm will hurt for a while, but he looks much better. "And I'm not teaching you how to do that either." He smiles and heads to his room. I collect my bunny slippers from where I had left them by the couch and check to make sure that the special rune stones I used to speak with Red, Green, and Blue are there before retiring to the second bedroom. I pile everything in a chair and go and sit in the shower. The water is as hot as I can take it, and then, for extra punishment, I make it a little hotter. *You never answered him.* I repeat to myself in torment until the water goes cold.

Afterwards, I dress in a sweater and jeans I keep stashed here and go to check on Alan. I catch him quietly making his way to the door. "Where you going?"

"Ah, I thought you might be asleep."

"Thought about it. Where you going?"

"I asked Millie to open the bar, but I should get down there."

I'm surprised. "With everything you saw today. Everything that happened, you want to work?"

He stands there for a moment and then shrugs. "I think I need to, you know." He pauses.

I see the weight of what he witnessed today in his eyes. "Alan -"

"Will I see you down there?"

I want to say so much, but all that comes out is, "In a bit."

This makes him happy. He looks like a kid who just asked his dad to watch him make a dive.

An hour of me not knowing what to do with myself passes. I decide to go downstairs. It's a busy night. I hear that before even stepping into the place. Even still, Alan has kept my stool open. There's a tumbler of whiskey waiting for me. The first sip is divine.

I only have to worry about one neighbor from my corner, and he gets up soon after I sit. A few minutes later, a middle-aged woman takes his place. She has a stylish bob mostly pulled to one side and is wearing a sleek dark-blue dress – nothing fancy, but nice for an evening out. I wonder if she's meeting or looking. My glance becomes a stare – and I stare trying to look like I'm not – because I realize I recognize her.

Alan is working at the bar and sees her. She nods, he nods, and he seems to know what she wants without asking. He doesn't question this. He probably doesn't even realize he's poured a glass of eighteen-year-old Glenfinnan. I take another sip of my whiskey.

"Anything more?" Alan asks me as he delivers her drink.

"The bottle, if you please, Alan, thank you." There's no judgment. A simple nod, and the bottle is set next to me. I close my eyes and rest my elbows on the bar. My forehead leans against the chilled rim of the glass. I sink into the moment of silence – my mind is quiet. My eyes open to the sound of her voice.

"You handled yourself well today," the lady says as she sips her scotch after Alan moves off to help someone else.

I give her a side glance and then close my eyes as I down what's left in my glass. I don't say anything as I pour myself a refill.

"I'm sorry, Aedan. You have to understand - by the time I knew, it was too late. The game had to be played out."

"The game," I snort and down my drink and then refill it. I'm surprised. I sense the regret in how she shakes her head, maybe a smidge of self-loathing.

"I'm not asking for your understanding -"

"I don't care, Brigit. If you've made one thing clear over the years, it's that you don't have to explain yourself." I'm not looking at her. I refuse to look at her. There's a long silent pause as we become just two people sitting beside one another drinking in a bar.

"You and Persephone spoke a lot during this adventure." I think she's waiting for me to say something, but I don't. "I saw that Gregor was involved, too," at this, I finish off another round. "Did, did you get a chance to speak with him?"

I pour myself some more and slowly drink it before answering her – more to build up courage, but also pleased by the anticipation she is trying to hide. "We spoke."

"And?" she asks. The ring of her fingernail against the glass is almost hypnotic.

The room spins for just a moment. "And, it wasn't the type of situation where we play catch up." I blink and fight off a sudden haziness – the whiskey or her, I'm not sure.

She finishes her scotch and stands up. I sense reluctance. "He's on the board, Aedan. I can't hide that anymore."

"Do I need to worry about Lugh?" I asked soberly, still refusing to look at her.

"Lugh broke a lot of rules. Not the least of which is that his recent and numerous visitations to your realm had allowed for several demons to sneak across the boundary. Leaving things very untidy – and Father hates the untidy. If things had gone his way," she shrugs, "but as it stands, let's just say that Father is very unhappy." She leans in and slides her hand, palm down, over the bar top towards me. "I got you a present," she whispers. She lifts her hand, and I don't feel her step away, but I know she's gone.

I look down. It's a key. It's my key. It's my house key. The one that should be on my keyring. I stupidly pat at my pocket. There's nothing there. There's nothing there because the key, keyring, and house should be gone. Are gone. I slip the key from the bar and into a pocket. I sit, and I listen. I listen to Alan speaking with customers. To the snippets of conversation floating around the bar. To the cheers directed towards the teams on the TVs. I listen as "Should I Stay or Should I Go" by The Clash begins to play over the sound system. I listen, and then I take another sip.

9 7 9 8 2 1 8 8 0 4 1 8 3